# TURMOIL IN THE RENAISSANCE

A Historical Fiction of Ludovico Sforza-Duke of Milan

E. F. Palermo

Published by BookLocker.com, Inc., St. Petersburg, Florida.

Printed on acid-free paper.

This is a work of historical fiction, based on actual persons and events. The author has taken creative liberty with many details to enhance the reader's experience.

BookLocker.com, Inc.
2017

First Edition

# Dedication

To Diane, My love and companion through life

The sun slithered through the bars, finding a resting place on his table, illuminating the open book that lay on it. How had it come to this? How did his future evaporate like dew on a warm summer's morning, leaving nothing but empty dreams? Looking around, he saw an empty cell, the dirt floor scattered with a few shreds of straw, the walls chipped and broken by years of damage by former inmates, yet still sturdy enough to become, he was sure, his living tomb. No one was there to serve him, to love him, to envisage a future with him. He had wanted to become a stalwart in saving the Duchy of Milan against those foreign powers that threatened his birthplace. Now, he thought, all was lost; he was lost; the dream was gone.

*****

He remembers his years as the son of a peasant, working the brown ecru-colored fields with his father to eke out sufficient food to sustain him, his father, mother, and younger brother on the small plot that his family was allotted. Life was difficult but they managed to reserve a little grain over and above what they usually needed for the year. There was love here despite the monotony of each day, the inevitability of dying young like many of his neighbors, the harshness of the overseer and the constant sense of oppression from the lord of the manor. The field was often barren but the earth was rich in color the way his ancestors liked it, and the stone pine trees enclosing it on three sides brought the only color into his otherwise dreary life, a place where, on occasion, he could relax under the sun, plopping himself up against the trunk of a tree. He enjoyed watching the newly formed sun rise in the morning and often wondered how many others were also watching it with him. What made it rise every day was a question that puzzled him?

There was only a past and a present here. Dreams of a future were as scarce as a butterfly in winter. Risk was a constant. He did not know what to call it but it haunted his past, burdened his present and blocked his future. It existed for him as much as did the lone ass that plowed the field. He remembers the crop failure that deprived his family of needed food one winter and which transformed the family from one living on the edge of starvation to one living on the edge of death. Change was not something that he or anyone in his circumstance considered because the line between subsidence and death was thin; a mistake could jeopardize the entire family, and the reward was neither obvious nor immediate. But looking back now the day he met the Duke was extraordinary, changing his life in ways he could never have imagined, allowing him to experience the luxuries that only a few privileged people could but, ultimately, leading to his present state of despair, leading to a slither of sunray falling on his cell table.

Outside his village the world had changed: the last vestiges of the Black Death had left the population depleted by halve throughout Europe, inspiring a devotional excess of religious fervor; the savage Hundred Years War between England and France had ended, leaving unemployed soldiers ravaging the countryside in France, seeping into the Italian Peninsular and introducing a type of ferocious and unforgiving fighting to which the Italians were not accustomed; the Papal Schism had been mended and the Vatican had returned to Rome, a city that was devastated

6

over the years that the Pope resided in Avignon and was desperately in need of rebuilding. And despite these setbacks, a new spirit of renewal had emerged on the Peninsular, a spirit that had its origins in the $14^{th}$ century, first taken up by Petrarch, then finding a welcome in Florence and spreading throughout the Peninsular. This was the humanism that relished human existence, that saw optimism in the human spirit, that was not tied to the pedantry of Church scholars.

*****

In this emerging world, Gianni was brought to the monastery of San Gelsera, a monastery some distance from his home, by his father, a tall, gruff, but mostly kind, man given to occasional bouts of drunkenness to relieve the weariness of life. Children were sometimes accepted by the Order of Cistercians and quartered in return for work and the prospect of future initiation into the order, a life that would ensure the boy's freedom from want and survival in a world of deprivation. On that day, the chiming of the church bells could be heard as he and his father approached the walls of the monastery grounds, walls that had stood for 300 years despite the violence that had surrounded those very same walls periodically for 300 years. The boy was not afraid to be leaving home; his father had prepared him for this change and, in any case, life could not be any harsher than the one he had lived for 12 years. Yet, he would miss his mother, kind and caring as much as she could be but consumed in trying to keep the family alive, and thus, having little time to devote exclusively to him.

On arrival at the monastery his father knocked on the two huge wooden doors, carved bas reliefs of St. Gelsera on each door looking out onto the visitors, world-weariness carved into his face. Yet, something else struck the young boy, something that he had not experienced before, a feeling that arose from the face of the carving. There was serenity in that face, serenity that he would later learn came from devotion to a cause greater than his own. Below the reliefs, smaller human figures plowed the field in the background. Gianni looked at the carvings, stunned by their beauty, beauty that he had never seen before but he also sensed from them that beyond these doors lay a life of drudgery not unlike what he was leaving.

As he stood by his silent and serene father, he was ready to face the life that was hidden behind the doors. They were opened by a brown-robed monk, youngish in appearance and slow and mechanical in his movement, who was not surprised by the man and child before him. The monk gazed at them, first briefly meeting the eyes of the taller man, then quickly lowering them and gently indicating by a turn of his body to follow him. An immediate flood of color hit the boy's eyes, the colors of red and yellow tulips, blue hyacinths, and purple asters intermixed with acer and camellias; all combined with the flagrance of the flowers to soothe him. He had sometimes seen these flowers scattered along the dirt roads that ran through the countryside but never arrayed in the interlocking patterns and intricate designs that lay on each side of the path. Tall eucalyptus trees provided shade at various places along the path, shade that would be welcomed during the scorching summer months that often accompanied the season.

As they walked along, they soon came upon a church that was unlike the small village church that he and his family visited. A small spire jutted into the sky from each side of the façade like the arms of an infant reaching for an object much taller than itself. Decorated doors beckoned visitors to experience what lay behind them. Above the doors, a frieze of intricately carved religious figures enacted scenes from the history of the church that he did not understand. The physical structure of the church, the alternating pink and grey colors of the limestone blocks that comprised the structure, impressed him like nothing had in the past. He knew, he felt that he was in the presence of an extraordinary passion that somehow elevated his feeling of content. Adjoining the church, he could see a garden enclosed by a loggia type walkway, religious and everyday activities carved into the capitals, small fountains in each quarter of the garden spurting water into their basins, benches of intricately wrought-iron designs along the paths that crisscrossed the garden, flowers in full bloom in the areas immediately behind the benches, and small shade trees located in a way that provided a respite from the heat.

A larger, simpler building lay behind the garden and this was where he and his father, accompanied by the friar, were walking towards. They entered a doorway, his father motioning for him to enter first, then followed the monk to a room far down a plain hallway, somewhat dark but not entirely uninviting, unadorned with any ornaments save a few pictures that hung on the walls, the floor tiles containing a design of chrysanthemums of an alternating orange and blue color. Upon entering the room, they were met by Abbot Garganega, a short, wide girthed man, partially bald with a welcoming smile on his face and a man Gianni Cortese would discover had more substance than his appearance would indicate.

"Good day," said Abbot Garganega while motioning both his father and him to sit in front of a large, plain desk. "Hope your journey was pleasant."

Gianni could tell that his father was uncomfortable and restless in front of the abbot. He had seen this behavior in front of the landlord many times, his father's shoulders slouched and his demeanor withdrawn. After some pleasantries passed between the two men, the abbot left the room, saying, "Brother Nino will be in to show the boy to his room."

Brother Nino entered in a slow, yawing gait that made him look like he would tip over at any moment. He had what some would call a listless face, certainly not expressive by any means but not quite apathetic, a face ready to spring into action only with a good deal of prodding.

The boy's father put his arms around the boy, hugging him with a great show of affection. "The brother will show you your duties. I know this is hard but here, yes, you will work, but you will also be free from hunger, and you will be taught to read and write. This is better than anything I can give you."

Gianni accepted this pronouncement without any show of emotion. Just as his father was about to release him from his embrace, Gianni noticed a painting on the wall to one side of the abbot's desk. It was a painting of Christ rising from his tomb, encircled by several men and women, his white garment contrasted with the cloudless, bright blue sky behind him. Christ's arms were extended outward seemingly beckoning Gianni to him. The faces of the followers looked upward toward the risen Christ with obvious rapture. One figure in the background, though, looked not upward but out from the painting, seemingly, at Gianni with an expressionless face. It became a comforting scene throughout his stay at the monastery.

That evening Gianni had his first meal with the brothers. Unlike the members of the group, he wore his own clothes since he was neither a novitiate nor a member of the Order. After being introduced to Brother Matteo Grechetto, he was led to a large hall by Brother Matteo where long wooden tables were set-up in well-ordered rows facing the front of the room. Up on stage was a very long wooden table where the Abbot and other officials of the Order sat. The hall had three windows set about 12 inches into each of the two side walls. Only minimal light protruded through the windows because the sun was receding in the sky. Several tall candelabras were placed around the hall which threw out flickering shadows onto the walls. Most striking, however, was a large fresco on the wall behind the head table on the stage. In later life, when reflecting on his time at the monastery, he would be befuddled by the content of the mural, which contrasted so profoundly with the Leonardo mural of the Last Supper in the refectory of the convent adjoining the church of Santa Maria delle Grazie in nearby Milan. This mural was more appropriate for a Roman pagan festival than an ordinary evening meal at San Gelsera. Arranged across the fresco with a background pastoral scene were an array of nymphs and satyrs with some of the lesser Roman gods, all in playful, earthy positions with humans, overseen by a very playful-looking Dionysius. "We eat in silence here; there is to be no talking," Brother Matteo said, beckoning Gianni to follow him. Gianni took a place at one of the tables with Brother Matteo. Around him, sitting in silence were brothers of various ages; older, bearded, white-haired men; younger, robust-looking men along-side some pale, frail-looking men, and some men who looked not much older than himself. It was unlike his meals at home where there was always chattering going on, especially on those rare occasions when a neighbor would dine with the family. It was a simple meal; some crusty bread, a plate of vegetables that consisted of asparagus, beets and fennel, all steamed but with a very appetizing flavor from the herbs in which the vegetables were cooked. Future meals were to be primarily vegetables, occasionally with small portions of meat. Bread was always served, always delicious, and always freshly baked.

That night in his cubicle, which contained only a bed, a small table, a chair, and an ewer and basin in which to wash, Gianni had an opportunity to reflect on his day. This cell was to be his home; he did not know how long he would occupy it nor how long he would be in the monastery. His father and the abbot obviously believed that he was to remain here many years, maybe for life. But he was unsure, wanting to obey his father's desire but filled with an unease that he could not describe. He never wholeheartedly agreed with his father's decision but abided by it because he was his father, and Gianni knew that his father was not placing him in a monastery out of ill-will but out of dire necessary. He did not know what to expect from this life nor was he sure that he wanted a religious life. He had never thought of his future previously, and now it would be settled for him in this monastery by people he did not know. He had never felt religious despite attending the village church with his mother. He never had an emotional attachment to it and its rituals. As he sat on the edge of his bed, he thought, I must make the best of this. I cannot return to my family. There is little enough food to go around now. But what does this new life hold in store for me? I suppose I will find some answers tomorrow.

*****

Brother Matteo, who was to be his spiritual guide and teacher, woke Gianni at 4:00 AM for Vigils by knocking on his door. "Our primary purpose here is to serve the Almighty with prayer, reflection and work," Brother Matteo said as they walked to chapel. "Nobody is slothful here. You are expected to rise each morning at this time to attend chapel and services. Breakfast follows and then the brothers will separate, some going to the library to archive and copy the ancient books, others doing household chores, and some will go out into the fields to cultivate our crops. There will be time for reflection throughout the day. Your routine will be somewhat different because you are newly arrived and will be a student for a time before you are expected to work more fully. You and I will find time for study and discussion during the day. At dusk, we will all sit for dinner in the refectory and conclude our day with prayers."

Gianni had immediately developed a warm feeling for this kind, gentle man with a reassuring face in front of him. Brother Matteo moved in a smooth, graceful manner and talked without any sharp or disjointed hand motions. His words would linger in the air as if they had physical weight to them, appearing heavier than the man from whom they originated, yet they were as soft and comforting as a butterfly on a summer breeze.

"Brother Matteo," Gianni said, "I am well capable of work. I have been in the fields most of my life. But I do not know what you mean by reflection. When is their time to reflect. At home, we spent from sunrise to sunset working the field and then barely have enough to survive."

"You will learn that, apart from the few morsels of food that you need to exist, reflection is the substance of eternity," Brother Matteo said as they walked together toward the dining hall, crowded with brothers returning from the fields. As they entered the hall, Brother Matteo nodded politely at several monks. Gianni, however, saw an almost unnoticeable flinch from Brother Matteo towards one of the monks.

As the months passed, Gianni became comfortable with his daily routine of early morning prayers, followed by breakfast. A sense of security eased its way into him, a feeling that became noticeable only when it was fully vested within him. Schooling took place after breakfast, and he looked forward to his time with Brother Matteo. He found that he had a penchant for learning that Brother Matteo encouraged with enthusiasm, gently prodding him without being overbearing, indicating in his subtle manner that he was special to Brother Matteo. He taught him subjects that he would not have introduced to other students, subjects in addition to those of ordinary religious topics.

Many monks went into the fields surrounding the monastery walls after breakfast to tend the crops; carrots, fennel and peppers were the primary vegetables farmed. Farther from the monastery, wheat was farmed, and sheep were raised. The monastery was self-sufficient in all the foodstuffs needed to sustain it. Gianni discovered that the monastery was much more productive than the small plot of land that he and his father had farmed. The methods that the monks used to farm were much different than those that were used outside the monastery. The plots were quite large so that it allowed division of labor, crops were rotated every other year so that the land remained fertile longer, and natural fertilizer from the sheep flock was saved and applied to the plots. Near starvation had never been a real possibility at the monastery.

After lunch, Gianni would go into the cloisters where he would have time to reflect, sometimes walking the paths, other times sitting on one of the benches to contemplate some of the concepts that Brother Matteo had been teaching. Over time he learned that Brother Matteo was the youngest son of the wealthy Grechetto family located in the Lake Como area, renowned for its silk industry and not far from the city of Milan. The family had operated a silk weaving company for over a century, first started by his great-grandfather but made prosperous by his father into one of the leading companies in the region. Matteo would work alongside the pickers, harvesting the leaves from mulberry bushes, carrying the baskets to the edge of the field for delivery to the plant where they would feed the caterpillars. After being hatched for six weeks, they would attain about 50,000 times their initial weight, shedding their skin four times. The caterpillars would then attach themselves to a compartmented frame or twig or tree where they would later weave their cocoons eventually to be immersed in a hot bath to loosen the threads and to kill the caterpillar. A single thread would unravel into one long, shinning thread of up to 4,500 feet, one of many other threads which woven together would produce a magnificent garment of singular beauty.

Matteo loved walking among the bushes planted along the slopes of Lake Como, finding a place where he could rest and gaze down into the sunlit, shimmering deep blue lake. It was here where he first contemplated his future, and realized that he desired to serve the Almighty. His father would be unhappy with his decision but Matteo knew that he would understand. Matteo was convinced that a monastic life was the one he intended to pursuit.

Brother Matteo was well-schooled, having attended the University of Padua, the second oldest and one of the most prestigious colleges on the Italian peninsular, taking a degree in theology but supplementing it with private study of ancient religions, before completing his schooling in Rome in the Vatican after joining the Order. His learning touched many areas, including those that the Church would not have approved, if known. Gianni remembered Brother Matteo speaking about the origin of the world, how countries had similar stories about its origin.

Gianni was comfortable here because he was free of the constant pressure that, even though a boy, he felt along with his father from the landlord and from the vicissitudes of nature. Yet, he always retained somewhere in his being an inner anxiety and restlessness that he could not explain. It was not always present but it would appear periodically during his reflection-time. When that happened, he could not prevent it from overwhelming his thoughts. As much as he would try to focus on God and the meaning of a good life, the more the thoughts of a different life, a life away from the monastery, a life of forceful activity entered his mind.

The silence did not bother him; it was not much different than it was at home. He and his father did not talk very much. He knew that there was love; there was just no need to express it verbally. One day while he and Brother Matteo were enjoying a short conversation, an activity that was not encouraged in the monastery, Gianni asked Brother Matteo casually, "Is there something awry between you and Brother Aurelio? I could not but notice that each time you pass him, you seem to have an automatic flinch."

"Do not be concerned about that but be aware that Brother Aurelio is not the sincerest of monks here. In fact, I would say that he is most inauthentic, possible dishonest, not adhering to the vows that he has taken."

"What do you mean by that, Sir?"

"You will learn in time that life is composed of different kinds of people; some wishing to serve the Lord with honest good work; others wishing only to serve themselves. Brother Aurelio is one of the latter."

After a hard day's work in the fields, the brothers would have their evening meal followed by a time of solitary reflection. Gianni would take his time in the cloisters. This area became his favorite place to relax and indulge his thoughts. He liked being among the flowers that, except for winter, were always in bloom or about to bloom. The colors changed with the seasons and brought a bit of relief and expectation into his life.

Occasionally, Brother Matteo joined him and would continue their religious discussions. One time, Brother Matteo remarked how, "the One and only God brought into being the world from the chaos that existed previously and how He kept calm over the earth. For preventing the world from receding again into chaos, the Almighty expected mankind to serve him."

"But Brother, this expectation prevents mankind from being truly free," responded Gianni. "If mankind is dependent on the good graces of the Almighty, it would create anxiety as well. Would not mankind be freer and less anxious if they did not believe in an Almighty and had no expectations to follow?"

Gianni would often notice Brother Aurelio in the cloisters, always neatly dressed, over in one corner with several Brothers talking quietly but excitedly. In those early years, he was not able to learn the substance of those conversations, but he could not suppress the feeling that something was awry. The contrast between Brother Matteo and Brother Aurelio was striking. Brother Matteo had a soft, easy-going ambience, eyes that set upon you with a gentle touch, which could be interpreted only in the most unthreatening manner. Brother Aurelio, on the other hand, had a deeply rutted, stern face, deep-set eyes that fixed on one with no empathy at all. It was a face that wanted to be feared but not loved.

As time passed and as he grew more confident of his position in the monastery, he was able to understand that there were activities being conducted that were not done in the interest of serving the Lord. He was able to learn more of these activities once he began working in the fields outside of the monastery.

Brother Matteo's disposition changed over time also. Gianni noticed the change but it was subtle at first. Only when the relationship to Brother Matteo grew closer did Brother Matteo confide his despondency to Gianni. Brother Matteo was having a crisis of faith, a disappointment concerning the course of his life and his dwindling faith in the teachings of the Church and of the behavior of the clergy, especially those in authority. His life was not proving to be what he expected.

Gianni, too, was dissatisfied; his future was blank, a series of endless prayers extending forever with a reward only upon death. This is what the Church preached. This is what the laity believed. His only respite was his work in the field and Brother Matteo's lessons. The lessons, yes, the lessons he thought, as he sat alone in the cloister hands clasped on his knees, eyes unfocused on a distant object, the lessons extend my world. I live for the lessons, for the knowledge they impart. Beyond the walls, I occasionally hear of events from visiting pilgrims to San Gelsera. They tell stories of Milan fighting against Venice, of Milan fighting against Florence, of some of the smaller states joining the larger states, of Florence against Pisa. The turmoil seems constant, unrelenting. Is this what you seek, Gianni? Is this what you want to break your ennui?

One day as they sat quietly in the cloister, Brother Matteo remarked, "Have you noticed the offerings that we give to the saints? We offer flowers and alms and beseech the saints to assist us in some pursuit. Each saint has characteristics that differ from another, some thought to be concerned with eyesight, another concerned with travel, still another concerned with the protection of the home. You should know, Gianni, that ancient pagan Rome had polytheistic gods, many of whom they acquired from the Greeks. These gods also had distinctive characteristics ascribed to them. Temples were constructed to honor them, their purpose not unlike the purpose of our present-day churches. Offerings were made to satisfy the gods and to beseech them to provide for some favorable outcome or to provide for a continuance of good fortune. Just as our priests perform rituals for their congregation, the priests of Rome performed rituals for their congregation. These rituals were expected to be performed each day or at specific times of the year in a prescribed manner; ceremonies were held by the priest in the gods' temples and festivals were celebrated at certain times of the year; all to honor the god. For example, the goddess Vespa was the deity of the hearth and the man of the household was expected to honor her each day in the home in order to bring good fortune to the inhabitants. Does not this seem similar to what we do today? The offerings and rituals are different but they are given in anticipation of the same outcomes. Our saints are like the pagan gods of old. Many

20

emperors were made gods after their death, Caesar and Augustus the most prominent, just as some of our religious servants were made saints after their deaths."

Gianni, reflecting on Brother Matteo's statement, said, "But Brother, despite all the saints we have, we still have only one God."

"Ah yes, Gianni, Jesus Christ, the Son, came down to earth to tell us that there is only one God, God the Father. But have you ever heard an explanation of why he came to earth. Yes, to expunge our sins. But intelligent humans have existed for thousands of years before Jesus arrived, practicing a polytheistic religion; wars and lascivious behaviors were just as prevalent then and, yet, God found no reason to appear at some point back then. Why, Gianni? A belief in the supernatural has existed for thousands of years. Does it really matter to which god we show our allegiance?"

*****

Ludovico Sforza, called "Il Moro" because of his swarthy appearance, was born the second son of the Duke of Milan, Francisco Sforza, a condottiere who usurped the realm from the recently formed Ambrosian republic in 1450 and established the Sforza dynasty. Francesco was instrumental in forming the Peace of Lodi in 1454 between Milan and Venice, which kept the peace for 40 years between them and the other three major powers on the Italian Peninsular, the Kingdom of Naples, the Papal States, and the Republic of Florence. They and the smaller states formed the Italian League to defend one another in

21

case of attack from foreign powers invading the Italian Peninsular.

After Francesco's death, Ludovico's older brother, Galeazzo Maria, inherited the domain. In the service of his brother, Ludovico learned the duties of a ruler, and performed them admirably, always, however, harboring the thought that it would take an extraordinary event for him to inherit the throne from Galeazzo's young son, Gian Galeazzo. Like his father, Galeazzo started a vast building program, always with the idea to keep the populace at bay. New public buildings were built in the style of the high renaissance, new piazzas were constructed that encouraged new neighborhoods, artists were invited to the city. Ludovico enjoyed overseeing some of these construction projects, the details involved in them, the people who sought his favor, the praise upon their completion.

*****

The moon hid behind clouds on the night of his brother's assassination, darkening the narrow, cobblestoned streets like a dark cover concealing an unwanted, marred object. Yes, the people resented the imposition of high taxes to support Galeazzo's lavish and dissolute lifestyle; his cruel behavior was widespread, particularly to the nobles and their females who were the main recipients of it. They harbored a deep, long-lasting resentment to his reign. They, together with subversives who hoped to reestablish the republic that had been usurped by Galeazzo's father, plotted his murder on this dark cloud-covered Saint Stephen's Day of December 26, 1476. Three men hid in the dark shadows of Saint Stephen's Church as Galeazzo Maria knelt in church. The attack was vicious and quick. One of the men approached him, bending over as if to address him and with a quick hard thrust dug a knife into his chest. The other two assailants then added their daggers to the attack. Galeazzo fell gasping for breath, his blood ebbing onto the tiles of the nave. Two assailants were captured as they ran from the church and killed immediately. The remaining assailant scurried into the street, unsure where he was headed, turned a corner, pursued by the Galeazzo's guards, finally cornered and dragged away from the narrow, unlit street. Later, nearly all his bones were broken, and he was flayed alive but not before he died with one of the most memorable last sentences. "Death is bitter, but fame is everlasting." Above them the moon revealed itself from behind a cloud; Ludovico's beaming smile hid behind palace walls when he heard the news.

Upon Galeazzo's death, his seven-year-old son, Gian Galeazzo, became Duke with his mother, Bona of Savoy, acting as Regent. At 24 years of age, Ludovico yearned for leadership, feeling that the time he spent in his brothers' employ, had prepared him to be the successor to his brother's title. His vigor, he believed, was essential for safeguarding the realm and advancing its interests, interests that were always in danger from the city-states and republics surrounding Milan. For a time, he was conscientious in avoiding any conflicts with Bona, feigning sincerity as best he could while gathering support from trusted conspirators. He made no changes in lifestyle, living as evenly as he could, and complacent in his behavior and interactions with Bona. He walked the same paths he always walked, met the same people he always met, drank with the same people with whom he always drank. He was aware, however, that Bona was probably spying on him for fear of just what he might be contemplating.

Ludovico sat in his apartment enjoying a glass of wine several weeks after his brother's murder, looking at a painting on the wall above the cadenza, fine silver candelabra and ceramic vases beneath it spread out in a neat arrangement. Flames from logs burning brightly in the fireplace flashed on the walls, highlighting the painting. It was one of his favorites. It depicted the myth of Zeus disguising himself as a white bull to seduce the beautiful Europa, painted in the bright colors and technique recently introduced in Florence with the use of oil paints. The myth tells the tale of Zeus coming across the beautiful Europa in a meadow, turning himself into a bull after his rejection to whisk her away to the island of Crete. Ludovico's wine had grown warm in his hand. His thoughts wandered to the best way to move on his desire to fill his brother's position. Was force the way to proceed, either deadly or otherwise, or was subtlety and flattery, coupled perhaps with seduction the way to proceed?

As he sat there pouring another glass of wine, his thoughts turned to his father, Francesco. He had lived a life of adventure, led men in war and commanded attention from all around him including his enemies and had turned Milan into one of the most powerful states on the peninsular. He wrested the Duchy from the Ambrosian republicans, who briefly captured the city after the death of Duke Filippo Maria Visconti and was successful in maintaining the balance of power in the region, often with the support of the Medici in Florence. Ludovico not only admired his father but, even as a child, had an intense desire to emulate him, to succeed where he had not. He remembered his father confiding in him his desire to protect the Duchy and to expand it as a means to defend it. Francisco Sforza always felt that expansion would protect his lands by providing a buffer for the city and would make available more men to enlarge his already substantial army. Just as necessary, he emphasized the importance of defending the city with new weapons and innovative defenses. "Always be vigilant in seeking creative ways to protect the city," he remembers his father saying as they walked the gardens together. Francisco inculcated his dreams to his young son among the eucalyptus and cypress trees, the flowering hyacinths and geraniums. Ludovico took to heart all of his father's lessons and carried them with him for the rest of his life, never doubting their relevance to his own future.

Ludovico believed the populous would be less accepting of the Mother Regent than they were of his brother and, therefore, provided an opening for him. She would have to prove herself. Although she inherited the same counselors that advised her husband, all generally good men in their fields, Ludovico had noticed in private that she was petulant and overbearing. Would her behavior bring disfavor on her from these counselors? Then again, would one have to secure the favor of all the advisors? Is one more important than the others? The cinders in the hearth were crackling, their grey and red glow easing into flaky grey, dissolving into the already fallen ash.

*****

He stood looking out over the piazza below his window, the kiosks lining three sides stocked with various kinds of silk clothing, hats, and accessories, some shoppers milling about between the various kiosks, others relaxing on intricately constructed wrought-iron benches scattered throughout the piazza. A painting of the "Transfiguration" by Giovanni Bellini hangs high up on one wall of his study below which hangs a smaller painting of the "Crucifixion" by Antonello da Messina, both displaying the new oil medium introduced by Messina. He thought, how I love this city, its energy and beauty, the narrow streets in the old quarter, each side shielding the other from the scorching sun in summer, the cacophony of sounds that infiltrate the air morning and night like a band of ghosts playing invisible games. Some people love to be introduced to a new morning by the sounds of birds. Me, I like sounds of commerce, each sound, I know to be followed by a concrete action, reaching an identifiable conclusion.

His close friend and advisor, Giorgio Filanghina, sits in deep thought, legs crossed by his friend's desk savoring a glass of red Nebbiola wine. "I much prefer the paintings of Antonello da Messina," he says, glancing at the smaller picture on the wall. "The realistic expressions of grief and agony in his characters has to move any viewer with a modicum of empathy, his colors are exquisite, and the intimate detail transfixing. I believe he acquired the technique from the northern countries via Sicily, and it is being adopted by many of the Florentine painters."

Giorgio had been a friend since childhood, his father once the captain to Ludovico's father's palace guards. He died in the service of Francesco, and Francesco felt an obligation to the boy whom he found bright and energetic and who was the same age as his son. Giorgio and Ludovico would race through the palace together always getting into mischief, only to be retrieved from the repercussions of their actions by his mother, Bianca, and his governess, Lady Lucretia. They were educated together in the arts; weaponry became second-nature to them, often taught by Francesco himself. Both were dedicated to Francesco, admiring his masculine demeanor and the reputation that he carried with whomever he dealt.

Ludovico admired his father's love of the arts. A man of strength and bearing but also a man who appreciated the new humanistic learning that was replacing the scholasticism of the Church and capturing the minds of many young scholars, learning that looked to ancient Greece and Rome for guidance into leading their lives. An optimism of man's future, that man was the master of his own destiny, suited Francesco's philosophy and was accepted by Ludovico wholeheartedly. Francesco saw himself as a practitioner and sought out leading authors like Leon Battista Alberti and was particularly fond of Alberti's "Book of the Family."

Ludovico turns from the window and addresses his friend, "I remember walking the streets as a little boy with my father. He taught me to love this city, to guard its history with honor, to always advance its interests with strength, to never neglect its problems, and to always be aware of the people. I want to make this city one of the great artistic communities. I want to attract the great artists, composers and architects, artists like Leonardo, attract them from other cities if need be. I remember the trip I took in the entourage of my brother and Bona to the court of Ludovico Gonzaga of Mantua several years past. His domain is small compared to ours, yet Gonzaga manages to have one of the most respected courts on the Peninsula, chamber after chamber of paintings by some of the most prominent artists. Andrea Mantegna was the court painter, and he was just completing his frescos of the present and past Gonzaga family covering the walls of one of the rooms, now called the 'camera picta.' It is an example of trompe l'oeil, a method of producing illusionistic images. They seem to jump out of the wall. It is already considered a masterpiece. If I were Duke, I would have a court that surpassed the Gonzaga's and would be the envy of the world."

"Ah, yes," says Giorgio, placing his wine glass on the desk and looking at Ludovico, "but first you must become Duke. You need the substantial income from the realm to do what you contemplate. Only the income of the Duchy will give you that."

"The Mother Regent has no ambition. She wants the power to do what... merely advance her son, of course, but especially her own material comfort. She has no concern for the safety and prestige of Milan. She leaves those concerns in the hands of Cicco Simonetta, and I have no respect and less confidence in him."

Giorgio rises from his chair, walking first to the window to peek out, then approaching Ludovico, saying softly, "You must overthrow Bona, if you want to achieve those objectives and you must control Cicco and you must do it quickly with surprise. Don't you remember when your brother was ill with small pox and near death how resourceful Bona was, getting her brother-in-law, Louis XI of France, to support her and enlisting the assistance of Ludovico Gonzaga of Mantua. She and Cicco will never relinquish their power willingly. Are you ready to show cruelty or mercy?"

"Giorgio, it is never a question of cruelty or mercy. It's always a question of when cruelty, when mercy."

The sun was setting on the piazza, the vendors were closing the shutters of their kiosks, and the sounds of the day were abating into the advancing nightfall.

*****

As the years passed, Gianni noticed a change in the monastery. Increasingly, he preferred to be away from it, to have a measure of privacy that it was difficult to find. He enjoyed the morning trips to the fields, taking in the diverse and changing scenery, the mountains in the background, jagged and grey, the fields unfolding before him like a bright green blanket, and the birds awakening to the sunrise with their lovely singing. Even his time in the cloister did not satisfy him as much as previously. His dissatisfaction with the monastic life grew, the long, strenuous days followed by the tedium of life in the monastery. Only his daily journey to care for the sheep brought him any joy. He also noticed, however, that the monastery itself had change, not just physically, but some unexplained cloud of unease oppressed the air.

By this time, Brother Aurelio had taken on more duties, as a result, Gianni learned, of Brother Aurelio's family connections, a connection he became aware of only recently. The elevation of Aurelio's brother to a Cardinalship the previous year ensured that advancement for Aurelio was inevitable. Even before Brother Aurelio was accorded the new position, Gianni noticed changes in the monastery; power was ebbing from the Abbot, sometimes not so subtly. Even more ominous was the increasing neglect of maintenance on their properties and, according to some, the nearly complete abandonment of recordkeeping for properties that the monastery held, the farms, lands and livestock.

The world of monastic life was changing. This, he knew from the sparse conversations he had had with monks that he sometimes met along the way to the fields. A long gradual decline had accelerated in recent years, becoming more obvious to those interested in it. The donation of lands to monasteries by the nobles continued unabated, lands that had to be cleared and worked if they were to produce, a practice that had been ongoing for several hundred years. After all, there was never any shortage of sin to be absolved by donations. Like many other monasteries, however, it was becoming increasingly more difficult to recruit novices and to meet financial commitments. The needs of the brothers were slight, but the monastery was required to feed pilgrims and provide sleeping arrangements for those who visited the site. It was also involved in providing funds for several local charities in the surrounding area, especially for the indigent of the community. Some farmland went unused, and some livestock had to be slaughtered for lack of sufficient resources for their care. Even land that was farm-ready lay fallow. Abbot Garganega was forced to rent even more properties to supplement the monastery's income.

Gianni walked slowly to the fields, an hour's journey or more. On his way, he would often meet pilgrims making their way to San Gelsera to view the saint's relics and he occasionally entered conversation with them. On one day, a group of five pilgrims were resting by a large eucalyptus tree on the side of the road, eating a morning breakfast of bread and cheese. Their conversation was animated and excited. They seemed to be in awe of a Saint, Asclepius, they called him, who had traveled the countryside preaching, now recently deceased. His sermons were said to be electric, inspiring, raising listeners to levels of frenzy and joy that they had never before experienced. He was impervious to snakes; he could be bitten by a poisonous one and be unaffected; he was purported to perform miracles. One story had it that an adder had hung from his hand with its fangs imbedded in it with no harmful effects. People were awestruck by his powers. He had heard this story intermittingly over the years from several pilgrims, but the story seemed to have gained momentum and embellishment, new features of his powers being added, it seemed, each time he approached and spoke to passing pilgrims. He was not surprised, then, when one day he discovered a monument along the side of the road, flowers laid by a saint-like figure with several pilgrims knelling before it, reciting a prayer he had never heard before.

In the years since his youth and with the education he had acquired from Brother Matteo, Gianni had won the confidence of Abbot Garganega and was sometimes consulted by him on affairs of the monastery. The Abbot had grown old and frail; his mind was still active, however, and he was capable, but his stamina was encumbered, and he was frightened by simple obstacles that would not have disturbed him in the past. On one morning prior to Gianni's excursion to the fields, the Abbot called him into the office.

"Gianni," the Abbot said, "I'm concerned about the survival of the monastery. Our income is not sufficient for all the activities that we have traditionally done. Each year we have a shortfall and Cardinal Bonvino is threatening to reduce our status to a priory if we are not able to fund our own programs. We would lose our independence and fall under his supervision if that happened. And our income would flow to him, to be administered by him."

"Abbot Garganega, are you confident that Cardinal Bonvino has only the concern and revival of the monastery at heart. There are always rumors about his profligate ways, his fondness for food and wine, and, some say, women and that he has little concern for the flock. Should you not talk to Brother Aurelio? After all, Cardinal Bonvino is his brother." Walking toward the door, Gianni finished, "I will ask around about Brother Aurelio. I have always had a suspicion about him." He noticed the Abbot did not object to his statement.

Brother Aurelio always had the intent to legitimize himself and secure a future for himself through the Church. This was a path that many high-born sons had taken, especially second born and illegitimate. He was the illegitimate son of Count Antonio Corvina, but was raised by his mother until he was 16-years-old, she being a hardworking farmworker of kind disposition but unrealistic to the ways of the world. He seldom saw his father, but knew from an early age who he was and had no expectations for his future. He worked the land next to his mother, always craving, however, for some other life. His half-brother was Roberto Bonvino, who also entered religious life and had advanced quickly with the assistance of his father, eventually becoming Cardinal Bonvino, an emissary of Pope Sixtus IV. Brother Aurelio worked diligently at the abbey, becoming Prior with the aid of his brother's patronage.

Sitting in his room quietly one evening soon after his conversation with Abbot Garganega, the finances of the monastery still on his mind, Gianni felt that others must have some impression about Brother Aurelio, might even know about some of his activities. He knew those brothers who were associated with Brother Aurelio. He would avoid them and casually ask others about Brother Aurelio's behavior. Have they noticed suspicious behavior? Also, he noted to himself that the renters might have observed aberrant behavior of Brother Aurelio. He must somehow get an account of the monies that were passing between the farms and the monastery and the outflow of those same funds.

Gianni was observant enough to understand that money fueled most behavior. Perhaps the only desire that engendered extraordinary behavior more than money was sex, and he knew from his discussions with others that both money and sex were as prevalent in religious life as was bread and wine.

One of the periodic means that the Church gained money was the Jubilee Year. A Jubilee year was first mentioned in the Jewish Book of Leviticus. The first Jubilee year was proposed by Pope Boniface VIII to be celebrated during the year 1300. The aim of the Jubilee was to grant indulgences and absolve pilgrims of their sins if they made the trip to Rome and visited the four cathedrals, St. Peter, St. Paul, St. John Lateran and St. Mary Maggiore. Tens of thousands of pilgrims, including many of the privileged classes throughout Europe, attended the Jubilee in Rome. Boniface promoted it to collect money to refurbish the Church's decaying physical structures but, inevitably, much also went undisclosed. His intention was that it become a centennial event. Dante, alive at the time, was so incensed over the perceived abuse of the Jubilee that it became one of the reasons that he placed Pope Boniface in the seventh circle of hell in his "Inferno". Pope Sixtus IV was proposing a Jubilee year for the same purposes as the initial Jubilee, now to be held every 25 or 50 years. The Church was always looking for new sources of income.

*****

With the morning sun streaming through his windows, Ludovico awoke full of confidence of gaining his prize. The shutters of the kiosks in the piazza had not yet been completely opened, the clerks were nonchalantly milling around conversing with their neighbors, from time to time arranging merchandise neatly for viewing by passing customers who were soon to arrive. He could hear the horses clomping on the cobblestone streets around the piazza. It was a splendid day, like many other splendid days this time of the year. However, his ebullient feeling was heightened with the rush of expectations coursing through his mind; making his demand to the Regent for her voluntary abdication, leading his band of rebels, if necessary, through the palace halls to overcome the security guarding the Mother Regent and her son, and repulsing the inevitable counterattack by Cicco's palace forces.

The day had come. Ludovico's men, under Giorgio's command, lay in waiting for his instructions. He thought that only a small force was required to confront and, if necessary, overcome Bono's guards. He hoped that she would surrender peacefully but did not have great expectations for that outcome. Cicco could be a problem, but he would be able to raise only the palace guard, a force, perhaps, of 50 men, spread over the palace and not easily assembled into a single unit in the immediate aftermath of the coup.

With a small party of men, Ludovico entered the palace on the pretext of a council meeting, believing it would not arouse suspicion. Giorgio and the remainder of the men were scattered in the courtyard, the repository of the coat of arms of many of the nobles in the Duchy. They hung from one wall of the courtyard, stone plaques announcing the illustrious families of the province, symbolizing their aggregated intention to oppose any foreign aggression. At the end of the wall were steps that led to the level of the palace where the servant quarters were located. When alerted, Giorgio's men were to enter by this door, which was guarded only on special occasions.

Bona, the Mother Regent, was of the French House of Savoy and the sister of Charlotte, Queen of France and wife of King Louis XI. Ludovico had sent word that he had an urgent message of statehood that he must discuss with her that related to her alone. As he entered the stateroom, a room he had admired since childhood, its parquet floor always shining so brightly, even more so today as the large crossed-hatched renaissance windows immersed the room in sunlight, its walls covered in paintings purchased by his father and brother from well-known artists of the day. He always had an empathy for Andrea Mantegna's "St. Sebastian" painting hanging on one wall, the saint tied to a column, his body pierced with arrows, head tilted, the painting's perspective distorted to allow for a more emphatic presentation of the saint's agony. Just how was my brother able to wrest that painting from Ludovico Gonzaga of Mantua, he thought. That question always tweaked his curiosity. But his curiosity was quickly extinguished this day. Standing by Bona was Cicco Simonetta, already with a vaguely perceptible, yet darkly ominous smirk on his deeply lined face. Ludovico knew immediately that something was awry as his mind quickly searched for alternatives to his original intention. He quickly set on completing his original agenda regardless of the consequences. After all he thought, he controlled the situation with his men in the courtyard.

Bona spoke first, greeting Ludovico in a strongly confident manner, her words tinged with noticeable disdain from the months of dissention between the two. "Welcome, Ludovico. I invited Cicco today because your message sounded urgent, and I treasure his council. What is it you want to discuss or should we get right to the crux of this meeting? I have no time to waste on trivialities." Just as she finished, the doors to the room were opened and the captain of the guard approached her and delivered a written message. She read it with clear pleasure, a smile crawling over her face like the newly risen sun laying its morning rays over a field. She seemed to gain an even more confident manner.

"Bona," Ludovico started, bracing himself for the unexpected that was now more apparent from her behavior, "you and I have had our disagreements that we have never been able to resolve. I treasure Milan and her history. Under my father, it was a well-respected Duchy. He took command of the Duchy from the Ambrosian republic because he believed that the republic was not capable of protecting all that he had won for it on the battlefield, and he feared for its future. Under his rule the recognition of the Duchy on the Peninsular was enhanced even over that which the Visconti had left upon his death. It became a true power, one that could not be intimidated by its neighbors; he brought prosperity to it as well and he welcomed artists into his palace. Today, it is still recognized as a leading state, but I fear that you are not concerned for its future, for the safety of its inhabitants and do not value the significance of the Sforza name. You put too much trust in your sister and the French to safeguard the integrity of Milan, but I am not as confident in the French and have my suspicions about them. The safety of the state requires innovation and creativity, new ways of defending itself and new ways of enhancing its recognition. We must first be able to defend ourselves before we call on others to defend us. You are not capable of furthering the state and I am. Henceforth, I will assume the Regency, and

I will protect little Gian Galeazzo. You are surrounded now by my men, and I ask that you abdicate your regency voluntarily."

"Don't be so sure of yourself," interjected Cicco as he moved closer to Bona, his face now with a wide smirk and taking command of the situation himself. "We have been watching you for some time and know of your every move. We are not surprised by your attempted coup."

"Yes," said Bona standing tall, arrogant and unafraid, her disdain for Ludovico unconstrained. "Your men in the corridor have been surrounded and disarmed and those in the courtyard have been either killed or captured. Your friend Giorgio has been maimed but is alive."

Moving to the window, Bona gazed out, beckoning Ludovico to approach. "You are the one to leave, Ludovico. Your choice is exile or death."

Ludovico turned to look at the picture on the opposite wall, San Sebastian's body pierced with arrows, and smiling thought, I wonder if he felt the arrows as acutely as I do at this moment.

"You must leave the city tomorrow," said Bona as she moved from the window and walked toward the doors. "You can bring Giorgio with you, if you like. The monastery of San Gelsera is expecting you. If we discover you have left the monastery you will be sentenced to death. Tomorrow, Ludovico, Tomorrow."

Leaving the room accompanied by a detail of palace guards, Ludovico thought, this exile will not stand. I will be revenged, and she will regret letting me live to see another day.

Once outside the room, he requested to spend a few moments in his favorite room. It was his father's also, and Ludovico enjoyed his father's quiet comments on the pictures that covered its walls. Francisco was so proud of his acquisitions. He often commented to Ludovico of his devotion to the Virgin Mary. This small room was dedicated to paintings of the Madonna and Child. Ludovico had acquired his father's interest in the cult of the Madonna, and both men had a keen sense of the influence that she exerted on their people and followed the rumors of her intercession with God on behalf of the needy. These rumors of miracles were pervasive throughout the Peninsular and had existed for centuries, giving people hope when little else was available to them. Many people, especially women, felt the more human history of Mary was closer to their own life and more easily relatable than that of the Almighty. Francesco and Ludovico, too, embraced her story as strongly as did their subjects.

On the wall opposite the entrance, Giovanni Bellini's "Madonna with Blessed Child" immediately faced Ludovico, acquired only a few years before his father's death. Ludovico stared at the painting facing him and remarked to himself, all of the renderings of the Madonna in these paintings display her beauty but Bellini's impresses me with pure, serene beauty. Of all of the Madonnas, this is the most exquisite. Not even Aphrodite can compete with this divine presence. The Christ child stands on a balcony in a somewhat awkward pose embraced by Mary. His eyes are unfocused but peer out knowingly from the picture away from the viewer but at nothing specific. A plain black background presages the Child's ominous fate, a fate he keenly understands. Despite the sadness that the painting evokes, Ludovico walks from the room enraptured with the image of the Madonna, satisfied and full of hope for his own future.

*****

After months of investigation, Gianni's review of the financial accounts had not produced any financial impropriety that he, with his lack of knowledge of financial accounts, could notice. He was, however, acquiring little twitches and nervous movements that he had not experienced before. Life in the monastery had been so calm for him up to this time, his meditations in the cloister and his work on the farm were like salve for his bouts of restlessness and his obligation to the monastery and deep gratitude to the Abbot infused his attitude. Gianni could see the disappointment in the Abbot's aged and furrowed face. He had looked at San Gelsera's accounts surreptitiously, gaining access to the accounts-room in the evening when the brothers were asleep but, despite his intense scrutiny, found no deceptive practices. He did notice one somewhat odd aberration. The rents recorded for some of the properties did not seem to him to be sufficient for the quality of the properties rented. Some properties had already been cleared of forest, been in use for some time and near a water supply; others were still in woodland and at a distance from water, yet properties of relatively equal size were charged similar rents. Some properties did not command a premium that reflected their convenience and earning power. But he was not an expert in this kind of financial affair and thought that, perhaps, he was merely being overly suspicious. He had no one to whom he could turn for assistance and concluded that the best he could do was to travel to their locations at some time, question the renters as best he could, and record their rent.

*****

Anxious to travel to the farms, he had Brother Garganega's permission but was wary of many of his fellow brothers, in particular, Brother Aurelio. Gianni waited until he had an excuse to leave the monastery for a short period of time. When in his cell, he paced his small space, wall to wall with his hands clasped behind his back, unable to sit for any length of time and unable to move on his alternatives, his anxiety reaching uncomfortable levels. His calm, uneventful life had become disjoined, and he had no reservoir of similar experience from which to draw. From time to time he would stop and brush his hair from his eyes with little awareness of his actions. His small table became as unneeded a piece of furniture as a cat in a hen house. His anxiety would not abate with time no matter how often he berated himself for what he considered his cowardly behavior but, he thought, was becoming a normal part of his daily routine, as normal as his daily prayers, a time for prayers and a time for anxiety spells.

Gianni's travels took him to properties in the outer reaches of San Gelsera's domain. He heard similar stories from many farmers. The rental agent had changed the agreement some years ago, requiring the annual fee to be paid in bushels of grain rather than in ducats as was the requirement in the past. The agent was not a member of the monastery and was always reticent about himself and his activities, although he had the requisite authority to collect the fee. Several of the more perceptive farmers related to Gianni that grain prices had soared in recent years because of the bad harvests in the south but they could monitor prices only sporadically. There were rumors that much grain was being shipped south to the Duchy of Florence and the Kingdom of Naples. One farmer had even figured that the amount of grain that was required to satisfy their rental agreement was worth considerably more than the fee that previously was required. Could the agent be ciphering off the surplus cash from the sales for themselves? And why would the prior of the abbey, Brother Aurelio, not know about it?

*****

"Ludovico, our informant in Florence tells me that Giuliano de Medici has been murdered, and Lorenzo injured but escaped," Giorgio says as he reaches Ludovico in the cloister of San Gelsera. They had arrived only a month prior, adjusting comfortably to the staid life of the monastery. Although a more serene place than either man had ever experienced, they were discovering a satisfying sense of inner peace in their new surroundings, divorced from the intrigues of court and the almost constant turmoil of the Italian Peninsular.

Ludovico rose angrily from his seat between two columns of the loggia, his muscles tightening, "I have been fond of Lorenzo ever since I visited him in the entourage of my brother. The Medici had been allies of my father and have always treated us well. Do they know who committed this atrocity, though I suspect that the Pope may have had a hand in it. He has been having a not so silent squabble with Lorenzo."

"It is not just the Pope, Ludovico," says Giorgio, a frown on his face. "The Pazzi are implicated. You're aware of the competition between the Pazzi house and Medici house for the Vatican finances. Finances always make for uncontrollable and sometimes vicious competition that can easily mutate into evil. There is more. And you will not like it."

"Come, come, Giorgio," says Ludovico as the tension initially shown in his face mounted to encompass his entire body. This is not something he needed so soon after his expulsion from Milan. "Tell me what is disturbing you."

"The husband of your niece, Caterina, is also implicated in the plot. Girolamo was not involved in the murder itself but his troops were ready to enter Florence after the plot had succeeded and his guard, Giovanni Battista da Montesecco, was involved. Girolamo never did enter the city because the uprising of the Florentines never occurred as was anticipated. On the contrary, just the opposite happened. The Florentines turned on the assassins. Montesecco, Cardinal Salviati, and Jacopo and Francesco de' Pazzi were captured immediately. The two priests assigned to kill Lorenzo were also captured. They were all hung in the public square as an example. Sandro Botticelli has drawn a picture of their dangling bodies as an example to posterity. Girolamo escaped and is probably being sheltered by Pope Sixtus."

"Where was Giuliano murdered?" his voice rising several more decibels in anger.

"In the Cathedral of Santa Maria del Fiore, the Duomo, one of the most sacred and beautiful churches in the world, during the celebration of Mass. What a sacrilege! The signal for the assassins was the elevation of the host," Giorgio's voice now reaching the same level of frustration as his friend. "What does this mean for the Sforza's?"

"Girolamo is Bona's son-in-law. She must be attempting to make amends to Lorenzo as we speak. We must emphasis to Lorenzo that Girolamo is her son-in-law and imply that she was sympathetic to the assassination plot. We will need Lorenzo's support when we make our attempt to gain authority in Milan again. And we will make another attempt. Send our agent, Carlo, back to Florence with these instructions. We will go ourselves later. We need Lorenzo to be at least neutral when we make our next attempt."

Ludovico recovered quickly from the news of Florence. And as his temper abated, his face slowly gained a determined look, his body now more relaxed than Giorgio had seen for months. Are Enrico and Danilo still in our employ in the Castello Sforzesco?" Receiving a positive reply from Giorgio, he responded, "Get word to them that a better position will be theirs when I return to Milan. We need them to quietly explore and recruit two reliable and loyal people in the palace who are near Cicco, perhaps disaffected workers of Bona's regency. We need them to assist us, especially on the whereabouts of Cicco when the time comes. We will need access to his home, when he is guarded and when he is unguarded. Offer the recruits sufficient money to entice them."

Ludovico turns to Giorgio. "I feel somewhat like St Jerome in Leonardo's painting, "St Jerome in the Wilderness". The difference is, he wanted to be there, however; he was a hermit. I do not." As vespers are heard floating through the air in the background, Ludovico nods confidently to Giorgio and says, "The world is not kind to those who dally and depend completely on others."

*****

"Gianni, my name is Gianni Cortese," he said when he first met Ludovico and Giorgio. Gianni was immediately in awe of him, Ludovico standing straight-backed and relaxed next to Giorgio in the cloister and impressive in his brocaded garments. It was Abbot Garganega who introduced Gianni to Ludovico, telling him beforehand of Ludovico's position and his place in the recent history of Milan. Gianni had not met anyone as notable as Ludovico, and instantly detected the camaraderie between the two friends, so at ease in each other's presence, a trait he came to admire.

It was not long before Gianni was accepted into the confidence of the two men. Brother Matteo had for some time noticed that Gianni was not suited to a life in the monastery. He was studious, kind and obedient but was more a man of action than a solitary servant of God largely hidden away in a monastery in the mountains of Lombardy. Both Abbot Garganega and Brother Matteo had mentioned the innate intelligence of Gianni, his hunger for knowledge and his absolute loyalty to those whom he respected. The two new residents also saw those qualities and commented on them between themselves. Ludovico said as he and Giorgio walked along the walls of the monastery one morning, "Gianni is somewhat naïve in the ways of the world, but experience would quickly erase that impediment and render him a worthy companion to us. I see much possibility in him."

*****

Pope Sixtus IV was enraged when he was informed of the tragedy in the Duomo. He was even more enraged when he heard that Cardinal Salviati was executed in connection with it. Yes, he desired to reduce Lorenzo's influence. Lorenzo had denied him a loan that he needed and was often an impediment to his plans but Sixtus thought he made it clear that he was not in favor of an assassination. "This was all Girolamo's doing," he said as he met with Cardinal Caramignano in his Vatican offices. Knowing how aroused Sixtus was, Cardinal Caramignano suggested a glass of Frascati to the Pope, knowing that it would soothe his anxiety more than comforting words.

"What will this mean to our plans, Caramignano," said the Pope, as he rose from his desk, inner tension clearly showing on his face.

"We have received the loan that we need from the Pazzi house. You're aware that the Pazzi conspiracy was a competition between the two families that had very little to do with our problem with the Medici. As far as our plans, we are on track."

"My nephew, Girolamo, has made me look like a conspirator in the incident. No one will believe that I was not. Where is Girolamo now?" Sixtus said, pacing around the room wildly flaring his arms as if he were a fledgling attempting to fly for the first time.

"He is on his way to his palace in Forli. It appears that he has avoided any repercussions, although the guard you had assigned to protect him, Montesecco, has been executed for being involved in the plot. He admitted to the plot and exposed Girolamo."

"Is his wife, Caterina, with him?" his appearance now calmer and his manner softer. "She is such a splendid person, intelligent and refined but still proven in equestrian and hunting activities and interested in the finer arts. And she shows a decidedly strong character, a person of resolve just like her father, Galeazzo Maria Sforza, a daughter to be proud of." Pacing the room in obvious better humor, he continued, "I cherished her stay here in Rome after she married my nephew, Girolamo. She would visit me often and our conversations were so pleasant. She was simply charming. She was more learned than you would expect for a girl her age and able to hold her own in discussions of art, and, surprisingly, even politics. Perhaps, I should not have been surprised. She had a shrewd understanding of the goings on around her, a facility she says was taught her by her father. You know her story. She is Galeazzo's illegitimate daughter but was raised with his legitimate children, treated no differently than them, and educated similarly. His wife, Bona, gave her all the kindness that she allotted to her own children. That's why she has such heartfelt feelings for her father and Bona also. Bona gave her much tender advice when it was needed and continues to advise her. What is surprising to me is how Galeazzo could be so tender and kind to her at the same time that he was so cruel and violent to many of his subjects. It is a puzzle of human nature."

Pope Sixtus looked at the painting hanging on his wall and let out a barely perceptible sigh. It was a fresco meant to commemorate the Vatican Library that he had commissioned and later transferred to canvass for hanging, "Sixtus IV Appointing Platina as Prefect of the Vatican Library" by Melozzo da Forli. Surrounding Sixtus on his papal chair are his four nephews, Cardinal Giuliano della Rovere (later to be Pope Julius II) and his brother Giovanni della Rovere with Cardinal Raffaele Riario and his brother Girolamo Riario, the husband of Caterina and a principal in the Pazzi scheme. Sixtus could not but think that the painting would have been better presented and the event preserved for history if Girolamo had somehow been excluded. "How could I have been so generous to Girolamo, giving him the town of Forli for his control as well as the income that comes with it. His cruelty follows him around like the black plague. But I so love Caterina."

Returning to his desk, he motioned Cardinal Caramignano to sit. "Enough of this talk. How is the transfer of the monasteries to priories coming along? We need them under our jurisdiction. And the funds, are they still in safekeeping and collecting interest? Are you giving them your constant attention? The Pazzi loan is only a temporary loan which should be repaid with the next Jubilee monies that we take in. I am putting my trust in you and the Almighty Father is as well. It is for his glory that we have initiated this endeavor."

"Your excellency, since our last discussion, we have converted two more and are proceeding in three others. We are proceeding cautiously in some because they are supported by local nobility whom we do not want to arouse. The funds are well invested."

"Fine," said the Pope. "And the plans for the Jubilee year? Are we ready to launch the pageant? It will bring much needed monies for the infrastructure of the city, the churches and the Vatican. The excess, which we will determine, will go to our fund. We must keep the Canelleria Apostolica in line, especially my nephew, Cardinal della Rovere, and Cardinal Cybo and Cardinal Borgia as well. You know that this is not a short-term project, and we need them for the future of it. There will be pitfalls but we must prevail for the glory of God and the Church"

As Pope Sixtus looked from his window at the pretty collection of cirrus clouds that had gathered in the sky, tinted pink by the setting sun, his silent thought was, I know I will not survive to see God's victory but I can begin the process and can lead it in the correct direction and put in place the men and ingredients to claim final victory.

*****

After eating his evening meal, Ludovico was sometimes able to engage a reluctant Brother Matteo in polite religious discourse. Ludovico was a religious man, inculcated from birth with a strong sense of the spiritual, especially of the Virgin cult, but was always looking for affirmation of his religious beliefs. He struggled but always returned to them. Looking around him at many of the clergy to which he had been exposed, he abhorred the behaviors he had witnessed, behaviors that were so unlike those of ordinary field workers or merchants for example. He was often confused about which men were truly practicing the ethics taught by Christ.

Ludovico could sense that Brother Matteo was interested in conversation with him but was hesitant to remove himself from his evening prayers. Intellectual curiosity sometimes prevailed, channeling the two into a quiet corner of the cloister away from the other brothers. Gianni and Giorgio would sometimes join them, but would as often simply walk silently outside the walls of the monastery, savoring the foothills of the Alps in the distance, covered in the shadows of an invading sunset.

If Ludovico believed that his faith would be affirmed by conversations with Brother Matteo, he was to be sadly disappointed. After years of devotion, Brother Matteo was experiencing a crisis of faith. The years of silent contemplation, often leaving him in a frenzied state in his cell, was producing a fundamental change in his relationship to the Church that he had so assiduously followed for over 30 years, producing not a complete abdication of the way he viewed the Almighty and approached his faith, but creating an intermittent anxiety that often incapacitated him. Over the years, he had expanded his knowledge of the early era of Christianity that he had begun during his days at the University of Padua, and this new knowledge had unsettled his beliefs like a seagull floating on a downdraft of wind. One night during one of his conversations with Ludovico, he asked him, "Do you believe that the Church as presently structured is the only manner in which to view Christ and his teachings? Are the fathers of the Church the only teachers to be believed?"

Ludovico walked slowly by the side of Brother Matteo, hands clasped behind his back, comfortably enjoying the cool, clear darkness, stars doting the blackness. "Well, are their others to be believed?"

"Ludovico, the scriptures that we know, the 27 books that comprise the New Testament, are not the only scriptures that were written after the death of Christ. The two centuries after his death were turbulent years for the nascent Church. It was in great flux. There were many Christian sects widely dispersed along the Mediterranean, all claiming to follow the word of Christ from scriptures that were written by people that are not now known in the Church, all part of the Jesus movement of the time. Some sects, like the Ebionites, believed that Christ was human, the son of the sexual union of Joseph and Mary but still maintained their belief in the Jewish rituals like circumcision, food restrictions and the Old Testament as the sacred word of God; others like the Marcionites, followers of Marcion, one of the most influential Christian thinkers of the second century and one of the arch heretics of his day, rejected any connection with the Jewish faith, disavowing the Jewish scriptures and Jewish God. He believed that there were two Gods, the wrathful, vengeful God of the Old Testament and the loving, merciful God found in the writings of Paul. The God of the Old Testament created the world and everything in it, including the evil that abounded on earth. The God of Jesus came into the world to save people from the God of the Old Testament. He was not human, was not actually born, had no flesh but only appeared to be human. Marcion's type of Christianity attracted many adherents, especially in Asia Minor, and persisted in some form for many centuries. The early elders of the Church understood the teachings of both the Ebionites and Marcionites to be threatening and found it necessary to refute them in written documents distributed across the region."

Ludovico looked puzzled at these remarks. He could not believe that a man as holy and devoted to the Church as Brother Matteo could expose his doubts so openly, and he was deeply touched that Brother Matteo would trust him with such an intimate piece of his feelings. Stopping by the side of a bench near a sheltered corner of the cloister, Ludovico motioned to Brother Matteo to rest and sat next to him. "Please, go on Brother. This is knowledge that is completely unfamiliar and surprising to me, if true."

Brother Matteo could see the distress and disbelief in Ludovico's eyes. He motioned quietly to Ludovico to remain silent. "There is one other group I want to mention to you, perhaps the most dangerous group to the elders of the Jesus community," said Brother Matteo as he shifted his weight slightly on the bench in apparent discomfort in order to continue his conversation in a more intimate position.

Ludovico could not withhold his disbelief, and his annoyance clearly reflected on his face. Straightening his back, he was about to reply to the Brother.

"Wait, Ludovico, hear me out," Brother Matteo said, himself now distressed by Ludovico's reaction but continuing in a quiet, calming voice. "There is one group, the Gnostics, whose thoughts still linger in the world and who became the greatest threat to the orthodox thinking of the Church in the first two centuries. Their beliefs are diverse, but there are several common themes that created great anxiety and particularly alarmed the leaders of the Church. The Gnostics believed that Christ did not rise bodily from the grave. The resurrection was merely a symbolic resurrection, reflecting a rebirth of the spirit. They also spoke of God in both masculine and feminine terms, allowing women to practice alongside of men. In fact, Marcion also appointed women on an equal basis as men as priests and bishops. Orthodox groups prevented women in these capacities and pointed to scriptures to justify their exclusionary practice."

Brother Matteo remained silent for a moment to assess Ludovico's mien, then continued with his discussion. "Perhaps the most important distinction between so-called orthodox Christians and the Gnostics was the idea of "gnosis". To the Gnostics, gnosis was sort of knowledge, self-knowledge. In simple terms, it was self-knowledge of the idea of Christ, gained through one's trials to personally understand Christ. It is the idea that people in general are asleep to the realities of the non-real world. They drift through life without breaking the bonds that tie them to this world. The orthodox Christian Church believed that only the leaders of the Church could lead their followers to Christ and then only when they believed in the organization and the hierarchy of the Church (Pope, bishops and priests), the creed of the Church and followed the rituals of the Church. It is easy to see that the orthodox Church needed structure to unite many of the disparate groups that practiced around the Mediterranean into one catholic group that transcended country and ethnic affiliation and had the means to survive over the centuries."

"It was not until the late first into the second century that elders of the Church like Irenaeus and Tertullian, called apologists, tried to expose these "heretics" in their writings. These 'heretical' writers were part of the Christian community of the time, all praying together, all honoring the Almighty. The Nicene Creed, which we have all come to recite, was developed in response to these aberrant beliefs, but it took decades for the current orthodoxy to prevail."

"Ludovico, consider the Nicene Creed," Brother Matteo continued. Lowering his head slightly and nervously adjusting his sitting position again, Brother Matteo went on. "Almost all of these orthodox professions of faith had alternative interpretations that were critiqued widely by the leaders of the Church and expunged from the teachings of the Church."

Brother Matteo suddenly began reciting the Nicene Creed in a slow, calm, soft voice, which seemed to carry a far wider distance than that between the two men, and seemed to be imbued with an unworldly essence.

"We believe in one God, the Father, the maker of heaven and earth, of all that is, seen and unseen. We believe in one Lord, Jesus Christ, the only Son of God, eternally begotten of the Father, God from God, Light from Light, true God from true God, begotten, not made, of one Being with the Father. Through him all things were made. For us and for our salvation he came down from heaven: By the power of the Holy Spirit he became incarnate from the Virgin Mary and was made man. For our sake, he was crucified under Pontius Pilate; he suffered death and was buried. On the third day, he rose again in accordance with the Scriptures; he ascended into heaven and is seated on the right hand of the Father. He will come again in glory to judge the living and the dead, and his kingdom will have no end. We believe in the Holy Spirit, the Lord, the giver of life, who proceeds from the Father and the Son. With the Father and the Son, he is worshiped and glorified. He has spoken through the Prophets. We believe in one holy catholic and apostolic Church. We acknowledge one baptism for the forgiveness of sins. We look for the resurrection of the dead and the life of the world to come. Amen."

"Brother, I cannot believe what you are telling me. Are you saying that what I have believed all these years is wrong, that the Church elders have tricked their flocks?"

Brother Matteo rose from the bench, lightly clasping Ludovico's arm, concern growing on his face. "Ludovico, you must understand that the early Church was like any other institution, trying to organize and structure itself into a unified whole to preserve the values for which it stood. The elders knew that having a Church of contrasting tenets within the body was a prescription for disaster. The Gnostic teachings were particularly troubling, for example, the belief that the "gnosis" could be gained without a leader, that each individual had within him or her the power to achieve it through self-knowledge. That kind of belief would exclude the need for leaders, priests, bishops and popes, to lead the Church."

Ludovico looked up at Brother Matteo, quietly absorbing what he had just heard. He rose and stepped away from Brother Matteo and then returned. "Brother, isn't the New Testament considered to be the word of God?"

"Yes, but in gathering the gospels together many other gospels were excluded, for example, the gospel of Thomas and the gospel of Philip that were so favored by the Gnostic sects. The Gnostics remained a force within the Church for several centuries but were then expunged from history along with the scriptures they admired. We only know of the Gnostic gospels from the attacks by the "apologists" for the Church. Portions of them are included in their books in order to refute them."

Wiping his brow, Brother Matteo turned to Ludovico and continued. "The New Testament scriptures as we know them were collected by St. Athanasius of Alexandria in 367 A.D. in one of his annual letters, becoming the first person to establish the 27 books of the New Testament. The Nicene Creed reflects those gospels but remember that it was the reigning church elders that decided what it meant to be a Christian, what to believe, and what was included in the Creed."

Darkness was falling over the cloisters, and the two men were clearly ready to end the conversation. "One other comment to consider, Ludovico. Is it necessary to believe in the Creed to be a Christian? After all, it is only theology developed by the first Church leaders. Read it carefully. It does not assist a person to lead a good life, does it? It is not like the philosophical teachings of say, Plato, to examine the meaning of a good life. Perhaps, it is better to look to the ethics of Christ, the way in which he led his life and interacted with others, that makes us worthy of Him and teaches us which practices we should follow."

The two men slid into the darkness, some early owls hooting into the darkening sky, one man more puzzled but more stimulated about his beliefs than when he entered the cloister in fading sunlight.

*****

"Gianni, walk with us outside the walls. Giorgio and I are hiking into the woods. The sky is as clear as a newfound truth, and the air is as fresh as a newfound love this morning. It is on days like this that you want to believe in a physical afterlife that will be eternal."

Gianni was eager to accompany the two men. In recent days, he had glimpsed an approaching event that appeared imminent, and he hoped that they would take him into their confidence.

"Gianni, why have you not committed to the Brotherhood?"

"Sir, I just do not have the dedication in my heart that Brother Matteo has."

Ludovico smiled slightly at this comment without expressing any emotion. He motioned to Gianni to follow him as the men walked to the entrance doors. There, Ludovico stopped to appreciate the carved figures on it. He always found them comforting and always wondered if anyone ever achieved the respite that they evoked.

"I have tried to find my future here but I am forever restless. Brother Matteo has been a kind teacher to me, but I have come to feel that my life would be better spent in some other pursuit away from the monastery, perhaps, learning some trade in the city. Brother Matteo's kind counsel has expanded my horizons beyond anything I could have expected before my arrival."

"Well, would you consider leaving the monastery with us and serving as our aide?" As Ludovico said these words, they entered a clearing and an eagle left a high tree branch. All three men raised their heads to view this majestic creature soaring into the sky.

"Yes, I would like to accompany you. But I would like to tell Brother Matteo myself."

"Of course, of course. Remember, this conversation is for Brother Matteo's ears only. Do not say anything to him yet. I will tell you at the appropriate time. And do not mention this conversation to anyone in the monastery. You could put us all in jeopardy if it became public knowledge."

"Sir, there is one question I would like to ask you about the finances of the monastery."

"Please, go on."

"You have no doubt noticed the deteriorating physical state of the monastery. Abbot Garganega has asked me to investigate the noticeable drop in the income that the monastery is receiving from its rental properties. I have examined the monastery's books as best I can and can verify Abbot Garganega's observation. I thought to go to several of the properties and speak to the tenants."

"Who collects the rental money," Ludovico asked, "and how does it find its way to the monastery."

Just as Ludovico asked the question, a deer darted from the wooded area in the distance, trailed by two fawn, all hopping across the clearing in an apparent playful mood. The men stopped to gaze at them with a small degree of admiration and envy.

"There must be an agent who collects the money, either some brother or some trusted individual outside of the monastic community," Giorgio said, "but who accepts the money here?"

"He would be Prior Aurelio," Gianni said.

"Ah," both Ludovico and Giorgio intoned at the same time. "Now it becomes a little clearer."

"Giorgio, do you want to accompany Gianni on his trip to question these renters? But let's be careful how we describe our visit." In an unusual sarcastic voice, Ludovico went on. "We do not know which of these renters may be collaborating with our kind Brother Aurelio or even if they are collaborating."

"Gianni, let Giorgio and me return to the monastery alone. I have something to discuss with him."

\*\*\*\*\*

"Perhaps it is time for us to return to Milan, Giorgio. There is a hint of sweetness in the air like Pinot Grigio ripening on the vine. That is always a good omen and, if nothing else, makes for a good harvest but let's hope that it presages a successful return to Milan. Has Giulio reported back to you?"

"Yes, he's said that he is being especially cautious about his assignment but that he is near completing it. He has found several people to approach concerning Cicco Simonetta. If all goes as he expects, it should be completed in a few weeks. He has also employed a group of mercenaries to augment our own forces."

"I dislike mercenaries. They cannot be trusted. They are almost as likely to plunder you as they are your enemies. If they are in danger of defeat, they turn on you, and if they are victorious, the only reason they do not plunder you is that they plunder your defeated enemy. There are many examples of a principality being worst off with mercenaries than without. One could argue that one of the major reasons for the collapse of the Roman Empire was their increasing reliance on the Goths as mercenaries. Enough of my pessimistic babble. Our own troops will outnumber those in the castle, so we should not have a problem. Keep them in the dark as long as you can. We do not want to give one of them the opportunity to betray us."

"Giulio is a good and loyal man and has exceptional perception in these matters," said Giorgio, brushing his blond hair from his eyes and looking at the eagle returning to its nest, its chicks' meal in its beak.

"Good, good, we must go to Florence to shore up our relationship with Lorenzo. We will need the Medici to support us, if not publicly, at least privately. We have to be careful when we are out of range of the monastery. No one who knows us must be aware of our departure. But first, you must go with Gianni to collect information about this rental income issue. It is very suspicious. Perhaps we should also examine other monasteries as well to determine their state of affairs. This, however, is trickier and, we can postpone that search. In any case, disguise yourself as a brother when you are with Gianni. When you return, we will make plans for Florence. You know, Brother Aurelio is the half-brother of Cardinal Bonvino, so it could be a very delicate affair."

"We will leave tomorrow under darkness," said Giorgio, eager to be involved in some activity for his friend and acknowledging his instructions. "It will be good experience for Gianni. You and I can already anticipate the result, can't we. The only question is what happens to the money when it reaches the monastery."

With that the two men returned to the trail that led to the monastery, enjoying the fragrant air peppered with the pleasant chirping of warblers and the mellifluous cooing of doves, fully engaged in their sense of commitment to the future.

*****

On their first night on the road, the sky was as dark as pitch tar with a half-moon hidden behind invisible clouds. Giorgio and Gianni left the market town of Imola the day before, gathering vital information about the scheme that someone, as yet unknown, was perpetrating on farmers renting monastery property, information that exposed the essential nature of the scheme.

Giorgio was engrossed in his own thoughts as the two men rode along hurriedly on the road the following morning, both men eager to arrive at the monastery as soon as possible. In front of them, they were confronted by four horsemen, swords drawn threateningly. Giorgio stopped abruptly. Gianni, startled and still not comfortable on a horse, warbled to a stop; he had neither sword nor dagger to draw. Both men believed they were being accosted by brigands since this area was known to have such men roaming about harassing travelers, probably unemployed French mercenaries and, therefore, to be taken seriously. As the horsemen drew closer, Giorgio did not need to talk to these men to know that he and Gianni were in danger, and his reaction to danger was always to respond first. Quickly, without thought, he sliced one rider with his sword, dismounting him in pain. As the now fallen rider rolled over the ground in agony, Giorgio lunged at one of the other riders, missing him, nearly taking a blow himself.

"Ride, Gianni, ride," he shouted as he struck his horse forcefully. "Follow me."

Both men took off, followed by the brigands who would not take their assignment so lightly and abandon it so quickly. Gianni, however, not being accustomed to riding, let alone riding at a gallop, swayed on his saddle like a ship tossed about on an ocean gale. Giorgio, realizing that Gianni was likely to be separated from his horse at any moment headed into the forest, stopped to collect Gianni and proceeded on. Neither man could ride at the pace they had being riding on the road but neither could the brigands. At a point where the forest grew thicker and where they had put some distance between them and the brigands, Giorgio jumped from his horse as he indicated to Gianni to proceed on, released his horse and scampered up a tree. Noticing that the brigands had become separated, Giorgio waited for one to pass under him.

In the distance, Giorgio heard one brigand shout, "I've got one of them." At that moment, another rider approached, giving Giorgio the opportunity to unmount him. In an instant Giorgio was on the rider with dagger in hand and with one swift thrust sent him to the ground dead. Giorgio heard some rustling in the area where Gianni had apparently been captured. Walking gently to the sound, Giorgio assessed the situation, knowing that at least two brigands were with Gianni. To Giorgio it seemed like the birds had stopped singing and the crickets had stopped chirping, as his anxiety rose and concern for Gianni mounted. He was already regretting allowing Gianni to travel with him. Once within eyesight, he followed the men out of the forest onto the road where they gathered their injured companion.

Fortunately, Giorgio's horse made its way out of the forest to the road also, allowing Giorgio to follow Gianni and the brigands at a safe distance. It did not take long for the men to stop at a house some way off the road sheltered within an ancient olive tree grove. To Giorgio, the gnarled trees seemed a fitting metaphor for the situation in which he found himself. Crawling up to the house, he waited until an opportunity presented itself to rescue Gianni. He was not prepared to leave him without an effort.

Giorgio realized that the injured brigand would not present a danger to him because he could see that he was incapable of rising from the cot in which he lay. His wounds were unwrapped, and it was not likely that he would survive more than a few days without attention. Surveying the surrounding area, he noticed a well about 100 feet from the house near a row of old, large olive trees, good cover if someone were in need of drawing water. I can easily lay in wait near the well and surprise the person who comes for water, he told himself. If I am unsuccessful I can retreat into the grove. But these men are not brigands, else they would not have taken Gianni with them. They would have simply robbed him and left or killed him. I would like to hear what they are saying to Gianni but I cannot risk it.

Hours later, night had arrived and Giorgio, still crouched behind a tree, heard someone approaching. The time was perfect for a stealth attack as the moon was still hidden by clouds. As soon as the brigand reached the well and his back was towards him, he sprung on him with his dagger, piercing his chest three times, blood gushing from his chest, some emptying into the well. The man fell forward with the upper part of his torso resting over the wall of the well. Giorgio now crept towards the house slowly, reaching one of the windows. He felt invigorated. This was not the first time he had killed a human, but he was a realist, knowing that actions of this sort were sometimes necessary. In his life, order was more often produced by violence than by mercy.

He knew that at some point the man inside the house would grew curious about his companion and leave it or, at least, open the door to gaze out. Giorgio decided the best approach was to stand by the door until it was opened and, then, accost him. When that time came, Giorgio grabbed the man but did not foresee his strength. Giorgio was thrown down hard and stabbed on his arm as the two men grabbled on the ground, each trying to gain the advantage over the other. Giorgio knew that he would be unable to sustain his effort much longer before he was overwhelmed. Suddenly, the man rolled off of Giorgio and lay unconscious next to him. Standing over him was Gianni holding a truncheon, his face swollen and red from the beating he had taken.

"Gianni, these men were after something other than money. I believe there is a connection between our visits to the farms and this attack." With that, they both climbed on Giorgio's horse and sauntered off to the monastery.

*****

On their arrival in the dark of night, they waited outside the monastery walls where they tucked themselves into a small clearing surrounded by several wide-spanning poplar trees until the monastery doors would open in the morning. Their trip had been successful, and they were eager to relate their findings to Ludovico. While resting by a tree content with themselves, they ate some crusted bread with Bel Paese cheese they had purchased at a farm along the route. The food was a perfect complement to the bottle of local red wine made with an unusual blend of Barbera and Dolcetto grapes, according to the farmer who sold it to them.

Giorgio turned to Gianni while holding his cup of wine and briefly seemed in a trance. "Simple pleasures make a man whole," he said. "One can lose himself in the world's chaos. It's only simple pleasures that return him to himself. This is what God intended, not the chaos we see and experience around us. If you believe in God or some other Deity, the Almighty made the world out of chaos. Why, then, would the Deity let the world revert to the chaos whence it came?"

"Gianni, you will enter the world very shortly, and you will be astounded at the people you meet, the events you attend, the creative energies, paintings, statutes that will inspire you. But remember, they are but a small respite from the chaos that surrounds them. Each person, each event, each painting, each statute has its own whirl of chaos, hidden or unhidden."

Giorgio turned from Gianni, raised his head to the sky for a brief second, then peered intently at Gianni. "Gianni, life is short, death is sure," he said.

In the morning, they awoke to the singing of warblers, both men spirited from the refreshing sleep they had. Looking to the sky, Giorgio saw clouds floating by to reveal a bright blue sky. "Gianni, I know this sounds obvious, but I take this to be a good omen."

On meeting with Ludovico in the monastery, Giorgio allowed Gianni to convey their findings about the farms. Nino, who rented a farm quite some distance from the monastery, had a newly arranged agreement, about three years ago, that required a fixed payment in bushels of wheat. He was compensated in cash at a price that the agent determined, supposedly based on the market value.

Nino was suspicious that he was being underpaid but could not prove it because he did not have access to a market price, being so distant from a market town. He had heard, however, that wheat was in short supply, especially down south in Tuscany, and suspected that wheat prices had increased in the last several years. Through his wife's cousin who lived with him several weeks, he learned that the weather had not been kind to Tuscan farmers for several years.

At Enrico's farm, an equally distant farm from the monastery, they heard the same story. With this information, Giorgio decided to check wheat prices in two market towns that they purposely passed through on their return and discovered, not surprisingly, that market prices were higher than the price that the farmers were receiving. Equally interesting, Giorgio and Gianni had discovered in one market town that the monastery's agent, a man called Julio, had been negotiating with the buyer as a monopolist. He controlled most of the wheat available in the two adjacent counties.

Ludovico smiled at both men. "So, Julio is skimming from the renters as well as inflating prices at the market. But is the money going to Brother Aurelio? Check on whether this man, Julio, has a connection with Brother Aurelio. If he does, as I'm certain we all suspect, we can also assume where the money goes after leaving Brother Aurelio. Straight on to Pope Sixtus or to some account which he controls. But why all this subterfuge? Pope Sixtus must have some ulterior motive in mind."

"Gianni, I agree that these brigands who accosted you have something to do with the mystery of the farms from the questions you were asked, probably employed by the person who is organizing this plot. They obviously wanted to know who sent you and were willing to play rough. We have to follow up on these leads and most definitely have to discover if Brother Aurelio is involved. He is the key. If he is involved, perhaps he can lead us to the Pope."

*****

Ludovico, Giorgio, and Gianni were on their way to Florence in a manner that bespoke their humble conditions at the moment. Gianni was quite happy riding along with the two men, not knowing the circumstances in which the two men had traveled to Florence years earlier in the entourage of the Duke of Milan, Ludovico's brother, Galeazzo. On that trip, the entourage consisted of Galeazzo and his wife, Bianca, his children, including his daughter by another woman, Caterina, in addition to Ludovico and Giorgio, a hundred armed guards in full armament and the sundry attendants needed to travel in style and comfort, the women traveling in covered coaches. When near the city, they stopped in camp so as to garb themselves in the latest brocaded garments that were the current fashion, all to impress Lorenzo di Medici and the Florentines who were renowned for their appreciation of fine clothing and pageantry. Bianca wore an ermine-lined mantle over her crimson-colored and embroidered dress. Her horse and Galeazzo's horse were caparisoned in a gold colored cloth with brocaded hems and precious stones. They meant to project a majestic entrance.

"Gianni, when last we were here with my brother and Bona, Lorenzo gave us a magnificent entrance to the city. We were greeted at the gate with musicians playing such sweet music. Jugglers entertained the many Florentines lining the streets as we moved towards the palace. A stage was built in Piazza della Republica for the enactment of religious plays and Lorenzo, himself, recited some of his poems to us in his home. He is a quite good poet, a facility of which few people know except his close humanist friends. This, of course, will be a quit different entrance for us."

This trip, devoid of the fine clothing and pageantry, had a different purpose in mind; to consult with Lorenzo and obtain his support to the idea of Ludovico wresting the Regency from Bona. Although Lorenzo's support was not a necessary condition for this move, Lorenzo would add a large degree of credence to the attempt; it would provide a patina of legitimacy to Ludovico's action. Florence, particularly the Medici, was respected throughout the Italian Peninsular. It would be a delicate negotiation. He felt just as strongly as he did before his previous failed attempt to replace Bona, that he was the most appropriate person to guide Milan under the guise of the Regency. He was his father's son and the blood of quick, decisive action ran through his veins like rapids over a waterfall.

The men were enjoying the fine June day, lazily riding along as the birds mimicked them and rested lazily along the limbs of trees, occasionally abandoning their places only to remember to return in a few brief seconds. Along the road, Spring painted the fields with green. Ludovico turned to Giorgio and motioned him closer. "The peace that my father and Lorenzo's grandfather put together at Lodi has held for the most part all these years and has kept foreign intruders out. This is the point we must make to Lorenzo. He and I have the legacy of our forbearers, a legacy that extends from them to us. I am more capable and, need I say, more trustworthy, of maintaining that legacy than is Bona who has French ancestry."

"All true, but will the Pope agree? Will he pressure Lorenzo," Giorgio responded?

"I think not. Lorenzo must still remember the Pazzi and the Pope's implication in the plot. That was not an incident that is easily forgotten. The Medici are long on culture and hospitality, but they are also as long in memory as a saint's suffering. Both last for centuries."

Gianni always listened intensely to Ludovico's and Giorgio's conversations. He was still awakening from years of Brother Matteo's tutoring that was long on theoretical knowledge but short on the practical application to life and, his new education was proceeding quite swiftly since his association with the two men. He could not remember ever talking in the ways that Ludovico and Giorgio spoke about matters nor ever previously hearing anyone talk in that way. It was still beyond him to conduct a conversation that considered the consequences of this or that decision. It was like another language to him, but he thoroughly delighted in the realization that they could affect their own lives and envied the ease in which they could participate in those outcomes. His was a naiveté that not only developed from unwonted innocence but also from a truly pure heart, both attributes that were sorely missing in the associations of his day.

"I get a feeling that we are being watched, an unease that has gripped me for some time," Gianni said, as he eased closer to his companions. "I don't know how to describe it, but it is an unsettling feeling."

Ludovico and Giorgio had not paid much attention to their surroundings. It was partly from the constant discussions they were having, partly from the lack of concern for potential danger, and partly from their generally casual attitude on most topics that were not immediate. Only the beauty of the dulcet tones of the birds' singing or an occasional deer crossing their path aroused them from their discussions. Looking at Giorgio, Ludovico said, "Ah, Giorgio, we must both open our eyes and ears wider to take in Gianni's suspicions." And then, with a little smile on his face and a twinkle in his eyes addressed Gianni. "After all, he is our saintly companion and has the saintly presence with him."

After dinner of roasted sausage with grapes in a red wine sauce at the Inn of Four Corners, they sat at their table finishing a fine carafe of local wine, a Sangiovese, that had a soft, smooth, long finish to it with overtones of cherry and a bit of blackberry. It was an unexpected and delightful surprise finding such an enjoyable wine in this somewhat shabby roadside inn but did produce the desirous effect of easing their muscles from the long day's journey. Giorgio, with more wine than he was accustomed to imbibing, was finding the female server much to his liking and was not above playfully patting her behind and intoning his admiration of her as she passed their table from time to time. She did not seem displeased with his attention nor was she above establishing a repartee with him. Gianni, having enjoyed more wine than he had ever had previously, was wide-eyed with admiration of Giorgio's confident advances and impressed with his newly discovered interest in the server, any server. He had seen attractive girls before but never in this kind of setting and never after drinking a half carafe of wine. He was besotted with puppy love, the first of his life. Brother Matteo would probably have said, "Gianni, how tempting are the ways of the flesh," all the while smiling gently and understandably at him.

Ludovico was shortly to put a stop to this happy evening for Giorgio and Gianni. He was growing concerned that their behavior was soon to jeopardize their principal reason for staying at this inn, to pass through this territory with as little notice as possible. They were in danger of exposing themselves. He could not allow this trip to fall into an excursion of futility.

"Enough Giorgio. You also, Gianni," he said quietly, shaking Gianni who had already placed his head on the table and fallen asleep. "We have much to accomplish tomorrow," but no one heard him.

He had never felt this way before. He and Giorgio had often pleasured themselves with an evening of wine and frolicked with all sorts of women. He wondered if he was becoming a bit prudish or was he just so concerned about the success of this mission. A failure to remove Bona this time would surely mean death to him.

Ever since Gianni mentioned his fear of being tracked earlier in the day, Ludovico had taken on a more concerned and conscientious attitude, careful to be aware of his surroundings and the people who inhabited it. He was often given to inattention in his personal life but never when it concerned state affairs. The room was crowded with diners, some huddled together in serious conversation, others talking with their tablemates with wide sweeps of their arms, some more raucous than others. Ludovico, however, could not but notice two diners sitting silently at a table in the corner under a mounted boar's head, a carafe of wine between them. They were rugged looking men with deeply furrowed faces and small deep-set eyes but unlike the farmers who made up most of the other men in the room. Isn't it odd, he thought to himself, I was concerned about Giorgio's behavior arousing attention, when, in fact, it is the quiet diners who are more noticeable here. The aberration always stands out, in life as well as science. As he passed the men's table struggling to lead Giorgio and Gianni up to their rooms, he glanced at the strangers. From a distance, he had not been aroused with anxiety but close to these men his suspicions rose like a hawk on an updraft of wind. He now felt fear hanging over him, and it was as tangible as the wine in his belly. Tomorrow, we must determine if we are really being followed, he thought.

Rousing Giorgio and Gianni from their bed in the morning proved just as difficult to Ludovico as placing them in bed the night before. Sleep makes babies of us all, he thought, as he shook them until they were at least mildly awake. Ludovico thought it more prudent for everyone to be in the same room, given the ever-increasing feeling of danger to

73

them. While they occupied his bed, he rested on a small couch, half-awake most of the night, considering alternatives for the next day. He woke the men early, before daylight, ready to leave without provoking suspicion.

Once awake, Giorgio bounded about with the energy and enthusiasm of a chirping bird in the morning, ready to continue the trip, ready to pursuit their adventure, ready to follow the sun. For him, this experience, as were other experiences with Ludovico, was as much about the adventure as it was about the politics of the situation. He had not recovered his senses sufficiently to remember the potential danger that they might have uncovered the night before and could potentially await them on the road today. Yet, he understood the importance of this trip as well as did Ludovico and was completely recovered from his previous night's binge as soon as Ludovico addressed him. "Giorgio, I noticed two men in the dining room last night who looked suspicious to me."

Giorgio's eyes grew wider, intense interest showing in them. He moved from the bed where he was siting to the table where Ludovico was, placing an arm on the back of one of the chairs. "How can we examine them? Might the innkeeper have some knowledge of them?"

"No, no, that is too risky," Ludovico said, "I'm thinking that Gianni and I continue along while you trail behind at some distance off the road. Perhaps, you can glimpse if any men are following us. But do not attack them alone. Catch up with us, and we will deal with them together, if need be."

As this conversation was proceeding, Gianni rose from the bed, looking embarrassed. He felt foolish in the eyes of the two men. They, on the other hand, only mildly acknowledged him with a quick nod of the head. At another time, they would have joshed with him about his conduct of the previous night, maybe, even embellishing it. Now, they had more serious concerns. Ludovico indicated to Gianni to sit at the table and explained the plan to him.

When they exited the inn, dawn was just emerging from its nightly sleep. The men traveled about a mile, their casual behavior returning to them along the way, Gianni now receiving the mild ribbing that was denied him at the inn and relishing it immensely. He recognized the camaraderie that was developing, a feeling he had never experienced in his life and it brought a wide, hopeful smile to his face.

"Certitude of action relieves a good deal of anxiety, doesn't it," Giorgio said to no one in particular, the reins of his horse in his hands as he turned him to enter the woods running alongside the road. "I will see you both later."

Ludovico and Gianni continued on, Gianni surprising himself that he was not more nervous than he was. He concluded that these two men not only brought fellowship but also a confidence that was inborn, that was as easy to them as it was to a hawk or eagle pursuing its prey.

They stopped at noon to relax and enjoy lunch off to the side of the road under a very large plane tree. "We cannot linger long. We do not know how much time we might have."

After a few moments, Ludovico said, "How often has this tree offered shade from the sun to travelers passing by it, and does it get any thanks, any appreciation...no, people just take the tree's kind offering of shade and ignore the tree. What can we leave for it?"

Gianni looked puzzled but thought he understood Ludovico's question. He was certainly not used to considering the feelings of a tree. "Sir, the tree has seemingly been very comfortable providing shade for all these many years and seems to enjoy its largess, after all, it would not have grown so large and wide if it felt unappreciated. Maybe we could leave something for the next traveler to sit here, something like a note from the tree wishing the traveler god speed. The tree would certainly like to have the next traveler recognize its contribution to the traveler's journey, and I'm sure the tree would appreciate the recognition."

"Very good, Gianni. Now, what should the note say?"

"What would a tree say, if it were alive," said Gianni immediately, feeling both amused and provoked by the situation in which he found himself, a feeling that lasted but a few seconds.

"Ah, Gianni, but the tree is alive, that's why it might have something to say, it is just not human," now tearing a piece of bread that the men had acquired at the inn before they departed?

Gianni sat dumbfounded. "Is the tree male or female?" inquired Gianni, taking the bread handed to him by Ludovico.

"Good question. I think female," Ludovico said. "A man would not spend several hundred years caring for passing travelers. He would be too selfish of his own time. And do not the branches of this tree resemble the outstretched arms of a woman caring for, perhaps, her child or someone close to her? Yes, a female I think."

Gianni was amazed. Here was a man concerned about their safety only several hours earlier, now questioning him on the language of a tree. "Something simple, probably. After all, no one could believe that a tree was very loquacious."

"Yes, yes, something simple."

This was the first occasion Gianni saw Ludovico puzzled. He had only seen him in command previously. "What if the tree wrote," 'I offer you my shade, the most valuable thing I can give you, gathered from two hundred years of earnest effort; savor it with my complements. Cordially, The Tree.'

"Perfect." With that Ludovico gathered his pouch and walked to his horse, stopping momentarily to glance back at the tree. "Let's go, Gianni."

They were not to advance very far before they noticed Giorgio standing by his horse in front of them. He gave a short wave of his arm once he recognized them and walked to them. "Morning."

"What have you to report?" Ludovico said as he dismounted and led his horse to the side of the road.

"Well, two men are following you," Giorgio said, as he unbuttoned his brownish colored doublet to relieve himself from the oppressive heat. June was the first of the summer months, and it was living up to its reputation. The field beyond the trees lay before the men like a blanket of green, waves of heat seemingly emanating from the blades of grass. "By your description, they are the men you noticed in the inn last evening. They are not very far behind now. The only way to discover if they have a mission concerning us will be to question them or to follow them ourselves."

Ludovico looked out into the field, the sun nearly directly overhead. Shielding his eyes, he said, "No, we do not want to follow them. Our primary goal is to get to Florence. We do not want to waste time following them. Let's move on until we discover a place where we can confront them. Perhaps, a little persuasion will open their mouths."

Several miles ahead they came across a place that met their expectations. The idea was for Ludovico to act as if he was relaxing by the side of the road. Giorgio would lay hidden behind the men, and Gianni would enter any fray only if needed.

When the men approached Ludovico, they appeared somewhat startled. They approached Ludovico and stopped before him, both men trying to seem relaxed in their saddle. Ludovico immediately recognized them as the men he saw at the inn the previous evening. One man inquired about Ludovico's condition as the second man dismounted and slowly approached him. "Good morning, you look familiar," he said in an innocent tone but without conviction it seemed to Ludovico. "Did you not stay at the Inn of Four Corners last night? I believe we saw you in the dining room."

"Yes, I was there."

"Did you not have two companions with you? They seemed to be having a good time."

"Yes, I did. They have gone ahead to reach Florence before me to tell our host I will be tardy. My horse is a bit lame, and I want to pamper him."

"Ah, Florence is your destination," each man approaching in an unconvincing but not yet threatening manner. They were attempting conviviality, but they obviously had little experience in social situations. It was not simply the frayed pants' bottoms and jacket cuffs; hard working, god-fearing farmers often appeared in similar clothing. No, it was the harshness of their faces, the deep furrows combined with an unbecoming awkwardness, an awkwardness not arising from innocence but an awkwardness arising from a deep-seated inner unbalance bordering on maliciousness.

Ludovico suddenly did not want to be caught siting. He wanted the freedom of his legs. Rising from his place, he said to the men. "I must go now. I do not want to be on the road when evening approaches." But he could see that the men were not going to allow him to pass. One grabbed the reins of Ludovico's horse and pulled it to him. The other man whose face had turned to hatred in an instant rushed Ludovico with a knife suddenly unsheathed. Then the second man also rushed Ludovico with a knife.

Ludovico quickly fled behind a giant boulder situated about 30 feet from him, a field opening behind it, sword drawn. He could now see Giorgio running towards him. Recognizing that they were now outnumbered, the men ran toward their horses which were now being scattered by Gianni. Awkward as these men were, they were not the kind of men whose first impulse was to surrender when directly confronted. Without their horses their only alternative was to face Ludovico and this they did with swords drawn and with their inner maliciousness overt. They held a strength advantage over Ludovico and Giorgio, but the latter two had the finesse that came with hours of instruction and practice in fencing.

Giorgio was always a better swordsman than Ludovico and quickly placed his opponent in peril, forcing him backwards on his heels, yet the attacker's strength almost compensated for his lack of skill. Both men fought ferociously, each man having his moments. Giorgio's usual good nature now suddenly turned to heated anger, an anger that matched the attacker's maliciousness. At this point the attacker realized that his strength would not prevail in this contest, turned to run but had nowhere to go without his horse. His escape exit was preempted by Gianni. With instant recognition Giorgio sliced through the attacker's arm with such force that he severed it above his elbow. Blood gushed onto the ground like a mountain spring releasing its water, as the attacker stood stunned and rigid momentarily, a white haze clouding his eyes before Giorgio's final blow, a thrust to his stomach that exited from his back, the sound of cracking ribs filling the air and competing with the chatter of the disturbed birds reviewing the fight from tree limbs.

Meanwhile, Ludovico was battling the second attacker and was holding him at bay until Giorgio could assist him. The attacker now faced the two men alone and accepted the futility of further effort, dropped his sword and waited to be told what to do. Once restrained, he was placed on his horse and led away by the three men.

After some time, Ludovico said, "This seems to be a good place to stop and interrogate our guess. We are out of the way, and he should have some interesting information."

Giorgio smiled slightly, his anger still not dissipated completely. He was never one to release it easily and was often criticized by Ludovico for his relentlessness.

"It hinders your intuition," he would tell him frequently, but Ludovico also knew that a less angry Giorgio would be a less relentless Giorgio.

"Yes, I also want to hear what our man has to say."

The attacker was at first reluctant to divulge any information and was enraged about his capture, but it did not take him long to know that these men were not ones with whom to be coy. His gruff and recalcitrant behavior was soon replaced by a more genial compliance after his head was placed in a loose noose wrapped around a strong tree limb.

"Why do we have any reason to keep you alive?" asked Giorgio, holding the reins of the horse on which the man sat. The captured man knew that Giorgio was not one to be ignored.

Gianni looked on perplexed and anxious, shaking nervously and twitching uncontrollably. He had seen lambs slaughtered on the farm and was unshaken by it, but this was a higher order of slaughter, one he was afraid would leave him scared forever, one that might challenge his faith in humans, a holdover from his monastery days. Yet, he could not turn from the scene; he was mesmerized by it. His fear slowly abated as he watched Giorgio and Ludovico act on the attacker. After each unanswered question, Giorgio would tighten the noose ever so slightly, enough to permit the attacker to be aware that each move portended a shortened life.

"We have a very reluctant guess, do we not," Giorgio remarked, brushing his hair from his eyes. "It is a shame that your employer will never know how brave you were. But the worms that eat your body will. They, no doubt, will gain strength from your entrails and live another day. But you, my friend, will not."

Gianni attempted to interrupt Giorgio with some comment but received a deep, forbidding stare from him. Gianni could only retreat and watch the remainder of the scene, however it played out.

Finally, the noose was tightened sufficiently that the attacker was gasping for breath and wriggling on the horse in an attempt to squeeze another breath of air into his lungs.

"If you want to live, you best control yourself or my horse may get away from me, and your life will end without any purpose," Giorgio said in a voice full of contempt.

The attacker, after several moments of fighting for each breath, gave up the principal piece of information that Ludovico desired, the name of the person who had sent him. Giorgio and Gianni's visit to the wheat markets in the two towns they had visited on their journey had aroused notice. It had eventually reached a man who was called Alphonso, and it was he who hired the attackers. They were meant to follow Giorgio and learn his destination. He had been followed since his return to the monastery. Initially, there were three men in the group, one of whom had already reported to Alphonso. Alphonso was the agent who handled the collection of rents for the monastery of San Gelsera.

Sitting away from the attacker, who had been tied to a tree nearby, Ludovico said, "So, it seems that someone in the monastery is involved. It does not seem likely that this Alphonso was simply skimming money from the monastery. And that person has to be Brother Aurelio or, at least, he is the prime suspect. He controls the accounts."

Once they were relaxed, Giorgio brought out a bottle of a red Dolchetto that he had picked up along the way. They passed the bottle around. After a few swigs, Ludovico looked at Gianni sitting quietly plopped up against a tree. "This was an unusual day for you, was it not."

"Yes sir, it was."

"You appeared bothered by our activities today. What bothered you? Was it the suffering that we put our brigand to? Do you not see the benefits of what happened today?"

"All I saw today was a man in agony, fighting for his life, a life given to him by God Almighty."

"Ah, God Almighty. That Supreme Being. Personally, I believe more in his mother than I do in him. But consider this, Gianni. Consider a territory rife with disorder, with savage killings and other terrible acts perpetrated on the population. What would be a more appropriate outcome to you, let the situation continue with all the horror that it entails to appease your conscience or to find a strongman who can end the horror even if it takes actions that might be unsavory? Who would your Almighty God reward? Would not more lives be saved in the latter contingency?" Isn't a stable community more rewarding to the people than one of unknown danger and caprice? Which community would you prefer to live in?"

Giorgio stood by amused. He was the man to enforce the presumed code of conduct, and he sided with Ludovico with obvious relish.

Gianni looked befuddled. But before he could offer a rebuttal, Ludovico continued.

"I have offered you an extreme example, one that is more weighted, perhaps, on my side. Today was not an obvious choice, but we do not always have time on our side. Decisions often have to be made in haste, without the long consideration that your side would encourage. I believe that what we are attempting to do is to the advantage of our people and that drastic methods are appropriate. Let there be no doubt. I would have disposed of this man today, if I had not obtained the information I wanted. I will release him in a few days because I don't believe that he can cause us anymore harm."

"Ludovico, Christ preached that the way to Him in heaven is to exhibit humility, to love our enemies. The meek shall inherit the earth, he said often." Gianni looked earnestly at Ludovico but could not discern any change in his appearance.

"Yes, Gianni, the scriptures and the Church do instill a conception of humility and meekness to its faithful. These behaviors are preached to be the way to eternal salvation. People are willing to endure the loss of their freedom and the degradations of life. Enter any church and what does one see, paintings of saints meekly being subjected to cruel punishments, bodies being pierced by arrows like St. Steven, or hung on a cross like St. Peter, Christ enduring his crucifixion. This Christianity celebrates and exalts only the afterlife. The ancients, the Romans and the Greeks, had a different conception. They celebrated men of great deeds in this life, men who exhibited honor, men like Achilles, Odysseus and Hector. These men were more likely to fight for freedom than the men of our day, and religion plays a role in creating that distinction."

"But still, Ludovico, is it not better to lead a good life free from the kind of behaviors you describe? Would not God be more likely to award the person with everlasting life in heaven?"

"Would he? Consider the early Christian sects that we have spoken about from time to time, the Gnostics, for example, or other Christian sects. The Church was no longer interested in simply writing polemics against them as it did in the early Christian period. No, the Church initiated an inquisition against heretics. It was called the 'Great Heresy', especially against the Cathars, whose believes were similar to the Gnostics and whose faithful were pursued throughout southern France and Italy for hundreds of years and nearly completely exterminated. It was started by Pope Innocent III in 1200 who sanctioned the auto de fe against them. The policy was followed by succeeding Popes. It was justified in the name of God; the Church was doing God's work."

Gianni sat stone-faced, unable to counter Ludovico's argument. He had had discussions with Brother Matteo before on religious topics but the discussion never had gotten so heated. Before he could respond, Ludovico continued in a calmer manner, looking at Gianni softly, "Gianni, I apologize. The people of these sects lived simple lives; what many people would consider godlike lives, quiet, dedicated religious lives. Were the Popes' behavior likely to represent what Christ wanted? The heretics were burned at the stake for professing doctrines that ran counter to the doctrines of the Church but their lives followed Christ's proclamations." Then holding Gianni's attention with a gentle smile, Ludovico said, "Their lives were ended with no great gain for the Church, no one was saved on this earth for this policy of the Church."

With evening approaching, the three men continued their journey along the Via Emilia, a major route on the way to Florence. Mid-morning the following day, as the men paused for a rest, all thoughts of the previous day slowly ebbing from their minds, an entourage traveling in the opposite direction greeted them. The leader of the entourage, a kindly-looking elderly man with soft features and long shoulder-length hair gently approached them. "Good morning, sir, addressing all three of the men, is there any assistance we can provide you?"

Given what had happened to the three the previous day, each man was reluctant to respond, even though the entourage seemed innocent enough. After a brief hesitancy, Ludovico stood to greet the leader, proffering a more appropriate and approachable demeanor. "No sir, but can we offer assistance to you?"

"No, thank you. Do you travel in God's graces, good sir? We come from a site that has witnessed a miracle from the Mother of Christ."

"Oh, of what miracle do you speak? We are unaware of such a miracle."

The leader held his hands together in a gesture of peace. "We are coming from Piratello, near Imola, where several years ago the Virgin spoke to a pilgrim on his way to the Marian shrine in Lareto. This pilgrim stopped at every shrine along the Via Emilia to offer a lit candle to the Virgin. At Piratello his candle fell from the small rough shrine of the Madonna and Child. When he lifted it to replace it on the shrine, the candle relit by itself. The pilgrim then heard the Virgin speak, 'I am the Immaculate Virgin Mary.' He fell to his knees in awe and asked her what he could do to serve her. She ordered him to go to the next town and order the people to build a shrine to her in Piratello." 'If they do not believe you, show them this.' His cape immediately filled with roses. This in a time of severe cold weather."

"That is quite a story. And you believe that this is not a fraud?" Ludovico said, looking at Gianni for some kind of acceptance.

"No, no, no fraud, no fraud. It is a small, simple shrine and the one to replace it is only a little larger, but there is hope of building a church there one day to celebrate the Virgin in her full glory."

As the group of pilgrims walked away down the road, Ludovico, who seemed genuinely interested, turned to Gianni, ignoring Giorgio because he knew what Giorgio's typical response would be. Ludovico always was perplexed that as alike as he and Giorgio were in most matters temporal, raised together with the same values and same experiences, they were opposites in matters spiritual. "Gianni, what did you think of these people? Do you find their story realistic?"

"They certainly appear honest. I do believe that they believe. I've seen many people like this at the monastery, those who make the pilgrimage to honor San Gelsera's relics. And they are moved by their experience, some are moved with the greatest of passion. Am I to say that they are simple minded. No, many are quite intelligent and quite lucid. Am I to say that they are gullible, tricked by the history of the relic. No, the church sanctifies the relics and often profits in their preservation. Am I to say that they are poor and destitute, looking only for a small sign that their life will be better in the afterlife. I say, why should they not snatch a few brief minutes of spiritual bliss from the relic, some hope to sustain them through their dreary life, their hunger, their thirst until the end overtakes them, until the dust of their body floats away over the trees, over the mountains, over the seas to rest until God finally gives them true rest. I will say this, Ludovico, I have more faith in the original purveyors of these miracles than those who come afterward, especially our bishops. Brother Matteo and I have often discussed this topic and at times like this I miss his understanding council."

To Gianni, Ludovico said, obviously impressed with his reply, "Well done, Gianni. You may make a true believer of me. My religiosity does not go quite that far." Then turning to Giorgio, he said laughingly, "Well, Giorgio, what have you to offer to the conversation. Do you agree with Gianni? What salves do you take to ease your dreary life?"

"Me....a bottle of the finest Brunello to sate my thirst, a good, well-rounded woman to give me warmth at night, and a clean, sharp sword to make it all possible."

"Let us move on," then looking at the sky for a brief moment, Ludovico said, "before the evening closes in on us."

As Ludovico ambled on, he commented leisurely, "We should arrive in Florence in a couple of days, just in time to celebrate St. John the Baptist Day on June 24, the patron saint of the city. Gianni, it is a very festive day. Everyone enjoys it, the nobles, the aristocrats, the public, even the priests of which there are many in Florence."

"What do the events look like?" Gianni shot back. He had never seen a festival, and his interest was keenly aroused.

"The event goes back a couple of hundred years. It starts in the morning with a parade from the main square, Piazza della Signoria, to the Baptistery, named after St. John, in the Piazza del Duomo where the Church of Santa Maria del Fiori is located. In the morning, flag bearers, dressed in their finest brocaded costumes of bright colors, hurling their flags in the air from time to time as they march down the streets, lead the parade, followed by the aristocrats of the city carrying oversized candles draped in fancy ribbon designs which are to be placed in the Baptistery. People line the streets frolicking in the merriment of the moment. Once at the Baptistery, the most beautiful doors in the world are opened, the doors of Lorenzo Ghiberti, comprised of 10 marvelously curved panels depicting scenes from the Old Testament. These, Gianni, were only completed in 1452 and are considered masterpieces by everyone who has had the good fortune to view them. Many famous Florentines have been baptized under the 13$^{th}$ century mosaic ceiling of the Last Judgment, Dante, for example. Across from the Baptistery is the Church with its magnificent campanile designed by Giotto in the 14$^{th}$ century. Giotto, more known for his paintings than his designs has many paintings scattered around the city, several in the Church of Santa Croce. You are fortunate; you will truly enjoy yourself. I, myself, have seen the festival only twice before."

"Much of the expense of these festivals is supported by Lorenzo de Medici. His family has incurred these expenses for decades. It helps him to stay in the good graces of the populous. An expense worth incurring."

Giorgio stepped in, speaking with muted enthusiasm to Gianni. "A mass will be celebrated in the Church, and the relics of St. John will be put on display."

"If you are still interested after mass, you can either proceed to the Arno to watch boat races or watch another parade from the Piazza Santa Maria Novella to Piazza Santa Croce where the finals of a very rough ball game consisting essentially of kicking and tackling takes place. It is called the Calcio Storico Florentino and has a long history. The teams are formed from different neighborhoods of the city."

"And the final two teams of the tournament will compete for the championship," interjected Ludovico. "Before the tournament begins the piazza is covered in loose dirt, so the game becomes quite messy and makes the game all the more interesting."

In the evening as they were sitting at their campsite outside the walls of the city, Ludovico addressed Giorgio in a very somber manner. "Giorgio, on our return to Milan we have several other actions to consider," then hesitated in order to invite Gianni into the conversation.

Repeating himself, he continued. "There are several other actions we must complete before we initiate our plan. Our reason to be in Florence, as you know, is to solicit Lorenzo's tacit approval of our plan. There is some discord over the regency of Bona among the population in Milan. I have heard it myself and from friends. We must encourage

91

and exploit that discord. It can only help the populous to accept our leadership more readily when we depose Bona. We need our friends, and you know which ones I mean, to begin to disseminate those rumors more widely. They will be paid but must not know anything about our ultimate endeavor. They must be kept in the dark. The fewer people who know our plan, the more likely the plan will succeed. This is going to take months before we can act. Once in charge, we must move quickly to show the people that we have their interests in mind and make it be known that we are planning public projects to enhance their lives. I know just the artistic people to entice to Milan: Da Vinci and Bramante for a start. Everyone is aware of these two artists."

Giorgio was nodding his approval. "Once back in Florence I will get our agents to begin the rumors and raise suspicions of her behavior."

"We have Cicco being followed now, but we must also determine the movements of the Captain of the Guard and his assistants. They must be disposed of also," Ludovico said, his voice becoming more impassioned and his body becoming more animated. "Our men must be professionals, must not hesitate to do what is necessary. We have to eliminate her immediate power structure. The rest will follow. We should put two men on each of them."

Gianni sat silently and intrigued, looking at the two men like a lion cub to its mother, not yet knowing his part in the plot, if any.

The next day the men arrived in Florence and Gianni's senses were assaulted by the sights and smells of an urban center. They rode through the Piazza della Signoria, pass the Palazzo Vecchio, the town hall of the city, whose campanile and crenelated cornice has overlooked the piazza and city's pageants and festivals held there since 1322.

"The Palazzo Medici is not very far from here," Ludovico remarked as he swirled around to look at the statutes arrayed in the piazza. "We must first pass the Cathedral and the Baptistery whose magnificent doors you will see shortly devoid of the crowds that will shield them on the day of the parade."

Gianni gave a side glance to Giorgio to detect his reaction to the sights. Surprisingly to Gianni, Giorgio seemed as enamored of the city as did Ludovico, lightly holding the reins of his horse and carrying a very pleasant smile on his face.

As they sauntered up the street, they could see preparations being made for the events of the next several days. Passing the Orsanmichele on the way to the Piazza del Duomo, Ludovico jumped from his horse and motioned for Giorgio and Gianni to do the same. "We will be unable to see Lorenzo until after the festivals. He will no doubt participate in it. You must see this building, the Orsanmichele, built originally as a grain market in 1337 but soon after, with alterations, turned into the church you see now. There are 14 niches in the facade, each exhibiting a statute representing a major guild of the city. The statute I'd like you to notice is that of St. George standing straight and strong, his fist clinched with determination, his shield resting upright in from of him, his body in heroic stance. Below is a small panel in bas relief, showing him slaying the dragon. This is the image that I often call forth when I feel my resolve wavering. It's one I want you, Gianni, to remember. It was sculptured by Donatello, an artist whose works we will see later at the Palazzo Medici."

"I can see how St. George could inspire someone," said Gianni walking around the façade and stopping before each statute. Gianni followed Ludovico inside the church and was surprised that it was smaller than he anticipated, its gothic interior consisting of two naves, a vaulted ceiling and a small alter with, perhaps, room for 200 worshipers. Gianni was not religious when he entered San Gelsera and was unimpressed by the spiritual sincerity of many of the brothers there. Brother Matteo, as well as several other brothers, however, had such obvious faith and innocent belief in and devotion to the Church and its theology that Gianni had come to gain an appreciation for it also despite Brother's Matteo's wavering faith in recent years. Gianni's faith included stopping into most churches he passed to say a prayer for the family that he saw so infrequently.

"Where is Giorgio?" Ludovico said softly to Gianni.

"He's still outside."

Giorgio stood in front of the church, holding the reins of the horses and surveying the area with curiosity, a product of his skeptical nature. Mulling a conversation from the previous evening, he thought, religion is a necessary evil, maybe not an out and out evil, more like an encumbrance to clear thinking. Last night, Gianni went on about the kindness we should show to all people. This is, he said, one of the lessons taught by Christ. He just could not see that kindness is just the opposite side of cruelty. But princes must show cruelty at times. The point is not cruelty but cruelty well-used. Well-used cruelty is the expression of kindness in many situations.

Mounting their horses, the men moved on past Lorenzo's palazzo to the Piazza di Santa Maria Novella where there was an inn in which they could stay for the next several evenings.

The morning they were to meet with Lorenzo, the men walked to the Palazzo, lingering briefly in front of the unfinished façade of the Church of San Lorenzo, the Medici's neighborhood place of worship. The façade belied the solemn dignity and grandness of the interior which was designed by Brunelleschi, also the designer of the Cathedral dome. As Gianni was lighting a candle inside the church, his senses were finally overwhelmed by the sights and sounds he had experienced in the last few days, and he fell into complete silence, briefly into a state of bliss. Once he recovered he met Giorgio outside the church. "The Calcio Storico was the most exciting event I have ever seen, the ruggedness and intensity of the action on the field totally absorbed my attention." Nothing, save a few religious experiences, had aroused this kind of reaction in him before.

"You sound perplexed, Gianni. Life is a series of experiences, if you are alive. And if you find your way into different settings and do not limit yourself to the same one continuously, you will emerge with a gradation of feelings, some which you will want to remember and others which you cannot forget. Some of those will not be pleasant at all."

Upon meeting Lorenzo in his offices, Ludovico commented on his trip to Florence and the palace with his brother years before. "I remember so fondly one of your gallery's. There was a picture of the 'Madonna of the Magnificat' painted by Botticelli that I admired very much. I believe your mother, Lucrezia, is the model for the Madonna and you, as a young boy, are in it as well."

"Yes, that is one of my favorites also. I still think of my mother as the Madonna, even though it may be a little sacrilegious. You must let me show you around my other galleries before you leave. I will show you some of my favorites."

Lorenzo was courteous without being supercilious, a man who knew how to engage someone regardless of his or her status. With the vast amounts of funds that he and his forbearers had committed to many charities in the city, he had a reputation for kindness and generosity which countered the equally held believe of his forcefulness.

"Did you enjoy the Calcio? I love festivals and the people enjoy them. We have them many times over the year. It is one of the benefits of my wealth." Despite being the richest man on the continent, richer than even kings, Lorenzo was an unassuming man with an obvious quick intellect, a rather good poet with an appreciation of all the fine arts but also an adroit diplomat.

"Very much so," replied Ludovico.

Motioning Ludovico to sit opposite him in an exquisitely upholstered chair, Lorenzo offered Ludovico a glass of wine. "You will enjoy this Brunello. It is grown in Montalcino, not too very far from here. It compares very favorably to your Barolo up north, perhaps a little lighter and softer."

Ludovico thought to himself, this is strange. Lorenzo is rumored to have no sense of taste or smell from that misshapen nose of his. Here he sounds like he does. Does reality not coincide with rumor?

As the two men drank the wine, Ludovico presented his case for displacing Bona and her son from power and requesting Lorenzo's tacit approval of the plan. "Can I count on your tacit support?"

Lorenzo paused for a moment, with a somewhat clouded appearance on his face, obviously deliberating his reply. "Sixtus, you may be aware tried to take Imola for that dissolute nephew of his with the help of Ferrante of Naples after I dismantled and dispatched the Pazzi and their co-conspirators for their unspeakable plot. He excommunicated me for disposing of Cardinal Salviati, that devil who murdered my brother and attempted to assassinate me. Milan provided no support for me against Sixtus, even though the Medici had a long, supportive relationship with your father, Francesco. I still do remember that Milan provided shelter for my grandfather, Cosimo, when he was exiled from Florence. My resentment of the

Pope lingers with me. The memory of my dead brother still infuses my thoughts."

"Yes, that was unfortunate and an aberration of our relationship. Bona and Cicco Simonetta were behind that policy. Our relationship will be restored when I become Regent."

The meeting with Lorenzo gave Ludovico the assurance he desired, a tacit approval of his plan to displace Bona as Regent to his nephew, Gian Galeazzo. In return Ludovico committed to his non-military support of any Florentine defense against the Pope and the Papal States. Lorenzo was wary of Pope Sixtus and harbored a lingering resentment against him for the still unforgotten Pazzi conspiracy. Moreover, Lorenzo related to Ludovico his growing suspicion of the Papacy's territorial ambitions. Exiting the meeting and entering the garden with ancient Roman statuary arrayed around the garden perimeter, Ludovico stared at Donatello's bronze David located at the center, the first nude statute to be completed since Roman times, and he thought it is a very feminine one indeed. He was so elated that he imagined the birds sitting aligned on the cornice of the roof to be singing to him alone. Approaching Giorgio and Gianni, Ludovico related the results of his discussion with Lorenzo; he seemed especially excited about Lorenzo's agreement to persuade Da Vinci to accept a proposal, which was to be made by Ludovico, to take employment in Milan.

*****

At the end of Via Largo, a man stood alongside one of the kiosks where merchandise was being sold. There they are, the three of them. Ludovico is the swarthy looking one, for sure. The younger one must be the fellow from the monastery. And the third must be Giorgio; he's the most dangerous and always at Ludovico's side. Look at them coming out of the Palazzo Medici. I thought they might have been in Florence to celebrate St. John's festival. But no, something else is going on. They were in the Palazzo quite a long time. Methinks my employer might find this an interesting tidbit of information. Well done, Ennio. I believe I owe myself a large goblet of claret for my effort."

*****

"Pope Sixtus will see you now, Brother Aurelio. Follow me."

Brother Aurelio followed the young page pass several galleries resplendent with paintings by the most famous artists of the day. One, recently finished by Da Vinci, entitled St. Jerome, showed him in the wilderness alone. They passed a new chapel commissioned by Pope Sixtus that was still under construction, called the Sistine Chapel after the Pope, and walked to the Belvedere Courtyard where the Pope sat in a secluded and shaded area. "Sit by me, Aurelio, and relax. What news have you brought me?"

"Your Holiness, it concerns our monastery and their rental properties."

"Yes, what is the concern," said Pope Sixtus tilting his head slightly to the sun. He was not one to be too concerned about setbacks when he believed that he was doing God's work. He had the conviction of a true believer.

"Your Holiness, two people dressed as Brothers, were asking questions of several farmers near San Gelsera and also questioning wheat brokers about one month past. I believed the situation curious enough to merit watching them and to trail them when they next left the monastery grounds. Two of my men were killed in the endeavor, and two others badly shaken. They were identified as Gianni, a member of San Gelsera and Giorgio Falanghina, a long-time friend and companion of Ludovico. Once they returned to the monastery, I had their future movements tracked. The two men along with Ludovico Sforza appeared to be traveling to Florence, perhaps, for the Calcio Storico."

"Did your men give up any information to Ludovico," asked the Pope in a sullen voice, not reacting very strongly to the incident. I know they went to Florence to visit Lorenzo, Sixtus thought to himself, not revealing this fact to Aurelio. Ennio had been tracking them for weeks.

Pope Sixtus was a quiet man not given to displays of emotion, but his quiet demeanor and behavior belied a thunderous ambition, one that began before his startling rise to the Papacy: head of the Franciscan order at the age of 50, made Cardinal at 53, and elected Pope at 57, builder of piazzas and churches and roads throughout Rome, and champion and procurer of the new Renaissance art for the Vatican. His ambition rose to including his family in the distribution of titles, lands and wealth. His desire to make his family one of the established families of Rome often led him to some very non-priestly decisions.

"My men were never in a situation to reveal any information," said Aurelio, withholding the information that was given up by one of them.

"Aurelio, keep an informant in touch with Ludovico and apprise me of the situation."

"I have men on them at all times now."

Brother Aurelio turned to leave the garden. "Aurelio, this could be an important development, and we do not want it to get away from us. Before we make any rash decisions, we must discover just how much Ludovico knows and how far we are willing to go."

Pope Sixtus lingered in the garden, enjoying the warmth of the sun that bathed him and swelled his confidence that he was on the right path. God will reward me for this. I do it only in his honor.

*****

Gianni sat in the cloisters alone, neglecting his duties at the monastery and pondering the events of the last several months. His thoughts were a confusing collection of conflicting emotions, the excitement of his journey to Florence and the sorrow of the unchristian behavior that he saw and in which he participated, intertwining like a vine twisting around the trunk of a tree. He did not notice the new blooms on his favorite flower in the garden, the geraniums, the ones that always had given him consolation. His life was moving at a pace he could not comprehend and the meaning of the events still eluded him. Yet, he did know that they were significant; he knew that his pulse was raised when he was around Ludovico and Giorgio and heard them talk; he knew that the Palazzo de Medici was a different kind of beauty than the arresting churches he had seen. It was a beauty that stretched his imagination, that enwrapped him in a soft, easing confidence. He knew that he could not consult Brother Matteo. And he knew that he had to go with Ludovico.

Ludovico and Giorgio entered the cloister and approached Gianni. Ludovico spoke first, looking directly at him. "We are ready to move on Milan. Are you with us, and know this, there are risks involved. Decide with this in mind. The next several weeks will be decisive."

Gianni was quick to reply. "I am with you."

Giorgio moved closer to Gianni and whispered, "No matter what happens, it will be an adventure."

To Ludovico, Giorgio said, "The men are in place. Cicco is covered as is the captain of the guard. We have one bit of good fortune. Cicco will be at his home and unguarded. Bona will be in the castle in her room. She is there every day with Gian Galeazzo and his nurse. There are only six guards in the hall leading to her room, one of whom is our agent. We will not fail this time. I will give my life for it."

"No need for that, Giorgio. One arm will be sufficient." Both men smiled at each other, as Ludovico grabbed Gianni lightly by the arm and pranced out of the garden.

On the walk to the monastery door, Ludovico looked first at Giorgio and then at Gianni. "We still have unfinished business with this monastery revenue issue. We must follow through with it. I do not want to forget it. Gianni, you must remind me, if I do not bring it up again."

Giorgio could feel his excitement rising just as he had on previous occasions. As a young boy, he had not known his father very well, who was absent from the house so often and killed in battle as Francesco Sforza's chief aide. One of the few moments he remembered strongly of his father was the visible excitement that showed on his face prior to leaving home. It was an indelible moment for Giorgio, one that carried him through life and fed his craving for adventure, one that linked him to the father he never really knew. He was dedicated not just to Ludovico but to the memory of his father.

Giorgio was not a divided man, pondering his every movement to the exclusion of action, yet he was not impulsive. His actions had a goal, perhaps not completely thought out but sufficiently considered to comprise a plan, one that usually had a decent chance to succeed and one that usually did.

The following day Ludovico said to Giorgio, "We need an excuse to be absent from the monastery. We do not want even Abbot Garganega to know our real whereabouts. What do you suggest as an alibi?"

"I think something religious. A trip to a pilgrimage site, say, the one in Piratello," said Giorgio without hesitation.

"Excellent." The sun, breaking through the clouds, filled Ludovico not only with a sense of warmth but also with a bubbling sense of anticipation.

\*\*\*\*\*

Ludovico stood, nervous energy animating his movements, reviewing all the elements of the next day that would solidify his position. He was not given to this kind of behavior, even in the most severe circumstances, but this was the most important situation that he had ever faced, his fate and the fate of Milan was about to be determined. Francesco had inculcated him in the proper behavior for a leader. Foremost among his advice was, followers must never see any outward indication that exposes your doubts. Everything was in place, only needing his command to begin. Yet, here he was awash in emotions that he seldom confronted, contemplating his future. A stray thought passed into his mind, "Would not I have been better suited as a Roman? Then, I could have prayed to the appropriate god, have a priest sacrifice an animal and extract its entrails to determine my fate, something solid and tangible rather than a prayer to an impersonal God."

Several minutes later, suddenly recovering his usual composure, Ludovico turned to Giorgio and said, "I can feel my munacielli telling me that everything will turn out in our favor. I can feel their energy overcoming my apprehension."

"Ludovico, I'm surprised at you. You, soon to be the leader of Milan, are deriving your inspiration from ghosts."

"Giorgio, you believe in nothing, not God, not the Pope and now you reveal yourself to be a denier of the munacielli. They have sustained people for as long as any Pope."

Gianni stood nearby, tension clearly visible on his face, pacing from time to time, trying to remember his mother and father that he had not seen for several years, trying to garner the courage that he knew they would exhibit if they were in a similar situation. But the experiences of the last few months were unique to him and would certainly be unique to them. There was no history for him to emulate. He could try to imitate Giorgio, but Giorgio, sitting nearby on a rock nonchalantly looking at the interplay of a flock of swifts that were circling in the sky like pieces of paper caught in the wind, was unique. Gianni could not possibly believe that he could produce that imperceptible combination of indifference and conviction that Giorgio wore like a thin skin appended to his frame.

The three were followed from the monastery, this time by one man. They had discovered him soon after they left the monastery but decided to wait on any action until they could be sure he was alone. They surmised that he was sent by the same people who sent the other men after them. It was impossible to keep the tracker alive. There could be no one who could know their movements and certainly no one who could associate their trip to Florence with their subsequent assumption of the Regency. If their trip became apparent later, it would be of no consequence. Giorgio made quick work of the man, ambushing him and with one powerful swipe of his dagger had his blood streaming onto the ground, staining the brown earth.

Ludovico woke in early morning, the sky still darkened with night and not yet easing into daybreak, birds not yet singing their way into morning. The plan was to go into effect before dawn. Word had been sent the previous evening that Cicco and Sergio, captain of the guard, should be detained in their homes as the plan stipulated. Neither man was guarded, and Ludovico's men quickly entered their houses. Cicco was already awake working at his desk, which startled the intruders at first, but they recovered and constrained Cicco with ease. He tried futilely to resist but his age promptly showed, and his resistance faded like a lioness in heat.

Meanwhile, Giorgio and Franco, a long-time associate, tried to break stealthily into Sergio's home. The captain, however, was known for his perceptiveness and forcefulness. He needed only one creak in the old wooden flooring to jump from bed and grasp the sword hanging on the bedpost. Surprised by the quickness of Sergio's response, Giorgio swiftly engaged him, rushing to confront him on the stairway. Swords clashed with the sound of metal, both men maneuvering on the stairway for best advantage. Sergio nicked Giorgio slightly as he jumped two steps to the floor, tripping over a foot stool, a trickle of blood staining his shirt. The captain tried to make his way to the door, but was at first prevented by Giorgio's accomplice, but he easily slew him, first with a parry move to counter his attack, then with a flunge move to leave him lying on the floor for a few moments before expiring. Sergio ran into the breaking daylight, then turned to confront Giorgio chasing after him. The captain was not one to retreat from an opponent, honor being as important to him as duty. The fight moved outside and regained momentum by the brightly flowered garden fronting the house before advancing into the garden. Birds were singing, unaware of the death contest taking place beneath them. Finally, Sergio, exhausted from combat, barely able to lift his arm, was put down by a riposte that plunged Giorgio's sword into his stomach. He fell to his knees before falling face down onto the ground. Giorgio, also exhausted, first fell to his knees before raising himself and finding a chair in the house on which to rest.

Ludovico and his men, separated into two groups to reduce suspicion, entered the palace through a servants' entrance far from the main rooms of the palace. Two of his men, dressed as guards kept the entrance free of pedestrians. Once in the palace, each group advanced by different routes to Bona's room and Gian Galeazzo's adjacent room. The six security guards in the hall had one of Ludovico's men in their group and, once he glimpsed Ludovico's men walking in step down the hall, grabbed one of the guards, holding him at knifepoint. The remaining four guards at first lowered their lances in unison and briefly considered resisting Ludovico's men but then spotted the second group approaching from the opposite direction. They decided that their only recourse was to surrender to Ludovico.

Ludovico stood before Bona's room and, oddly, knocked before entering. Bona stood from her desk, only now aware of what was occurring but, nevertheless, looked sternly at Ludovico, fear slowly seeping onto her face from a depository that had never before been tapped. Her life had been one of luxury, first as daughter of Louis, Duke of Savoy, then as Duchess of Milan.

"Ludovico, what is the meaning of this intrusion," she said indignantly, quickly playing possible scenarios through her mind.

"Good morning, dear sister-in-law. I have returned to replace you as advisor to Gian Galeazzo."

"This is nonsense, Ludovico, you have no standing here and no support among the people. You will not prevail in this ludicrous adventure. You must know that."

"Ah, but dear Bona, I will. You have no recourse but to yield your authority to me. And I advise that you do without delay."

"Cicco will soon have my forces here to rout you and your men and the people will not allow it. Your stint as Regent will last only a few hours, then it will be you who will have his body swinging in a hangman's noose. I hope you enjoy the wind blowing through your dead body as your guts are exposed."

"Yes, Cicco, the man who humiliated me just last year. Well, he is now in my custody, no doubt considering his fate. And the people.... you should walk the streets on occasion, Bona, to see how your subjects have turned on you in just the last months of your regency. You should have been more concerned with their welfare."

Bona paced slowly around the room contemplating her next move, not looking at Ludovico. She was not yet ready to bargain with Ludovico, unsure as yet of how severe her position was but also not quite prepared to concede her position. Outwardly, she held her back stiff, her head high as becomes a Duchess. "What are your plans for me, then? And what of Gian Galeazzo?"

"Do not fear, Bona, I merely want to guide Gian Galeazzo. I have no plans of disposing of you, if that's what you are thinking. You can live your life here with your son, that does not have to change, provided that you adhere to my authority."

Bona understood that her position was now undermined, that she was unlikely to prevail and was now subject to Ludovico's whims. All she could do was to wait until such time that an opportunity arose to reverse the situation. She did not particularly care for her future but she was not going to relinquish her son's patrimony to his uncle without an effort to restore it later.

Giorgio, with Gianni in tow, arrived as Ludovico was leaving Bona's room. "Ludovico, is it completed?"

"Yes. She and Gian Galeazzo are under guard. She understands her position."

Ludovico, now with an ever so slight smile on his face and a relaxed posture, threw his arms around Giorgio and Gianni and strode down the hall, down the circular flight of stairs leading to the huge castle entrance and into the courtyard. Word had already circulated about the coup, and Ludovico's accomplices were circulating into the crowds praising Ludovico's character, foresight and empathy for the people of Milan.

As Ludovico, Giorgio, and Gianni walked in the courtyard, Ludovico took Giorgio aside. "Where is Cicco being held?"

"He is being guarded in his home."

"Cicco is the power center here. He can bring us more harm in the near future than can Bona. We must dispose of him. We cannot have him representing an alternative to us. Can you do it quietly? Also, have all of the palace guards been subdued?"

"Of course, it will be done immediately and discreetly. The guards have accepted the transfer of power. There are no signs of a counterattack."

As Ludovico sat on a bench between two tall cypress tree, he said to Giorgio, "I also need to call the privy council together. We know that several of them stand with us. The others will come along. My Regency is a fait accompli. They would not be so foolhardy as to oppose us at the moment. Also, begin looking for somewhere to relocate Bona and Gian Galeazzo. Give them several months here and then move them. Perhaps, the palace in Pavia will satisfy her and Gian. It has all the comforts of Castello Sforzesco as well as the benefits of country air."

The summer sun was now beginning to fill the earth with its warmth. Trees and flowers were awash in morning light, enjoying the sun's rays before the scorching heat regained its domination over them. Ludovico looked at the sky, a growing sense of contentment filling his spirit. He had plans for his Duchy.

*****

Sixtus walked in his study reviewing the progress of the remodeling of the Sistine Chapel. He was surrounded by his architect, Baccio Puntelli, and the construction manager, Giovannino de Dolci. This new chapel was to replace the original, which had served as the location of the Papal Chapel and Papal concaves. Sandro Botticelli, one of the original artists commissioned to paint wall frescos was also present. Sixtus was excited that the construction project was nearly finished and that the fresco painting phrase could begin. As he was indulging his enthusiasm, an aide entered and whispered in his ear. Sixtus excused himself and left the chapel calmly.

Outside the door, Brother Aurelio waited for the Pope, twitching energy visible on his person. He addressed the Pope politely and immediately proceeded to reveal the reason for disturbing him.

"Your excellency, we have been tracking Giorgio Falanghina. We know he is a friend of Ludovico Sforza but we have lost contact with our man. All we know now is that they have left the monastery and have not returned, and we do not know their whereabouts. Also, I fear that Abbot Garganega is growing suspicious." Aurelio's overwrought behavior belied his usual stolid and stern facial appearance, the furrows on his face seeming deeper than usual. It was odd that, although standing in one place, he appeared to be moving from side to side of the Pope.

The Pope stood emotionless, not looking directly at Aurelio but pass him to the picture hanging on the opposite wall, Domenico Veneziano's "Saint John the Baptist in the Wilderness." How alone St. John appears but he will recover, he thought to himself. It was befitting that the Pope who had only recently given start to the Spanish Inquisition was not moved by Aurelio's report.

"Aurelio, calm, calm. The solution is simple. Return to San Gelsera, keep an open eye for the return of Giorgio or Ludovico, most probably Ludovico. We know they started their journey on Via Emilia. So, locate your men at the monastery to follow them and station other men somewhere along Via Emilia to pick up the trail if they come along it."

The Pope, experienced in leading men from his earlier position as head of the Franciscan Order, continued to remain confident that his scheme was for the greater good of God as were his actions to promote civic improvements in Rome. Returning to his study, Pope Sixtus mused to himself, essentially reconfirming to himself his many previous confirmations, The Peters Pense does not bring in sufficient monies for my purpose. I must expand our revenue without arousing the kind of curiosity I am receiving from Ludovico.

*****

Ludovico met Giorgio and Gianni in one of the secluded gardens scattered around the palace grounds. It was several weeks after deposing Bona. The coup had gone well; no disturbances had been reported in the general population; Ludovico had been accepted by the Privy Council, and he was in a reflective mood. Gianni had reminded him of San Gelsera, and this meeting was to discuss the next moves they would undertake.

"Gianni, you should meet with Abbot Garganega. See if the situation has changed at all, visit the farms one final time and add visits to farms associated with other monasteries. Try to determine if the situation is the same at these other monasteries? You will need some time to do all of this. Giorgio can accompany you for part of that time but I will need him here. I am sure you will want to see Brother Matteo again and spend some time with him."

"Yes, Ludovico, I will enjoy that. I have several questions I want to pose to him."

"What would they be?" asked Ludovico curiously, thinking that Gianni would inquire about some moral dilemma that may have arisen over the last several weeks that bothered his sense of religious deportment.

"Questions about the life of Christ that has been told me in the past."

"Gianni, if you want to understand the life of Christ or just the nature of man, you must go to the Scrovegni Chapel in Padua. There, you will see the frescos painted by Giotto of the life and passion of Christ. In the fresco, "Lamentation," you will see the emotions of agony and pain in the contorted faces of Christ's disciples as they hover around his dead body that will imbue you with a keener sense of life than any description that someone can impart to you, expressions that were produced for the first time, bodies that were real life bodies rather than the stilted, lifeless bodies of Gothic painting, and all of this painted in the first decade of the 14th century. You must go. You will be enlightened."

Gianni stood, eagerness painted on his face, ready to go immediately. He was visibly moved by Ludovico's description. His life had accelerated and expanded in the months he had been associated with Ludovico and Giorgio.

On his father's farm his life was always of the moment; at the monastery, his life was always of a static future; now his life whirled about like a sirocco off the African desert. Very often he was unable to incorporate these new experiences into his life. He had not as yet reached an equilibrium with them.

"Hold on, Gianni, your time will come to visit Padua," Ludovico said, looking calmly at Gianni's face and feeling a sense of satisfaction in his eagerness.

The men moved off, each absorbed in his own line of thought.

*****

I'm the Regent of Milan, Ludovico could hear from the inner voice that often drives us forward. However, an equally strong voice would countermand the first, counseling patience and restraint, reminding him that it's best to proceed slowly. Despite his father's successful career both as a condottiere and patron of the arts, he moved forcefully but with deliberation. It is what made him stand apart from the many failed condottieri that passed through the 15$^{th}$ century. Had he not captured Milan for his progeny and at the same time been instrumental in creating the Treaty of Lodi, which secured a modicum of peace on the Peninsular between the major powers?

Ludovico was convinced that he had the same future as his father, that the blood of his father ran through him with the same intensity, that his destiny was to be the crowning achievement of his father, anxious to prove to the people of Milan that his Regency would not be a reprise of his brother's harsh reign, a regime that dehumanized both aristocrat and peasant alike. He contemplated a civic improvement agenda, an expansion of the silk industry, followed by a drive to attract noteworthy artisans to his court, a court that would follow where his father had ended and would make proud the citizens of Milan.

There still existed an anxiety in him, an anxiety that had always driven him, that he could not, would not want to dispel. His father, so secure in appearance, once only, once in a moment of unabashed honesty, had told him that he had an anxiety that was like a brother to him, that counseled him and that he trusted over any other counsel.

"Ludovico," his father said, "risk is omnipresent in life, in anything you do. Risk can be high, risk can be low, but it is always there with any action one contemplates. The trick is to assess the level. It not always simple. Coming to terms with it, however, can help one determine the level of risk one is willing to accept. Being unaware of it can jeopardize even the best of plans."

Ludovico was puzzled over his father's pronouncement at the time. It took him years of practical experience to realize the astuteness and truth of his sentiment. Assessing the risk level, however, always proved to be the first and most important step in developing a plan of attack. And he found as he developed it over the years that risk changed over time. A successful campaign early on could reduce the risk level later on. It made him more comfortable with his actions, and he came to accept it as the brother his father always cherished.

*****

Eos rose easily, riding her chariot once again across the rising sun, and longing for the energy of the day to imbue her earthy subjects. Ludovico strolled in the garden of his Castello Sforzesco, reminding himself of the good fortune he had experienced since his return to Milan and the progress he had made, continuing the remodeling of the castle, widening some streets and writing his first letter to Leonardo in Florence, praising him profusely and inviting him to Milan, and reminding Lorenzo in another letter of his kind agreement to place a word with Leonardo. Bona and Gian Galeazzo had been moved to Pavia some 20 miles from Milan and were being accorded the respect that they deserved. Gianni had proven to be a valuable addition to his close associates, loyal and energetic to learn, someone who would take on nearly any assignment, still shy, however, of some of the darker and necessary aspects of governing, someone Ludovico enjoyed tutoring on cultural affairs. Giorgio remained his chief counsel, aware of current events, offering solid appraisals of them and solid recommendations of alternative policy actions and always available to enforce those actions, and someone with whom he could relax with a glass of wine or two. The situation with San Gelsera was still unresolved, and a resolution had not been advanced. Ludovico, however, could not envisage a scenario that would affect him and, therefore, did not consider it an urgent matter, certainly not urgent enough to forgo other matters of state. However, he continued to believe that Pope Sixtus was involved in some underhanded activity, and he resolved to keep that piece of information available for the future.

\*\*\*\*\*

The evening sky sat brooding over Milan, pouring its tears of hope onto the city. Ludovico and Giorgio sat by the window of his office relaxing, each with a glass of newly released Amarone, a wine that was made around the Lake Garda region and not very often available to them. They were savoring it and comparing it to the Barolo from the nearby Piedmont area. The heat from the fireplace provided the warmth that ensconced them in their friendship.

"Giorgio, the canals. Although I have begun some new construction, we have to be firm in our resolve to provide maintenance for the existing canals. They are so vital to the life of the city, especially the Navigo Grande."

"Yes, not only are the farmers in the countryside dependent on its waters but so much of our trade is also. There are not many landlocked countries that can get so far inland from their city."

Ludovico sat back glancing at the courtyard below, raindrops ticking at his window. "Yes, the Navigo Grande canal runs into the river Ticino which feeds the Po which itself flows into the Adriatic. My dream is to extend it to give us access to the Adriatic. And it also provides a connection to Lake Maggiore whose beautiful shores and islands I have always admired. We need the Lake Maggiore connection to continue to give us the marble from the Candoglia reservoirs that we need to finish the façade of the Cathedral. It will be a lovely cathedral when it is completed. All of the Peninsular will admire it as well as the people of Milan. The people can serve God with an overwhelming feeling of spirituality."

"Yes, the canals are vital but also an expensive item," replied Giorgio, rising from his chair briefly, needing to expend his nervous energy a bit.

"I'm considering how merchants would consider a raise in their tax, maybe calling it a maintenance tax, for the canal's upkeep. After all, the goods that they sell are transported on the canal and taxes are needed for its maintenance, upgrade and expansion. We may want to also include the farms that are supported by its water."

"Ah, I can tell you. They will not like it."

"I have to get Leonardo here, Ludovico said changing the topic of conversation. He is not only a splendid painter; he is quite an engineer, I hear. I have a few paintings in mind for him, something to honor my father and, perhaps, an equestrian statute to honor him also. I would charge him initially with finding some way to reduce the effort to open canal gates and to develop designs for new sections of the canals. Today, it takes two men an enormous effort to get a gate open. His genius and versatility would be a welcome addition to the court and provide us with a significant step in our plan to have the finest court on the Peninsular."

Giorgio showed little interest in Leonardo, hardly listening to Ludovico. His interests were more plebeian. "There is an item of some immediately concern," said Giorgio, pacing the floor slowly with his hands cupped behind his back. "Our agent in Venice reports that Pope Sixtus and Venice are collaborating to bring pressure on Ferrara for the salt monopoly. Ferrara is likely to be pushed into war over it. I don't see how they can win a war with both powers." Giorgio was now seated again and in a more relaxed mood.

Ludovico did not have to hesitate with his reply. "We want to stay away from any involvement. We are not ready for it or any involvement now. We need time to prepare. We are not immediately threatened. The Pope always seems to have his hand in things temporal. He is so aggressive. If he acted as diligently on things spiritual as he does on things temporal, God would be better served but that has been his way. Only the temperament of the man with the Papal miter changes the equation. But, if necessary, we will support Ferrara, as a Papal or Venetian victory will endanger us but let's wait on any involvement."

*****

When Gianni arrived at San Gelsera's he was full of a new sense of confidence. He was unsure of some of the actions that he had seen in the last several months. The killings of Cicco and the captain of the guard had shaken him. He was puzzled how Ludovico and Giorgio could be so nonchalant about their deaths. It seemed not to move them at all. Yet, Gianni could not dismiss the warmth that he felt for both men, and the warmth that he believed they held for him. Other than Brother Matteo, they were the first men with whom he had such a relationship. Was there some greater good he was missing that came about by the coup? Was there a justification that he was missing? His own life had improved markedly. His relationship with Ludovico had brought him unwonted attention. He was introduced to the

119

evening balls with their fanciful clothing and enchanting music, women in their brocaded gowns approached him, which at first made him uncomfortable but which he very quickly learned to accept with equanimity. He was in a world he never could have imagined sitting by a tree on his father's farm. And he felt secure, even more secure than he felt at the monastery.

He sat under an arch in the cloisters at his favorite place in the monastery waiting for Brother Matteo to return from a trip outside the monastery walls. Abbot Garganega had passed, his death seemingly suspicious, but Gianni could not gain any information concerning it. Aurelio had succeeded him. When Brother Matteo returned, he seemed more despondent than Gianni had remembered. Brother Matteo suspected but could not prove that something ungodly had and was happening at the monastery. Gianni was astonished how this kind and thoughtful man had succumbed to such a deep sense of melancholy. According to Brother Matteo, the monastery was in a continuing state of decline. He could not accept the selection of Aurelio to lead the monastery and lamented the future of San Gelsera.

After spending the evening with Brother Matteo discussing each other's history since they last saw each other, Gianni determined that there was little he could gain on his mission by remaining at San Gelsera. He left the following morning for the farms. His intention was to visit farms previously visited to verify information that he and Giorgio had gathered and, ultimately, to seek additional information from other farms. His intention was not to be fulfilled.

At the first two farms the previous renters were no longer tenants. Their whereabouts were unknown, or so it was reported by the current occupants of the property. They had a decidedly deceitful manner about them and were reluctant to divulge much information at all. Gianni took to the road again despondent and puzzled by the lack of cooperation he was receiving. His attitude had been shaped by his years at the monastery where most brothers tended to work in cooperation with each other to complete a project. In this dejected state, he trudged on to his next farm, pondering how to proceed when he arrived. He was quickly realizing that this assignment would be more taxing and require more subtlety and ingenuity than he originally anticipated.

Several days later as he was riding along trying to resist the temptation to slide into an extended state of despair and to bolster himself for his next destination, he came upon two men resting along the road with their horses. They seemed like any other men traveling along the road, dressed in ordinary garb, nothing distinguishing them from other men. They seemed to be relaxing and chatting amiably. Just as he was about to greet them with his brightest smile, they snatched him off his horse, threw him to the ground, tied and blindfolded him and led him away into the woods. His resistance was useless. He meekly accepted his capture.

Gianni's mind tried to focus on what was happening to him, but he was so overwrought that focus was impossible, his mind bouncing from one unrelated thought to another, none of which eventually made any sense to him. Anxiety did not intrude his person until he realized that the men were silent. If not for the tweeting of a few birds and the crackling of dried leaves under his horse's hoofs, Gianni could be suspended in the ether that some ancient philosophers write about.

It did not take very long for the horses to stop. Gianni was helped off his horse, grabbed by his arm and led into a farmhouse, an abandoned farmhouse in a clearing out from the woods. His blindfold was untied, and he was forced to sit in a chair in the middle of a room. The room was bare except for a table and two chairs by the window. There was a second room which Gianni assumed held beds. As his eyes continued to adjust to the light, he noticed an unusual contraption at the other end of the room. It was a thick, circular metal apparatus about three feet tall with dangling chains falling from its sides, the whole piece secured to a pulley tied to the ceiling beam of the room by another heavy chain.

One of the men finally spoke. "Gianni, is it not. I see you notice our 'Street Sweeper's Daughter', a device brought from the Crusades in the Middle East. It helps to loosen men's tongues. Let's hope that we do not have to use it on you. All we need to know is what your visits to these farms is all about. What are you looking for? Isn't that a simple question?"

"I don't know. I am just on a mission for Abbot Aurelio."

"Oh, really. Gianni, just because we are dressed as simple men, do not take us for simpletons."

Gianni hesitated, trying to look perplexed and innocent, his mind feverishly grappling with alternative answers.

One abductor moved closer to Gianni, grabbed his ear and twisted it fiercely, bringing a slight jump in Gianni's body. "Once again, Gianni, what kind of information are you seeking? Come, come, say something."

The second man moved in and spoke, glancing at his compatriot. "Perhaps he would like to know how our Street Sweeper's Daughter machine is used."

He moved to the machine, holding the top of it. "You will be undressed and placed in the circle kneeling. Your top torso will be bent over your knees with your head pointed downward, arms folded inward. Then you will be tied to the circle with chains and the circle will be tightened to compress your body. You will not be able to move one iota of your body. Then, you may be raised from the ground and left in that position. That adds a slight wrinkle to it. The more uncooperative you are, the tighter the circle will be made."

"Again, do you have any answers to our questions?"

Gianni nodded in the negative, still arrogant and steadfast in his resolve.

The questioning went on for about an hour before the men became frustrated with Gianni, had him undress and placed in the metal contraption. They tightened it only slightly at first, hoping to get a response.

Gianni could feel the cold metal on his skin; he could feel the metal compressing his body inward.

"By the way Gianni, after a time in that position the muscle cramps will begin, cramps you will not be able to relieve, then after several days your muscles will begin to atrophy, longer periods will see your bones fusing and your mental state will deteriorate. When you are ready to talk to us, let us know. Before we go, we will leave you a small gift and tighten it again since you seem to enjoy it so much. We'll be back in a few hours."

He's right, Gianni said to himself. I can feel the cramp in my right leg. If only I could move it a few inches, just a couple of inches, even one inch would help. I can't see around me. I can't turn my head. I can only move my fingers and hands a bit.

The men did not return in a few hours. They did not even return in the evening. Gianni, in his increasingly disturbed condition, muscles aching, hungry from a lack of food, already anxious about his future, stayed curled in over himself all night. His mind could not focus on anything, except the pain. If only he could think of some pleasant experience. He tried to think of the last ball that Ludovico had given. He had been outfitted in a fine costume. Ludovico and Giorgio had taken great pleasure in choosing it and seeing him in it. They chided him that he looked like a young peacock. Gianni tried so hard to remember the pretty girl he had met who instructed him how to dance. But he could only put his mind on these experiences for a moment before the pain reasserted itself and the agony came rushing into his mind again. Finally, exhausted, he nodded off but only for an instant. His life had become an instant of sleep, an instant of memory and a moment of pain. Night had fallen, reminding him of the bleakness and despair of his life.

The next morning the men returned and the process resumed, question, no response, another question, no response. Before they left for the night, the men tightened the circle again. Gianni counted three night-falls. His muscles were numb but the pain persisted. He was now reaching a state of total disorientation. Even pleasant thoughts could not stay in his mind. It was difficult to remember his own name.

*****

Giorgio remained two days in Milan attending to business that Ludovico had assigned before departing for San Gelsera. On arriving at the monastery, he learned that Gianni had already moved on. Not wanting to delay his rendezvous with Gianni, Giorgio departed immediately for the farms. This did not cause Giorgio concern because he and Gianni had preplanned a route in Milan before Gianni departed. At the third farm, however, Giorgio discovered that Gianni had not yet appeared, causing him to pause briefly and consider his alternatives. He decided to wait a day near the farm to ensure that Gianni was not simply delayed. When he did not appear, Giorgio became concerned that Gianni had experienced some untoward action which was preventing him from following the preplanned route. Gianni was lost somewhere between the two farms, he thought. Backtracking the route, he began inquiring from travelers and residents near the road if they had seen him and if there were other houses off the road. For two days, he was unsuccessful in his quest. On the third day, a man pointed him to a house, an abandoned house, that was a few miles away. This is where Giorgio found Gianni tied the Street Sweeper's Daughter in dire condition.

Gianni was alone, feeling forsaken in those brief moments when he was of clear mind. When Giorgio entered the house, his first response was extreme anger, followed by compassion. He immediately released Gianni from the machine, gently sitting him on the floor. Recognizing his disoriented state, Giorgio said, "Gianni, do you recognize me?" No answer was forthcoming. Giorgio tried to have Gianni lay on the floor supine believing that this position would relieve some of the pain Giorgio obviously saw in Gianni's face. Uncurling Gianni's arms from his body, however, elicited a loud cry of pain. Giorgio abandoned this approach.

Giorgio ran to his horse to retrieve water and food. Back in the house, he fed Gianni water and some small pieces of bread and cheese. He was concerned with Gianni but now he began to worry about the return of the person or persons who had placed Gianni in this condition. After several hours, he could see that Gianni had recovered some and asked, "Do you know me?"

Groaning, he said, "Yes, you are Giorgio. How happy I am to see you."

"Can you lay down. Perhaps it would relieve some of your pain. And your abductors. Are they around?"

"No, they return in the morning."

"Good. That gives us some time to leave. I'm sure you cannot walk yet. You look weak. If you can ride my horse, we can both ride it out of the woods. If not, I can tie you to it and walk the both of you out. But it looks like you need some time to recover. Tell me when you believe you can leave, and we will find a place in the woods for this evening. Try laying down for now."

Gianni, with the help of Giorgio, attempted to lay on the floor. He could hardly move his arms or legs. The pain was excruciating. He could unwind only inches at a time. Slowly and with great effort, Giorgio supporting him as he slowly uncurled, Gianni reached a state where he could lay flat on the floor. Relieve was painted on his face like fresh paint on a canvas. His strength was slowly returning. Giorgio could see that Gianni's biceps and calf muscles had already begun to atrophy, and Gianni was fortunate that he had been rescued when he was. His senses were recovering but he was still only able to speak in a slow, soft, staccato whisper.

Gianni, after lying on the floor for several hours, was still unable to sit upright for any length of time but could be placed across Giorgio's horse like a sack of potatoes and be tied to it. It was an ungainly sight but served the immediate purpose. With evening approaching Giorgio wanted to make a hasty evacuation of the farmhouse and find a place to pass the night so that Gianni could gain additional strength for the journey home. He knew it would be several days before Gianni would be sufficiently healthy to proceed home in even a subnormal fashion. Giorgio realized that they still had hurdles to pass before they could feel secure. He was hoping to find a secluded place in the woods to relax and recover, a place where they would be safe from intruders. He had sufficient food, some cheese, stale bread and half a bottle of wine, with him to feed Gianni and himself for a couple of days in a minimalist manner, and there was a brook nearby where Gianni could wash himself from the previous days' neglect.

Giorgio said to himself, this will not be the first time I have gotten by only on my wits. I can care for Gianni and myself quite nicely.

*****

Ludovico was intrigued and outraged by Gianni's story, his anger subsiding only when it seemed that Gianni's health was nearly recovered. Giorgio's anger, of course, could find no peace until honor had been served by the culprit's assassination. Gianni wavered between unwonted anger that he found hard to repress and his Christian belief in the ability to forgive.

Ludovico addressed Giorgio and Gianni one day as all three men sat in Ludovico's study. "I'm concerned about who initiated your torture, Gianni. It was an affront to all of us. More important, it remains a constant source of danger to all of us."

Giorgio, dreamingly looking out the window of the room at nothing in particular, replied, "True, we really should do something about it, and I can tell that is what you are getting at."

"Gianni, what do you think about it? Are you in a mood to do something and, if so, what might that be," Ludovico said, as he moved away from his desk to straighten a picture on the wall while expectantly wondering Gianni's response. "I suspect we are still being monitored by someone."

We can assume that this situation will be never ending," replied Gianni, "a good assumption I believe. We at least can show that we are aware and eliminate this immediate source of danger. If I returned to the farms, I will be followed again. I can play the abductor this time. And, in any case, we still have not gotten to the bottom of the farm situation."

Hearing the word eliminate, Giorgio's head turned toward Gianni with a facial expression somewhere between confused and amused. "When you say eliminate, do you mean eliminate as in slay or simply remove by other means? The required actions are quite different."

Ludovico was obviously enjoying this conversation between Gianni and Giorgio and thought to intrude but decided to let it play out, interested in Gianni's response.

Gianni's shoulders lifted and his back stiffened in a noticeable way, a slight redness coming over his face. "I mean eliminate, to take away, as in to take away his life, to end his existence, to turn him into dust."

"I've got it, I've got it. No doubt about it. You've eliminated my doubt," shot back Giorgio, smiling.

"Yes, Gianni, I believe that is the best alternative for the time being. You cannot do this alone. You are not quite ready for it," Ludovico said. "Giorgio should accompany you, do you think not, Giorgio?"

"Of course, but Gianni, does this not unsettle your Christian values," replied Ludovico interested in his response to this unseemly action. It was an anger with a decidedly bit of hatred at its center that Ludovico did not remember seeing in Gianni previously.

"Forgiveness is for those who deserve forgiveness, and, in any case, the Church is not above eliminating for what it believes is cause, like heretics, for example."

"Then we all agree. You and Giorgio will move forward on the San Gels era issue. I think I know where this all leads. But let's not get ahead of ourselves. Your abductor will follow you again, Gianni. You and Giorgio can work out the particulars."

*****

Pope Sixtus sat in his study alone, musing over his appropriation of the Medici family properties in Rome. The hanging of Cardinal Salviati, sitting Archbishop of Pisa, over the killing of Giuliano de Medici and the wounding of Lorenzo had continued to occupy his mind long after the incident had ended. Salviati's body was hung from the Palazzo de Signoria in Florence, an affront to the Church that Sixtus could not forgive and which required retribution to remind the world that he was not to be humiliated and ignored in such an arrogant and fearless manner. Yes, he had taken the Medici's Roman properties but there must be some other dishonor he could impose on them, he thought.

He had consulted with Ferdinand, King of Naples, about a combined assault on the province of Florence. Sixtus's nepotism knew no bounds, and he wanted to give to his nephew, Girolamo Riario and his wife, Caterina Sforza, the cities of Imola and Forli in Emilia-Romagna and the income generated. The long-standing vitriol from the Florence incident would give him an excellent pretext in which to begin the assault. He hesitated only because he was a cautious man, not given to rash action even when his anger consumed him.

Florence would resist him. This he knew. If Imola and Forli came under Sixtus's domain, Florence would be encircled by it and the Papal States, putting enormous political and military pressure on Florence. They deserve it, he thought to himself. Did Lorenzo's meeting with Ludovico have an accommodation with Milan in mind? If so, would it apply to the Papacy? The rumors of my accommodation with Ferdinand are already circulating. This I know. Lorenzo must be expecting it.

Sixtus raised a quill and rubbed its feather around his mouth for a moment. It seemed to provide an assuring presence to him. Ah, but the wheat, the wheat, that is a subtler attack on Lorenzo, it flies "sotto voce", like a gentle breeze, unrecognizable. Plus, it provides the funds I need.

*****

The snow fell wet and cold, covering the tree branches with a glittering patina of winter, the full moon augmenting the sense of serene mystery. Gianni walked alone in a glen near Milan surrounded by trees. He had displaced--he thought this a better word than eliminate or slay, it seemed

131

to lessen the nature of the act to him—one of the thugs who had accosted him, not before, however, having him experience the pleasures of the Street Sweeper's Daughter. At first, he had taken his own satisfaction from the retribution. But he now felt that he had dehumanized himself. His guilt had been slowly consuming his inner peace, leaving him in a periodic state of panic and melancholy. He pondered it so assiduously that it left him devoid of emotions at times.

As he walked along, Gianni could not help thinking about the one person who had given him support and council, both temporal and spiritual, during his days at San Gelsera, Brother Matteo. He wanted to visit him on his return to Milan from his visit to the farms but could not abide the sad and disappointed expression that he imagined Matteo would show after recognizing the shameful deed on Gianni's face, a deed that Gianni believed singularly marked him.

It needed to be done, he would often say silently to himself, never completely certain that he actually believed it. Sometimes he imagined that people saw him talking to himself as he walked the corridors of the castle. Maybe people are beginning to believe that I am insane. I occasionally feel insane he would sometimes say to himself.

At other times, he was happy and gay, enjoying the luxurious life that he found himself in the middle of, the balls, the concerts that Ludovico would hold for his court performed by notable musicians of the day, the extravagant banquets that filled his stomach and compensated him for the days of youth that he went hungry. The "mystery" plays performed in the castle by professional actors on topics of religious significance, sometimes with pagan figures as main characters, were always enjoyable and full of esoteric allusions. Savoring the panoply of foods of the evening, he would remember his father and mother, both since passed, sincerely regretting that he was never able to provide for them. He had long since lost contact with his brother.

The unfortunate trip that he and Giorgio had completed had brought much useful information and the thug, who was disposed, eventually related that his employer was Abbot Aurelio, confirming what they had learned earlier. From the farmers, they learned that not only were prices being manipulated on the San Gelsera rented farms but other monasteries were involved in the scheme. And wheat was being withheld from the export market, particularly now that Tuscany was experiencing a drought. Prices were steeply higher in Florence, arousing animosity towards Lorenzo de Medici who was being blamed for the increase in prices. One remaining question was, where is the money going and why?

The time between bouts of despondency grew longer and longer and, when they did arise, he was able to hide it behind the gaiety of the castle. Gianni felt more vibrant than at any time in his life, his mind more stimulated, his body more active, activity that was related not to the need to survive but for the purpose of pleasure, intellectual pursuits and affairs of state.

Ludovico had slowly given Gianni duties to perform, to report to either him or Giorgio. He was gaining a different view of life, a more realistic view that taught him that the world is not perfect, that cruel actions occur, either randomly or purposefully, actions that have myriad effects, positive or negative, but he, Gianni, could influence the outcomes. He had not completely surrendered the innocent, honest motives that Brother Matteo had taught him, but he was becoming aware of the manipulative atmosphere of the 15$^{th}$ century Italian Peninsular, the deceit of some of the actors, the hatred of many of the players for each other, the greed and arrogance that floated about irrespective of the clothe that men wore, priest or aristocrat, wealthy or poor; all performed their deeds under the same sky, overseen by the same God, never doubting their justifications for doing them.

As Gianni walked back to the castle, his depression dwindled, his mood lightened, the rays of the moon seemed to light the path home, yes home, that is what he called the castle now, that is where he felt comfortable now, that is where he planned his future to be, that is what he would defend with his life, there are the people who are his new family, there are the people he would defend with his life, there is his only home.

*****

The war had started between Lorenzo and Sixtus. The Pope had been able to solicit the assistance of Ferdinand, King of Naples, as well as the smaller states of Siena, Lucca and Urbino. He was a master manipulator, managing to feed on their fear of Florentine ambitions without displaying his own motives. From the start, the war did not go well for Lorenzo, and he was soon forced to seek a peace accord. Traveling to Naples, he was able, with a combination of cajolery and money and with his exceptional diplomatic skills to convince Ferdinand that the best interest for him was better served with a secession of hostilities, that the Vatican was a greater threat to Naples than was Florence and would become too dominant in the region.

Ludovico kept himself aware of the hostilities and sent a few of his own mercenary troops to supplement Lorenzo's mercenaries. Naples would have a claim on Milan if Ferdinand's granddaughter, Isabella, should marry Gian Galeazzo, and Ludovico did not want to anger Ferdinand. He did not want his involvement to be noticeable, but he also desired to retain Lorenzo's friendship, not simply for political reasons but also for the intellectual and artistic kinship he felt with Lorenzo.

Soon after the peace accord was signed, Ludovico discussed the now settled war with Gianni and Giorgio. The day was bright and comfortable, clouds sitting in the sky motionless and swollen like cotton balls. He advocated a walk in the garden now beginning to blossom with the colors of late spring. "What lessons have we learned from this confrontation of Florence and the Papacy?" Hesitating briefly, he said, "I know what I have learned. First, Sixtus cannot be trusted and will use any means to win. This in itself is not unique or particularly alarming. He actually must be given credit for it. Second, even the wealth of Lorenzo is not sufficient to win a battle. Wealth is necessary but not sufficient."

Then, stroking his cheek with his left hand while he simultaneously twiddled the fingers of his right hand on his desk, he said, "We must get Da Vinci here. Though young he is already considered a genius. He has responded to Lorenzo's prodding on my behalf and sent me a letter. It is the oddest letter. He is known for his artistic ability but in his letter, he expounds on his mechanical abilities like building war machines and other type of machines, yet nothing of his painting ability. I have many painting projects in mind for him, but we could use his engineering abilities more than ever. I will make a serious effort to get him here as soon as possible."

\*\*\*\*\*

The Peninsular was calm for the moment. No one was interested in pursuing intrigues by exaggerating perceived slights or advancing ambitious aggrandizements of territory, the various leaders going about their own business without the interference of others. Spying, however, continued to flourish as the premier avocation of the aristocracy.

Ludovico absorbed himself in the remodeling of Castello Sforzesco, and continuing the construction of the Cathedral. Canal improvements and expansion were in progress, opening new areas of transport. Against his own judgment, he had recruited new mercenaries to his army, mainly Swiss and German guards, which he integrated into his own army, being reluctant to take the time and energy to provide the training local men would require. To fund his programs, he had raised taxes, an action that did not find overwhelming support in the population. He realized he had to show his subjects that his improvements were not only necessary but would improve their life; this he had to do within a reasonable time.

His energies had been taken up mostly by cultural programs, work that he enjoyed immensely and had always been a part of his life, talking to musicians, composers, and painters. Painters were in the castle frescoing walls of some rooms. He planned and initiated several festivals during the year, emulating the actions of his friend, Lorenzo, who had told him that the people enjoy them, that they help to maintain the peace and that they bring much respect to their sponsor. Did not the Roman emperors and aristocrats do the same for the people, he thought, establishing the Coliseum for gladiatorial bouts and punishment of criminals, building new temples to their pagan gods, and eventually Christian churches when Christianity came into favor, and holding festivals for the gods throughout the year.

Ludovico had also been successful in finally attracting Da Vinci to his court, he of the enormous talent, a hiring that had prompted kudos for Ludovico. Da Vinci, whose energies surpassed Ludovico's, had already produced two festivals, assisting in selecting the theme, planning the details that made them distinct, orchestrating many of the events, and designing many of the floats that are always a favorite item. Da Vinci was also working on a mechanical design that would improve the opening and closing of the canal gates, improving the efficiency of moving cargo through the canals, an improvement that should mitigate the merchant's disapproval of tax increases.

Gianni, meantime, was growing more and more confident as his duties expanded. He often acted as a courier for Ludovico, transporting papers to foreign capitals on the Peninsular. He acted as an informal assistant to Da Vinci, overwhelmed by his genius, taken by his energies, and amused by his ability to move from one project to another, always leaving some projects brilliantly conceived and just as brilliantly unfinished. His genius seemed boundless. Ideas flowed out of him like a mighty river cascades down a mountain falls.

Time had assuaged his conscience over the slaying of Abbot Aurelio's agent, but he continued to remain sensitive to the incident and would avoid the topic in the presence of Ludovico and Giorgio. Although his confidence grew in matters related to activities performed for Ludovico, there lingered within him, just under the surface, a doubt concerning his spiritual being, that his route toward the Almighty was compromised. He could not completely relieve himself of this feeling, despite all the new pleasures he was being introduced to and enjoying.

*****

On a fine sunny morning that relieved the cold of winter temporarily, Ludovico gathered Giorgio and Gianni in his bright, warm study. "Giorgio, just how did you manage to discover from Abbot Aurelio the disposition of funds obtained from the farms?"

"Ah, the secret of love or lust. I can never distinguish the two." Giorgio stood by the window with a twinkle in his eyes, looking out at the melting snow dripping off the ledges of the castle window onto the partially cleared ground. "Even Brothers are not immune to the curvaceous body of a pretty woman. And Aurelio is less prompted to abstain than most."

"So, who was the lucky woman," shot back Ludovico laughing sheepishly. "Her way to heaven is more secure today after taking on such a hellish endeavor."

"She was well paid, Ludovico, but complained later that she should have requested twice the amount. She says that she will do more research next time we ask her for her services…. that she cannot take my request at face value anymore."

"Her information just confirms what we all suspected. Sixtus is skimming the money for some purpose. That is the next question we have to solve. The monasteries are the unwitting recipients of this deception. Lack of funds is causing many of them to deteriorate. I am hearing more and more of this. And I would not put it pass Sixtus to operate this scheme beyond the Peninsular. I have to sympathize with their plight. They deserve better. At some point, perhaps, we can do something to help them, or at least some of them."

The conversation ceased for several moments, each man in his own thoughts, Ludovico drumming his fingers on his desk, Giorgio staring out the window at a boy and girl hopping through the snow, clearly enjoying each other, Gianni leaning against a wall seemingly in a semi-trance.

Suddenly, Ludovico spoke without directing his speech to either of them. It was more of a stream of conscious thought directed to the room but with all in mind. "We have to try to get an agent into the Vatican. My brother, Ascanio, was promised a cardinal's hat as an adolescent by Guillaume d'Estouteville, who sought Galeazzo Maria's support for the Papacy in 1471. He did not reach that goal; the Papacy went to Sixtus. Sixtus attempted to procure a cardinalship for him in 1477 but that attempt failed. He is now Bishop of Pavia. We need a renewed effort. We could try through Sixtus. He is not yet aware of the extent of our knowledge of him."

"What can we offer him," Giorgio said, turning away from the window after following the boy and girl across the courtyard, musing to himself how pleasant the scene was.

Gianni jumped in. "Ducats are always an excellent currency with Sixtus. Perhaps, though, we can offer him assistance in the expected war with Ferrara. He is always trying to advance his family, always seeking to use the Vatican's influence and power to acquire new dominions for them. And this war is less about the salt monopoly than about his family. Venice is interested in the salt, and Sixtus and Venice are just complementing each other's interest."

"No, that will not do, Gianni", said Ludovico. If there is any assistance to be offered, it will go to Ferrara. If we are lucky, we will not provide anything but words. This war could be a tricky affair. We will wait on offering Sixtus anything."

"This reminds me, there is a project that has been on my mind for a while and I want you, Gianni, to get involved with it. Do you both remember the miracle at Piratello, near Imola, that involved the Virgin Mary. We met pilgrims on the road who related that the Virgin desired a shrine to be built there in her honor."

"Yes, I remember it," replied Gianni.

"Well, I am in a position now to pay her homage. I would like to build a modest church on the spot of the miracle. I want you to convey my offer to Sixtus and procure his permission. In addition to satisfying my own need for salvation, it should pay us dividends. If he hesitates acceptance and tries to squeeze another concession from me, tell him that I will give him design approval of the church."

Giorgio could not resist a rousing laugh, followed by a smile.

"Giorgio, Giorgio, do you doubt my sincerity? What is so horrible in satisfying two needs at the same time. I would have assigned you to the task but for my foreknowledge, which comes from great experience with you, that the end result would be a brothel."

Gianni entered the discussion by saying, "Won't Pope Sixtus know what you are doing?"

"Of course, he will. He's a shrewd man, gifted and experienced at these negotiations." Then he added, "This is a good offer. He will be satisfied. He'll receive most of the acclamation. He will make sure of it."

*****

The War of Ferrara had started, the coalition of Venice and the Papal States pitted against the little state of Ferraro, the immediate cause being the personal slight felt by Venice for the excommunication and banishment of Venice's envoy by the Bishop of Ferraro. Behind the confrontation, however, was a dispute over the rights to the saltworks at Comacchio on which Ferrara had been encroaching.

Pope Sixtus endorsed and encouraged Venice's action against Duke d'Este of Ferraro with whom he held a particular animus. The fray was soon joined by Gonzaga of Mantua, d'Este's son-in-law, and Ferdinand of Naples. Pope Sixtus's nephew, Girolamo Riario of Imola, the Republic of Genoa and Marquis of Montferrat joined Venice.

Ludovico, sitting in his office with Giorgio and Gianni but anxious of placing men on the battlefield in such an erratic environment, said, "We must assist Ferraro. A Venetian victory and control of Ferraro will upset the balance of power in the north. We cannot abide a stronger Venice on our northern boundary. Giorgio, you must bring a contingent of our men and join Ferraro. Ferdinand is attacking the Pope on his southern border, which should prevent the Pope's troops from joining Venice. It is not something that I want to do, but we have no choice. We cannot be compromised by Venice which is what a Venetian victory would do. They seem to be forever attempting to encroach on our Lombardy borders and our allies.

The usual political manipulations and duplicities of the principalities of the Peninsular applied. Alliances could change as easily as a snake shedding its skin. It had been such since the fall of the Roman Empire.

Ludovico had no territorial ambitions. His only goal was to prevent Venice from dominating the northern peninsular. Venice, however, proved to be a superb opponent over time, sacking and capturing several cities under the control of Ferraro before laying siege to Ferrara itself. Pope Sixtus, then apparently realizing that a more robust Venice would also be a threat to him, turned on Venice, allowing Ferdinand's son, Alfonso, to pass through his territory to engage Venice, excommunicating the Venetians and encouraging a peace agreement between the parties. Ferrara was eager to end the hostilities, fearing that it was on the edge of being absorbed by the Pope, and at the Treaty of Bagnolo, ceded its territory in the Polesine, and the war came to an uneventful conclusion.

"This war shows you just how fickle the leaders of this peninsular are. They never disappoint one," Ludovico commented two weeks after the signing of the agreement, as he and Giorgio were relaxing with a glass of 10-year old Barolo, the moon shining sporadically through the windows onto a multi-colored inlaid tiled table that held roasted lamb baked with an assortment of herbs in a red wine sauce, bread baked with rosemary, and an assortment of cheeses. They were in a very relaxed state.

"We were fortunate not to lose many men and were prescient not to offer many men. The lesson is poignant. Never trust any partner. They are as likely to abandon you as hot cinders are to scorch you."

*****

"Gianni, you have seen Da Vinci's plans for the canals," spoke Ludovico, the men now walking along a canal with the morning sun beginning to brighten softly, Giorgio slightly aside from the two and seemingly in his own dreamy space.

"Yes, and as he explained it to me, it again shows his genius. Such a simple plan. Yet so effective."

"Giorgio, do you know of the project," said Ludovico, rousing Giorgio from the inner conversation he appeared to be having.

"Only that he was working on something."

"As the canal gates operate now it takes two men to lift a gate vertically, requiring great effort. They have to overcome the horizontal water pressure of the river against the gate."

Ludovico continued. "Leonardo has designed a gate which consists of two halves, mitered at a 45% angle to form a "V", resembling an inverted "V" facing upriver with a smaller gated culvert below. In this way, the flow pressure of the river helps to open the gate. Ingenious, isn't it? With over 90 miles of canals in the city and surrounding areas, Da Vinci's innovation will speed the movement of goods. It will mean more transport on the cheapest means of moving goods around."

Ludovico stopped for a moment and gazed up at the sky, suddenly feeling alone. His moments of melancholy most often came over him when he was alone in his room and thoughts of his future comingled with thoughts of his past, neither one completely suppressing the other. His regrets would surface suddenly, like an arrow shot from a bow flying through the air at an unknown target never to directly reach its goal.

When his melancholy became particularly tortuous, he had the good fortune of being able to summon Giorgio. It was then that he and Giorgio had their most notorious and disruptive adventures. Only on rare occasions, however, did they become harmful to anyone other than themselves but always adding another regret to his arsenal of regrets. Oddly, it was Giorgio, the man with his own fearsome temper, who was able to mollify him and most often moderate both their behaviors.

Turning to both men, Ludovico said, "Sixtus has expressed his appreciation for the Piratello Church by approving Ascanio's cardinal's hat. He should receive it in several months. It will be an enormous benefit to us to have him in the Vatican."

Pope Sixtus IV passed away only days before Ascanio entered Rome invested with a cardinalship. Among his achievements during his Papacy were the remodeling of the Sistine Chapel, the modernization of many of the churches and monuments in Rome, the construction of many squares and new churches, and the first bridge across the Tiber since Roman times in addition to being a major patron of artists. He had also vested a cardinalship to six of his nephews, endowed his family with great wealth, and continued the sale of indulgences and offices.

"The Almighty will have a difficult time deciding his fate," Ludovico remarked on hearing the news of his departure.

"Sixtus is going to have to learn how to beg," shot back Giorgio, with a wide smile covering his face. "This is something he has not had to do for quite a long time."

"What does this mean for the monastery," Gianni replied in a palpably agonized manner. "Does this end our investigation?"

"No, Gianni," said Ludovico as he stood with his back to the window. "His mystery still lurks in the Vatican somewhere. And we have more help now with Ascanio there."

Ludovico moved from the window to approach the two men. "What puzzles me so much is why did he need this additional income? We know it is not accounted for in any of the official Vatican records. He had need for income to pursue the construction programs he was noted for. But he had many sources of income, the Peters Pence, the ordinary donations of his flock, the sale of offices and indulgences. Either his administration and projects cost more than suspected or his income was less than he needed."

"The monies from the monasteries have to be an off-the-book project, one that only a few people are aware of. It could not have been kept secret only to Sixtus," Giorgio responded, a serious look on his face. "There must be other participants."

Ludovico faced Giorgio thinking he had not often seen Giorgio this interested in affairs of the clergy or the church. He must have a hidden compartment within him that still has a few warm memories of his faith. Or is it simply that he prefers the underdog and in this case the monasteries are the underdog.

Ludovico moved to his desk and absent mindedly picked up a quill, "I agree, Giorgio. Sixtus's income sources were many but were mainly from the laity. Yes, nobles bought offices and indulgences and on occasion offered gifts but his taxing authority applied only to the lands that he held. Lands held by the aristocrats were taxed only by them. They had their own revenue shortfalls. This is why so many of them need bankers so often to bolster their regimes and so often are in debt to them."

"Skimming income from the monasteries all over the continent would generate a good deal of income, I would think," said Gianni almost hopping in the air.

"It would be another source of income of which no one is aware. I would think a major source of income," Gianni.

The three men were moving around the room almost in a circle as they pondered Sixtus's motives, trying to reconstruct his thinking, their movement mirroring their inner turmoil.

"Monasteries hold a good deal of land that they have accumulated over centuries. Much of it was donated to them from wealthy nobles to assuage their sins. They have a habit of remembering their deeds when they are near death and find solace in their donations," Ludovico threw out, forgetting for a moment that he was a noble.

"Do not forget the quid pro quo" laughed Giorgio, "a piece of land for entrance into heaven. If heaven is as pleasant as the priests say, I say it is a good exchange. And, let us remember that it is not good land, it's wooded and not always fertile. A good exchange. The nobles are always finding ways to cut corners and gain an advantage. I wonder if God appreciates their manipulations. Will they be rewarded for their cleverness?"

"Yes, Giorgio, yes, Giorgio, we hear you," snapped Gianni in exasperation. "The monks do have to clear the land and bring it into production. But many have proved themselves to be splendid farmers, and it would not surprise me if the lands generate more income than people believe. I remember my days on the land at San Gelsera, so I know of that what I speak. The farms at San Gelsera certainly generated a surprising income."

Ludovico interjected, ignoring Giorgio's remarks. "We have to wait to determine who is elected the new Pontiff. We know the scheme is in the Vatican. Will it still remain there after the papal succession? Will the new Pope take up the scheme or will it simply fade into the dark memories of the Vatican?"

*****

"Let's stroll over to the Cathedral and inspect the progress on the façade," said Ludovico, jumping from his seat. The Candoglia marble is flowing in again from Lake Maggiore, and I'm eager to see the work."

He was already on his way, as Gianni and Giorgio tried to keep pace with him. He enjoyed startling them from time to time just to record their facial expressions.

Giorgio finally replied, "This cathedral has been under construction for a century. It will still be there if we take a more leisurely pace. The Almighty resides there 24/7, doesn't he, or does he arrive only when the cathedral is completed?"

Ludovico smiled and shook his head, and Gianni, who seemed to be musing to himself about some unrelated topic, avoided eye contact with him until they were standing in front of it.

The approach to the Cathedral was dramatic, first walking along the narrow streets with cramped houses on either side leading to it, and then opening surprisingly to the wide Piazza del Duomo, in full view of the Cathedral and its spire in the center of it. "It can only inspire anyone who sees it," said Ludovico to Gianni, as they entered the piazza nearly empty of people.

The white marble of the façade shone with a pinkish hue, the sun prancing on its surface like a ballerina. Where marble had not yet been laid, the contrast was one of purgatory residing next to heaven, thought Gianni. It will be saved, but it will require time.

Approaching the entrance of the church, a stunning woman, stiff in posture yet supple in appearance and attired in an elegantly brocaded gold and blue dress with a fur-lined surcoat was standing on the arm of a tall, well-dressed man. Ludovico almost missed her entrance into the church. noticing her only after the sun sparkled from one of her gold adornments and attracted his eye involuntarily. His rapture was immediate, her alabaster skin at first impressing him indelibly, then almost fading into the façade of the church as he stood transfixed on her.

Giorgio immediately understood his friend's emotion, having seen it on several occasions previously. He was also impressed with the woman, actually had been impressed with her, having seen her on a number of occasions in the past. She was one of the best-known courtesans in Milan, Cecilia Gallerani, known for her wit as much as for her beauty.

Ludovico followed Cecilia into the church. "Giorgio, you must introduce me to her and who is the gentleman with her. I do not believe that I have ever seen either of them."

"She is Cecilia Gallerani and he is Luigi Cordisco, a wealthy merchant. He exports silk products and is known to be a gad about town and is generally well-liked by those who know him. He attends many of the fashionable events."

Once inside the church, Giorgio introduced Cecilia and Luigi to Ludovico. They recognized him immediately and showed the requisite deferential comportment to him, done in a natural and easy-going manner unlike many other people introduced to him.

Looking at the bare, severe and imposing unfinished interior, a nave and four aisles leading to the altar, the interior stood in stark contrast to the splendor of the exterior, even unfinished as it was, with its marble façade, gables, partially completed statuary adorning seemingly every nook and cranny of the exterior and stained-glass windows.

Ludovico said to Cecilia directly, "Does it not pay great homage to the Almighty?"

"Yes," replied Cecilia, "but one wonders if the Almighty needs such a splendid edifice. And have all the saints been carved onto its façade? It seems to lack no one. Is there room for anyone else?"

Then realizing that her remark could be taken for sarcasm rather than as a gentle, friendly retort, Cecilia said, "Would not a simple site for his flock to worship in be sufficient for them to show their love for Him?"

"Well, His flock needs such an edifice to attract them to Him," replied Ludovico.

Raising her head slightly without implying displeasure of Ludovico's remark, Cecilia said, "Is His flock so fickle and shallow that they need a lavish abode to say a simple prayer?"

"The laity really does need this display. They need a display that raises them from their dreary, ordinary life."

She looked directly at him and responded in a pleasant tone, "Is a prayer offered to God in a small, unimpressive, village church worth any less to Him than a prayer offered in this splendid cathedral of yours?"

"Ah, but do not women dress to impress men and attract them to their side?"

"Oh, but we are not The Almighty, are we," she replied with a twinkle in her eye and a wave of her hand.

Ludovico was stunned by her direct response to him but was truly in her power now.

"Giorgio, she is like a pleasant dream, Ludovico said after she departed. No, not a pleasant dream, like a dream floating before the gates of heaven."

As Ludovico walked from his office to the foyer a week after his introduction to Cecilia Gallerani, he turned to climb the circular stairway to the second level. At the top of the stairway to his left, he entered the large reception hall aglitter in mirror and gold trim, complemented by angelic gold carvings interspersed between the mirrors, high back chairs along both walls aligned with small tables beside them. He would often leave the confines of his office to sit alone in the hall to ponder current problems. His office, although spacious, sometimes felt confining at times, seemed to limit his thoughts. The spaciousness of the hall gave him a feeling that he could let his thoughts roam freely without constraint. He sat for some time considering affairs of state, but his thoughts would always return to a vision of Cecilia.

*****

As the days passed, Ludovico became more enchanted with Cecilia Gallerani, her beauty lingering with him like an enduring memory from childhood occupies our present, always there to enhance our mood and heighten our expectations. He had to meet her and his thoughts on current political events continued to be pushed aside, so occupied was he with thoughts of her. Even Giorgio had never seen him act in this manner before.

As he was standing one day in silent thought looking out from his window to the courtyard, now awash in color from the spring flowers arrayed along its edges, he requested that Giorgio and Leonardo come to his office.

"Looking at Leonardo, Ludovico said, "I want to give a ball, and it has to be lavish and fun but especially beautiful. Leonardo, I know your sensibilities are such that you can orchestrate an arrangement that will satisfy these requirements."

"Giorgio, invite Cecilia Gallerani. The purpose is for me to meet her again."

"She may be partnered with Luigi, Ludovico," Giorgio replied in an advisory tone.

"Well, then, invite both of them," Ludovico said, looking at Giorgio with a boyish smile on his face and a prankish twinkle in his eyes.

He certainly was not behaving in his normal manner, thought Giorgio, smiling as he left the room but not concerned about his behavior. As he was leaving, Giorgio stopped in the doorway and turned to Ludovico and said in the mocking voice that they used between themselves "The master really does need a new playmate."

Ludovico simply waved Giorgio off and returned to his desk to finish the paperwork scattered on it.

*****

"What, she's declined my invitation to the ball," Ludovico's anger flaring red hot when told by Giorgio about Cecilia's response, his anticipation deflated.

Giorgio, trying to appease Ludovico, quickly replied. "She seems to have a legitimate reason for the declination. Do not act impulsively."

"And just what is her excuse?" Ludovico looking calmer now, the redness in his face transforming into his normal swarthy color but still not fully recovered from his apparent rejection.

"She has prior plans and is traveling to Rome with Luigi. Even an eventual Duke like yourself can experience disappointment in life and in love occasionally," Giorgio retorted, his eyes sparkling with mischief like the Greek God Hermes who was known for his cunning. "Do not flatter yourself that you are Apollo. He was a prophetic deity and had his own Delphi Oracle. What have you prophesized lately?"

Ludovico could only shake his head and produce a heartfelt grin, as his rigid body receded like a balloon losing its air.

Ludovico paced the floor of his office, rubbing his chin sporadically. Finally, he said to Giorgio. "Invite Luigi to meet with me. I have an offer that should prove interesting to him."

"May I inquire of its nature," replied Giorgio, stepping closer to Ludovico. "You always have some way of turning a situation into your advantage, though often at a price that is not always apparent at first."

"You mock me, Giorgio. But your restraint on me is often for the best. Also, invite our Minister of Finance to the meeting, Tomasso Vermentino."

"Why do you bother with Vermentino. I don't find him trustworthy at all. My opinion of him borders on loathing."

"I know your feelings of him. You have made them very clear again and again. He is very knowledgeable about finance, however. He trained at the Medici bank. As for the offer, would Luigi turn down the offer of envoy to Venice to conclude our trade deal on our silk products. He has much to gain financially from exposure to Venetian trade."

\*\*\*\*\*

"Have we any news of the Papal Conclave to replace Sixtus, asked Gianni?"

"Only that it is proceeding," responded Ludovico, as he was seated at his desk. "Cardinal Giuliano della Rovere, Sixtus's nephew, tried for the miter but did not have sufficient support, according to information I am secretly receiving from Ascanio."

\*\*\*\*\*

Ludovico was enchanted by Leonardo's work that he had seen while in Florence. Lorenzo had warned him that in addition to being a genius, Leonardo was also an eccentric, his mind jumping from one topic to another, full of ideas that seemed improbable but which everyone who saw his drawings found intriguing. Gianni had already reported this unusual trait of Da Vinci to him, and Ludovico was anxious to spend time watching the process that Da Vinci employed in painting his subjects, just as Ludovico did with the composers he employed.

One day he summoned Gianni to accompany him to a room that Leonardo was frescoing, just to observe a genius at work. He wanted to experience the creative process. Gianni, walking along the corridor with Ludovico said, "You are in for an unusual experience. I'll say no more."

After exchanging the usual pleasantries, Leonardo sat at his chair facing the wall while Ludovico and Gianni sat behind him by the opposite wall. Ludovico was first struck that no images had yet been placed on the wall after nearly a month since the project had begun. The wall was bare.

After 15 minutes sitting calmly in his chair watching Leonardo and holding his restless feeling in place, Ludovico whispered to Gianni, "Nothing is happening."

Gianni responded in an equally low whisper, "Yes."

"I don't understand it. Do you understand it?"

"Is it any different than what you do when you plan an attack? You may look at maps, but you see the battle unfolding in your mind. And when it does not appear correct, you alter it in your mind. I see Leonardo taking the same approach; only he has just the blank wall."

Two hours later, Ludovico and Gianni were still sitting in their chairs as was Leonardo. Not a word had been exchanged between the men. The wall was still bare. Ludovico, finally, exasperated and restless said to Leonardo, "Why are you not painting?"

"Ah, painting.... applying paint to the wall or canvas is the easy part. Knowing where to apply the paint and which colors to apply. That is the difficult part. It makes little sense to apply paint until you know where you want each stroke to go. It will come, it always does."

Ludovico rose from his chair and politely left the room. Later he would say to Gianni jokingly, "We need another genius at court to determine if this is a genius trait or is just peculiar to Leonardo."

"Ah, but we also have one in Donato Bramante, known in the past for his painting expertise which has now been eclipsed by his recent architectural achievements. He seems to have abandoned his painting for architecture."

"True, we tend to overlook him. He has done wondrous work, and I agree about his architectural accomplishments. I plan to have him do work on the Church of Santa Maria delle Grazie. Surprisingly, his orchestrations of some of our festivals have been the equal of Leonardo."

\*\*\*\*\*

"Cardinal della Rovere and Cardinal Borgia have conspired to prevent the Venetian Cardinal Barbo from obtaining the Pope's miter," said Ludovico to Gianni.

"Was there anyone else in contention," asked Gianni, fixing his shirt sleeves before preening his hair, as he moved around the room.

Ludovico could not but notice that Gianni was becoming much more concerned about his appearance lately. He wondered if Gianni had a secret girlfriend hidden away somewhere.

"Despite their rivalry, Cardinals della Rovere and Borgia promoted the election of Cardinal Giovanni Cybo as a compromise candidate. He won consent and took the name of Innocent VIII. It took some bribes and the offer of benefices to entice the requisite number of cardinals to vote for Cybo."

"Do we know anything about him," Gianni said, now looking at himself in the large mirror by Ludovico's desk.

"He's a man of family wealth interested mainly in the material comforts of the papacy and furthering the fortunes of his family. He's also known by all to be a tool of Cardinal della Rovere, who supported him in his previous quest for a cardinalship.

"Both della Rovere and Cybo were appointed cardinals by Sixtus. Is this just a coincidence or are we also seeing Sixtus's hand reaching from the grave in having Cybo appointed?"

"It does seem strange, does it not? Sixtus to Innocent via della Rovere with Borgia appointed as Vice Chancellor. It does not need a lot of stretching to fit into a conspiracy theory. And Borgia is Sixtus's Vice Chancellor." Ludovico rose from his desk and walked to the window, looking out onto the courtyard pensively.

Gianni moved toward the window also, and said, "What kind of behavior do you expect from Innocent?"

"It does not appear that the Papacy will be changed materially by the investiture of Innocent. Cardinals della Rovere and Borgia, no doubt, will have an unrivaled influence. I just do not visualize in which direction they would move Innocent."

Then moving away from the window and turning, he said as he eyes suddenly appeared wider, "I do not know if I should feel gratified or not by his ascension to the chair. Ascanio tells me that he has seen and heard that there is an element of papal aggrandizement in his person. That always should put us on alert of his actions. The Papacy has seldom been kind to us, and I do not expect that feeling to change."

\*\*\*\*\*

The sun was rising a hazy pink in the sky, hidden from time to time by an occasional cloud. Castello Sforzesco was abuzz with activity, maids hurrying about to complete their duties, morning guards in quick step replacing the evening guards, delivery men at the service doors unloading their wares.

Ludovico was sitting at his desk, reading a dispatch from his envoy in Genoa. As Tomasso and Gianni entered, he rose, greeted them and walked to a large work table by the window, inviting them to sit with him.

"Tomasso, you have a report on our silk industry initiative?"

"Yes, the tax relief and subsidy for new silk weavers that you introduced are producing extremely good results. Just in the last half-year we have attracted 1000 highly qualified workers and inquiries from two firms interested in setting up plants here in Milan."

"It is also creating a negative reaction from Genoa," interjected Gianni. "They have lost the majority of those workers we have attracted; the Genovese Council is complaining loudly, as I am certain you have heard."

"And the education plan for the silk workers in our new school? Is it moving along, Tomasso? Are you keeping in touch with the guild? Are they still in accord with the agreement I struck with them? These guilds are so hard to appease but are so necessary for the regime's stability."

"Yes, they are quite satisfied at the moment."

Ludovico stopped for a moment, seeming lost in thought, then addressed Tomasso. "We should begin to consider training workers for the mulberry fields along Lake Como also. Though sometimes bothersome to us with their expansionary policies, Venice is willing to export our goods abroad." Ludovico rose from the table, leaning forward slightly with his hands palm down on it, and continued. "It will be good competition to Genoa. Expanded markets will require additional raw silk as well as additional weavers. It should be a beneficial trade for Venice as well as for us. The initial lost tax revenue will be more than compensated for in increased sales. Is that not so, Tomasso?"

Tomasso nodded his head in agreement.

Ludovico straightened his back and looked at Gianni. "You want to say something, Gianni."

"Yes, Genoa is quite upset.... well, more than upset," said Gianni, a grave expression on his face. "They are becoming quite aggressive. We should not be surprised if they attempt some counteraction that could include hostilities."

"I hear that from our envoy also. We are beginning to station troops along our border, we hope, without provoking Genoa. I am keeping the troops a distance from the border but within easy reach. I am hoping that it does not incite them. At times like this, they could use any pretext as an act of war."

Ludovico walked to the window, pausing momentarily, to gaze at the activity in the gardens, still recovering from its long nightly sleep. In the corridor, the sound of footsteps echoed off the walls as passing soldiers wound their way to their stations. He thought, war with Genoa is not something I want, but it might be the cost of advancing our state. And we must be careful. There is a French connection with Genoa, and I do not want to have the French participating in a war with us."

*****

*E. F. PALERMO*

The tension of impending troubles with Genoa affected Ludovico's mien, causing wide mood changes throughout the next several days, his mind focused on only this issue to the neglect of all other topics. Absolute certainty of all eventualities was an unachievable outcome which he understood but, nonetheless, strove to achieve. Even with the knowledge of this impossible goal, he could not relieve the tension that held his body like a vise clamped to a thought.

Giorgio would often join him in his study long into the night discussing current affairs. The moon's shadows would be thrown onto the walls as they alternately talked of affairs of state and personal remembrances of their youth, both men also discussing their current mistresses. Their remembrances relieved their stress as well as continuing the ties that bound them together. Before them would be several carafes of Amarone, small blocks of Belmonte and Branzi cheeses from Lombardy, marinated olives and thick, crusted bread to be dipped into local olive oil; all enhanced their discussions as the two relaxed together, making the mornings appear out of Ludovico's window that much sooner and welcome. Wine and camaraderie brought the only respite for Ludovico to his state functions.

Ludovico continued to be enthralled with Cecilia and could discuss her at length, her beauty, her intelligence, her manner, the way she curled her hair around her finger when in thought, the politeness she showed her servants. She was now installed in the castle and recognized by everyone as his mistress.

162

"Giorgio, I am going to have Cecelia pose for Leonardo as soon as he is finished with his current commission on the 'Virgin of the Rocks' that he is completing for the Confraternity of the Immaculate Conception. I have seen it, and it is a splendid painting of the Virgin, the baby Christ and young John the Baptist as well as the angel Gabriel painted in a style he calls, 'sfumato' that gives a sort of smoky patina to it. Leonardo is a very pleasant personality, polite and cordial and a good conversationalist when he has a mind for it and is not preoccupied with his own thoughts."

Then, almost as an afterthought, but in a very serious manner, Ludovico said, "Before I commission Leonardo, however, I want to dedicate a festival to the Virgin. She is such an important part of our world. It should be on August 15th, the day she rose into heaven, the Assumption. Gianni should be the one to oversee it, I believe, and Leonardo should orchestrate the participants and execute the floats and design any costumes that are needed. He has done an extraordinary job in the past on our events. I want stages constructed for the performance of religious plays and for music performances. I will have Franchino Gafforio compose appropriate music. I want the festival to be worthy of our people and an annual event that will inspire our people that they dwell in a leading city of the Peninsular."

"Yes, Gianni is right for it," replied Giorgio. He does seem to have a strong belief in her. His adoration of the Virgin is as great as yours. If someone did not know you as well as I do, they would think you and Gianni are searching for a mother."

"Giorgio, why must you always put our religious beliefs in such crude terms. One would think that you are attempting to be superior to believers. Your superiority is very much overrated. It does not annoy me so much, I know who you are, but Gianni may be taken aback. Your sarcasm is not humor and is only amusing up to a point."

*****

"Our agent in Milan reports that Ludovico's tax relief program for the silk industry has been so successful that Genoa is threatening him, claiming that Ludovico has not only stolen skilled workers from them but has also taken trade from them," the newly installed Pope Innocent VIII said to Cardinals delle Rovere and Borgia as they gathered on a sunlit morning in the Belvedere Garden.

"Genoa should be careful or they might get more than they sow with their aggressive words," replied Cardinal delle Rovere, always ready to assess an opponent's military weakness. "Ludovico is not known to ignore insults and accusations lightly. Genoa's wealth has been on a steady decline, and a severe setback would create unforeseen consequences for the regime. They are no match for Milan nowadays."

"They are not the power they were decades ago and cannot sustain a long combat," said Cardinal Borgia, joining the conversation and equally adept at assessing an opponent's weakness. "Venice has reduced them to a minor player, and they should not assert themselves unless they are unequivocally certain they can prevail or can come to a stalemate. A stalemate can provide some advantages to them. It might show Ludovico that they are not people that can be pushed around, and they may be able to draw France onto their side. That will alter the calculation."

"But it is Milan that would be the aggrieved party if Genoa attacked Ludovico, and he would have more than sufficient cause to strike back forcefully," interjected Innocent, then looking around at the garden beginning to show its rebirth after the desolation of winter. "We do not need such instability so close to our borders."

Cardinal delle Rovere noticed Pope Innocent's approval of his newborn garden and said smiling, "Persephone's return from Hades is always welcome. She brings such joy to everyone."

Innocent merely nodded, not wanting to seem to approve such a pagan allusion.

Innocent was a man of family wealth, a good deal of which was rumored to have been used to obtain the papacy. After three months as Pope, he was feeling much more secure in his position, and he desired one of his first actions to be a crusade against the Turkish Muslims. On this day, he broached the subject to delle Rovere and Borgia, who were becoming his favorite advisors, just as Pope Sixtus had hoped and planned through his conversations with each of them.

"You are not likely to receive the agreements you will need to mount a crusade at this time. There are only a few principalities that would join you. In addition, you should be more concerned with the Italian Peninsular than with far-off Turkey," said Cardinal Borgia, his ambition for his family just as evident, focused, and overpowering as was Cardinal della Rovere's. Ambition burned red hot for both men like smoldering embers. It exceeded the papacy for both men. A main difference between the two being della Rovere's pleasure in not only planning a campaign and engaging in the intrigue but also in leading troops into battle.

Pope Innocent, on the other hand, had a similar ambition but was just as resolute against the heretics that he believed were undermining the theological stability and administrative structure of the Church. He was to empower Tomas de Torquemada as Grand Inquisitor of Spain and to issue a bull for the extermination of the Waldensians, a Christian sect preaching a somewhat different theology. None of these concerns deprived him of his delight in the earthly pleasures, pleasures he enjoyed before his Papacy and would continue to enjoy afterwards. His wanton lust for the unclerical joys of this life showed on his person like a ship attracting barnacles and were never far from his mind.

*****

"Look at the Virgin's festival," shouted Ludovico enthusiastically as Gianni approached his seat near Ludovico in the reviewing stand. The festival was in mid-progress and the excitement in Ludovico's voice was contagious, attracting amusing smiles from all those around his box. Giorgio was absent, his whereabouts unknown but noticeable by Ludovico's entourage.

It was a hot, sunny, almost cloudless August 15th, crowds lining the streets enthusiastically. Men in brightly colored outfits were parading along the street hurling flags in the air, retrieving them before they hit the ground, twirling them in intricate patterns as they walked along, viewers applauding their moves, young children shouting their approval as energetically as Ludovico in the stands. The gold accessories on their red and yellow brocaded costumes gleamed in the sun like little rays of sunshine that danced in the air.

Floats followed the twirlers, floats honoring the Virgin, icons of her composed of roses and geraniums of various colors attached to the float, children sitting or standing by the icon as it was pulled along by men in brocaded costumes who were replaced at intervals as the floats progressed along the route by new, similarly dressed carriers.

"The Virgin will be pleased today. Leonardo has done a marvelous job," Ludovico said to Gianni and Cecilia on one side of him, then turning to Bishop Rhondinello, Bishop of Milan, on his other side to exchange a similar feeling with him. "Lorenzo de Medici would be proud of Milan today and could not have produced a festival any worthier than ours."

"Yes, I believe he would," replied the Bishop in as somber a voice that he could muster and obvious proud of what he was viewing.

On one of the seats near Ludovico, Leonardo, smartly dressed in a gold-trimmed brocaded outfit that complemented the outfits he had designed for the parade participants, sat with his attendant, savoring his accomplishment, and clearly enjoying the parade with the people around him. From time to time his thoughts would turn to his next project, a painting of Cecelia. He would turn to look at her several times to retain an image of her in different relaxed postures as the parade progressed. The more he viewed her, the more interested he found himself with her and the more eager he was to begin her painting.

*****

On a morning not expected to be eventful, the sky was heavy with the impending rain that was needed after the weeks of drought that Milan had experienced. Water levels had subsided along the canals and barge traffic had slowed to a trickle. Ludovico was sitting in his chambers finishing a leisurely breakfast of cheese and breads, as slow in thought as the clouds were in opening their heavenly faucet.

Giorgio rushed into Ludovico's chambers clamoring loudly as soon as he had passed the guards, "Ludovico, Genoa has attacked one of our guard posts along the border."

"Have there been any casualties," rejoined Ludovico, pushing aside his breakfast and jumping out of his chair, ready to begin deliberating on the incident.

"Several soldiers have been killed, and several other have been injured. But they held their post and repulsed the attack," Giorgio said as he took a piece of cheese off the table and wrapped it in a broken piece of bread. Both men walked to the table that was placed in a nook by the window, some paperwork scattered on it and sat.

"Despite the disagreement over our relaxed tax policy for the silk industry, why would Genoa take such a rash and hazardous action? They surely must know that the costs could be severe for them. Have they become so impervious to potential consequences or is something else going on?" Ludovico looked quizzical, sitting quietly for several moments. Then to Giorgio he said, "Have Tomasso join us. I want to know if our finances have at all changed recently."

Giorgio walked to the door and bid one of the guards to fetch Tomasso, frowning out of sight of Ludovico.

When Giorgio returned, Ludovico said to him, "Could this incident be unrelated to our silk policy, something trivial, not of national concern? I think you should go there immediately with some additional men and look into the incident. I do not want to act impetuously and without serious cause, although, whatever the case, this is an affront, but we must handle it judiciously. I want to avoid involving ourselves in a serious war, if possible. I am not ready for it. I don't want to show others that we are not as strong as they believe us to be."

"Genoa has never been the same since the Venetians defeated them a century ago at Chioggia. They have lost much of their long-distance trade to them. They remain a strong but reduced mercantile power but not a very threatening military power", replied Giorgio, now sitting at the table, legs crossed and eyes focused on Ludovico. "Banking is their main income source now. Maybe, this is more about Venice than it is with us, desiring to hinder the increased trade that will flow to them from our newly enacted policy." Giorgio was not one to become overly emotional about a minor incident that may have repercussions only in the future.

After several moments, Tomasso entered the room, slightly out of breath from rushing to Ludovico's chambers from the other wing of the castle. He addressed both men politely and sat where Ludovico motioned him to sit but not before pushing his hair from his eyes with his unencumbered hand. His other hand held two large bound books that summarized the finances of the duchy.

Ludovico looked at Tomasso. "Tomasso, what do our finances show for the past quarter? Is our tax relief policy showing any returns yet or is it too early to say?"

"It will take some time to recoup our lost tax revenue. The projection is still favorable. In fact, our revenue is slightly higher than the reduced revenue we expected to incur. We should achieve break even in about a year."

"Good, good," replied Ludovico leaning back in his chair and staring over the two men in front of him at, it appeared, nothing in particular. He was prone to this behavior when he was considering an alternative option. He did not enjoy staring vacuously at the person in front of him, thinking it could be misinterpreted as a purposely intimidating action. His option apparently considered and accepted through some internal mechanism, he dismissed Tomasso and called for Gianni to come to the room.

When all three men, Ludovico, Giorgio and Gianni, were together later that same day, Ludovico instructed Giorgio to the border with a contingent of men to supplement the soldiers on guard there. He ordered Giorgio to quietly attack the Genoese troops there in retribution for their attack on Milanese troops.

Gianni was given specific instructions. "Gianni, after our attack, I want you to consult with Vittorio Fiano, the Treasury Secretary. Offer him this proposal. 'We agree to provide Genoa with a transportation franchise of a portion of any increase in trade arising from our new policy in the western Mediterranean and the northern regions of the Holy Roman Empire for the next five years. This is a firm offer, not to be extended to additional concessions.'"

As Gianni was nodding his head, Ludovico rose from the table and addressed Gianni directly again. "You must not let this proposal seem that it is being forced on them, although I don't know how a proposal to their advantage could be interpreted as forced. Nevertheless, be cautious about your approach. This is of advantage to both of us."

*****

Giorgio rode to the border with a contingent of men. He was not as forgiving as was Ludovico of the incident, believing that there could be slight justification for the attack. People on both sides had been killed for little advantage. Genoa, if they are reasonable he thought, will retrieve a measure of self-respect but it was just as likely to have arrived at the same result without the bloodshed. After all, principalities were always altering their industrial and trade policies. He acknowledged the reason for Ludovico's hesitancy but was more concerned with the prestige of the troops. Giorgio was well respected by the troops, seen as one them, not unlike their respect for Ludovico but of a more ordinary nature.

According to the captain of the guards, a tall, angular, broad-shouldered soldier with a direct and simple style, who Giorgio knew well and whose conduct he respected, the attack was unprovoked and involved a small number of Genoese soldiers, perhaps 30 was his estimate. It occurred stealthily one evening without warning on his outpost. Milanese soldiers had not been anywhere near the border. Therefore, our intrusion on their side of the border could not be used as a justification for the attack. The captain could not offer any reason for the incursion; he was befuddled.

Fortunately, his men were well trained for this action. They were restrained in their defense, holding their line staunchly, and able to repulse the attackers after, in his words, a short, fierce skirmish that resulted in the casualties noted. The Genoese incurred somewhat larger casualties and withdrew from the field quickly. The captain allowed them to carry their casualties away.

Once completing his conversation with the captain and several of the men involved in the incident, Giorgio decided to examine the border area with a few of his own men, inviting the captain to join him with some of his men. They spent the day simply walking the border area closest to the access road to the Milanese campsite, leaving their horses in the supervision of the remainder of the troops.

Gianni remained in camp waiting for the moment he too would provide service to Ludovico, considering his presentation and forging his resolve. His appearance was slowly but inexorably growing into the role he was to play in the little drama that was unfolding. This was his opportunity to shine, and he intended to make the most of it.

Giorgio was confident that he was under surveillance as they walked the border. He wanted to be seen by the Genoese and was counting on them to bolster their defense by engaging more men at this contact point. Earlier, before his movement to the border point, he had ordered three-quarters of his troops to trek through the forest miles away from their present location in order to cross the border without notice and circle behind the Genoese camp. He hoped surprise would win the day when he initiated his attack. His confidence, which was never lacking, was especially obvious today because his purpose was not simply to show Milanese strength but to avenge the fallen Milanese soldiers of the previous week.

Giorgio wiped his brow, the sun beating down relentlessly this time of year, physically oppressing him like an unseen weight drawing him into the earth, his shirt wet with perspiration, his face red from sunburn. I'm thankful for the trees at the edge of the forest that provide a modicum of shade, he thought. It is almost impossible to think clearly in this weather.

The attack was set, not to be undone save for some extraordinary circumstance. He would fall on the Genoese guards, first having his Stradioti mercenaries advance on the sentinels stealthily, then when the signal is given, to attack frontally in force. The hope was that the Genoese troops guarding the rear would join their cohorts in the front. Giorgio's main force would then move in from the rear in a pincer movement, trapping the Genoese.

At dawn, the sun not yet risen fully in the sky, Giorgio led his men into the fray on horseback, slashing his way through the Genoese troops when he was felled from his horse by a foot-soldier, a deep gash in his right thigh. He hobbled to the side of the battle to regain himself and reentered the fight almost immediately, dragging his blood drenched leg along, his lieutenant by his side. The skirmish did not last long, ending as soon as his main force easily overran the rear guard of the Genoese. They then joined Giorgio's contingent to surround the full force of the Genoese, compelling them to drop their weapons, defeat in their eyes, blood on their suits, and sorrow in their hearts.

"Death comes quickly in battle, if one is fortunate," said Giorgio to his captain, as he lay propped up by a tree, his men gathering the remainder of the Genoese who had not fled. "Keep them under guard until tomorrow when we will decide what to do with them."

That evening, Gianni sat at camp envisaging his meeting with Secretary Fiano. His instructions from Ludovico were clear, and he intended to fulfill them precisely. He understood that Ludovico had trusted him with this assignment because he had gained confidence in his performance, and he also understood that his youthful appearance could prove an obstacle to completing his assignment. His confidence in his own abilities was not yet complete, but he was reminded of Ludovico's advice from his father, Francesco, "treat uncertainty as a brother."

Giorgio's injury took a turn for the worst in the evening. By morning he was hallucinating, burning with a fever that was dangerously lethal. An attendant approached Gianni, informing him that Giorgio required urgent attention. "He is calling out a woman's name, Magdalene," said the attendant, a nervous tick recurring between words.

Gianni, brushing hair from his forehead, looked at the attendant directly and replied, "She is, no doubt, just one of the many prostitutes that he favors," then realizing the unnecessary sarcasm and blatant insensitivity to his injured friend, hesitated for a moment and realized his error. "We have to save him, he is important to Ludovico as well as to me. We have been friends for many years."

"What should we do about his wound? Should we not have a physician attend him as soon as possible?" replied the soldier. Addressing Gianni in an almost pleading voice, he said, "There is one in the village not too distant from here. It would not take long to fetch him."

"Yes, yes, you must bring him here immediately and have Giorgio's wounds seen to. Do whatever you must to attend to him. I will complete my assignment today and will take him to Milan tomorrow to visit the court physician, a very respected one indeed, if Giorgio can be moved. Have the physician remain here until morning. We must get his opinion about transporting Giorgio. We must be positive that the travel home will not be too great a burden on him. If need be, we can spend a few more days here and send a courier to Milan with the result of my meeting. Gianni, whose mien was tightly controlled and almost frozen over his thoughts about his meeting with Fiano, suddenly seemed relaxed, his body unfolding like a flower spreading its petals to the sun.

Three days passed, however, before Gianni appeared in Genoa to meet Vittorio Fiano, Treasury Secretary for Genoa and General Octavio Catanzaro, Genoa's condottiere. Entering Vittorio's study, he introduced himself to him and his advisors gathered at a large rectangular table, the table top inlaid with pinkish-white marble, four legs shaped like the head and neck of a swan, located in the center of the study, a study of extraordinary beauty, heavily paneled embossed walls with gold trim and gold plated rosettes in each panel, paintings occupying all four walls on topics of various interest, portraits, agrarian scenes, religious scenes and several of very monumental church steeples.

Vittorio was a short, slim, youngish-looking man with a fair complexion and a full head of wavy black hair, a pleasant but, perhaps, prudish face known by reputation to be a reasonable and capable man. Octavio, on the other hand, was a short, muscular man with a swarthy complexion, originally from the southern part of the Peninsular, with a surprisingly jovial facial expression for his occupation.

"Good morning, your excellency, I am Gianni, Gianni Cortese, envoy of Ludovico Sforza, Regent of Milan. It is a shame our meeting has been postponed for these three days. But I know you are a man of vast duties, and I understand you need for time to attend to those duties." To himself, Gianni could not understand the delay of such an important topic, a cessation of hostilities. Milan's court spy, however, had conveyed to Gianni that there had been meetings with the French ambassador over the last few days which posed the possibility of French involvement, a prospect that would greatly compound the threat to Milan.

Vittorio addressed Gianni politely and bid him to sit at the table. "I must apologize for the delay but as you say, duty calls. I am confident that we can come to some accord on the subject that is at hand. We are neighbors and should not be adversaries. It is unhelpful for both our countries."

Vittorio paused for effect, then spoke, looking directly but without malice into Gianni eyes. The man has a soothing appearance, Gianni thought, a characteristic that has probably assisted him in negotiations in the past. I must not be taken in by it. "The confrontation between our troops is an unfortunate incident, don't you believe?"

"Unfortunate but provoked by your guards," Gianni replied immediately in a soft voice, trying strenuously not to avert his eyes from Vittorio's stare and to counter his opponent's relaxed attitude with his own soft but determined attitude, a battle that he was losing. He was resolute not to be intimidated by this man.

"My advisors tell me that our attack was an incomprehensible blunder on the part of our border guards, a mistake, a misunderstanding of orders given," said Octavio, both hands laying palms down on the table.

"But you must agree that it was, nevertheless, a provocation, one that may have ulterior motives, it seems possible," replied Gianni, now sitting uncomfortably in his chair and looking at an oddly misplaced drawing of a windblown landscape, a river bisecting it and flowers on its banks on the wall behind Vittorio.

"What may you be referring to?" said Vittorio, "blunders and misunderstandings are not uncommon in our profession. The trick is to resolve them before they become seriously uncontrollable."

Adjusting himself even more stiffly in his chair, Gianni retorted, "There is no reason to avoid the topic. There is evidence that you are dissatisfied with our new tax policy in regard to our silk industry."

Fiano hesitated briefly and replied, "Well yes, that is true."

"Surely, you understand that our policy is not aimed at you, and was not meant to harm you but is an effort to improve conditions for our citizens. Do you not wish to do the same for your subjects?" At this point, Gianni felt he was nearing the climax to this conversation and told himself to remain focused on his ultimate goal.

"I consider it an affront to Genoa who has been a friend to Milan."

"Again, I say, we meant it as no affront, and Ludovico does not see a cause for you to act in such a hostile manner towards us. We consider ourselves your friend also."

"Hostile, hostile," said Vittorio, anger rising in his voice, suddenly forsaking his calming appearance, his body visibly bracing against his chair. "We have reason to be hostile."

"Then again, friendships can be broken," Gianni retorted, looking sternly and directly at Vittorio, his resolve now visible on his face, his hands clasped in front of him on the table. "On the other hand, Ludovico has authorized me to offer you an alternative to this situation, one that I believe you will find attractive."

"Yes, and what would this alternative be," he said, his dour expression fading somewhat from his face. He was not yet convinced but appeared interested in the offer.

"He is willing to offer you the shipping rights to a percentage of the trade that comes from this new policy for five years, to begin in one year's time. Surely, this offer is more beneficial than the alternative. It would calm you merchants who are the ones most affected and would, we believe, gain favorability of your public. It is an offer that is costless to you."

"This is interesting but I need time to consider it, his anger disappearing as quickly as it seemed to have arisen. I will give you an answer tomorrow. Meanwhile, you and your friends will be my guest this evening and enjoy dinner with us."

"I look forward to your answer."

\*\*\*\*\*

For Gianni, the return to Milan was as joyous as a bird soaring over the countryside, first plunging to the earth with the wind, then rising to the clouds, all the time feeling the exhilaration that comes with success. Giorgio was recuperating nicely; the physician that attended to him proved to be very capable and treated his wound with the utmost professionalism. His negotiation was completed to everyone's satisfaction; his mind was free of the anxiety that accompanied him during his stay at the border, and he was anticipating a warm reception from Ludovico and the admiration of the court.

The time spent on the return to Milan was expected to be free from the pressures that accompanied Gianni on the original journey. The first day of the journey home was as clear and bright as any that he had ever seen. Spring had not yet arrived but Persephone was expected at any moment, hinting of her beauty by the early blooming flowers like the crocus and the arrival of flocks of birds from their winter respite in Africa.

"Isn't the day glorious," said Gianni with a wide sweep of his arm to the captain of the outpost who was accompanying him back to Milan.

"Yes, the anticipation of spring always brings a rise in my spirits."

Several days passed in this idyllic atmosphere when Gianni came upon an open field occupied by a large collection of people singing and dancing in obvious devotion to several statutes whose male image sat on elevated platforms decorated in brightly colored garments. They moved from one image to the other, dancing around the figures in alternating patterns, some of the devotees in semi-trance like states.

Seeing several people standing slightly removed from the dancers, Gianni approached them. "Morning," he said to one man leaning against a tree, "do you mind me inquiring about what is happening here?"

"No, this is a congregation devoted to the worship of Asclepius."

Gianni thought to himself, I remembered a group of hikers from years past who talked to me about Asclepius. This congregation has certainly grown and spread from the time I first saw them.

"What is the purpose of this celebration? I remember hearing about Asclepius and his exploits some time ago," said Gianni, talking to the man but looking at the dancers in the field.

"He has the power over the devil and protects his flock from the evil one," replied the man, gaining more interest in Gianni as the conversation progressed. "And he can bring salvation to believers who honor him."

"Is there any purpose to this celebration?"

"Today is one of several holy days devoted to Asclepius and celebrates the acceptance of several people into the community of Asclepius. It is also part of an initiation rite, but I can tell you no more. It is reserved for those individuals who are interested in the sect," replied the man now moving slightly away from Gianni, convinced that Gianni was only interested in casual information and not in pursuing a formal introduction to the community.

"One more question, if you please," said Gianni. "Is your sect found in other places?"

"Yes, there are many shrines elsewhere," he said in an obvious exaggeration.

Gianni could sense that the man did not desire to continue the conversation. He politely thanked him, and he and the captain moved on.

"What did you think of that?" asked the captain several minutes after they rode off from the field.

"As I told him, I was introduced to Asclepius a few years ago, when I met a group of Christian pilgrims along the road at a small shrine to Asclepius, and I am amazed at how quickly the community seems to have grown. I suppose it does not take much to become a god."

"Then I take it that you are not a believer," said the captain.

"In Asclepius, no. This community is not unlike the 'mystery' religions that came into being in the late Hellenistic era and ran into the early Roman era. The basic tenets were held secret, to be revealed only to members. For example, it was a prerequisite to perform time-consuming and expensive rituals to enter the sect, one being a purification to cleanse oneself of this world, to establish a rebirth, a reintroduction into a new world. These were meant to show the initiate's sincerity. Does not this sound somewhat like our introduction to Christ at baptism? Animal sacrifices could also be part of the ritual."

"Well, yes," replied the captain, feeling uncomfortable, not expecting Gianni to find any part of it comparable to Christianity.

"Periodic public celebrations, like the one we saw today, with processions, singing and dancing were also a significant element of the sects, often to attract new initiates."

"That seemed like fun," said the captain, trying to lighten the conversation and not sure how serious Gianni was.

"The reward for the member was to be protected from the blind power of fate, for the deity to advantage the believer. These sects often began as off-shoots of myths of fertility deities and their belief in the cycle of life, death and rebirth, later to be transformed into believes in salvation from fate. One aspect was giving the believer a feeling of a personal relationship with the deity and the feeling of being special for being a member of the community."

Riding in silence for a while, Gianni said, "Perhaps the most famous of these 'mystery' sects was the one devoted to Demeter, the goddess of the harvest, at Eleusis near Athens, Greece where a temple was built in her honor. Her daughter, Kore or Persephone, was abducted and raped by Hades, god of the underworld, and brought to his kingdom. Demeter, searching all the world, was unable to find her and fell into an extreme state of despair, leaving the earth fallow and barren and near famine. Finally, Zeus sent Hermes to Hades to demand that Persephone be returned to her mother. Unfortunately, Persephone, had just eaten pomegranate seeds, given to her by Hades. By law, anyone eating of fruit in Hades was destined to remain there forever. Zeus, however, ultimately exacted a compromise from Hades. Persephone was to spend 6 months of the year in Hades and the remaining 6 months with the gods in Olympus. Demeter was so relieved that she allowed the earth to become fruitful again, and Persephone now returns to her home every spring."

Gianni, holding his horse steady, turned to the captain beside him, and said, "You can see how the myth of Demeter can be associated with rebirth."

\*\*\*\*\*

"Gianni, have you seen Giorgio? He goes missing every now and then, and it's a mystery where he goes," Ludovico asked as Gianni entered the room. Fall was in the air and a bright sun took the edge off of this chilly morning lifting everyone's spirits. Ludovico was in such a fine mood that he could not be too upset with Giorgio. "I am going to have to have a discussion with him."

"No, I have not seen him for several days."

"I have news from my brother, Ascanio, and about my nephew, Gian Galeazzo," Ludovico said softly, directing Gianni to follow him into an inner room next to his office.

"Gian Galeazzo has decide to marry and the woman he has chosen is Isabella, granddaughter of Ferdinand of Naples. It is just as I have expected. The wedding is to take place in Naples in three months. It is fraught with danger for us. On the one hand, it can provide us an alliance with Naples. On the other hand, it could create a claim on Milan in the future. We can only wait and see what is to transpire, but it is good to keep this in mind."

"Perhaps you can send Leonardo to arrange and orchestrate the ceremonies for them as a wedding present," said Gianni, as he sat in one of the two comfortable chairs alongside the small table by the window.

"Wonderful idea, Gianni. Arrange for that to be done."

"Now about Ascanio. He has found evidence that there is a special fund in the Vatican, an off-book fund, that has existed since Sixtus's time, and he suspects that it is the money that is flowing to the Vatican from the farms and possible from other sources."

"One would have to believe that it is a very significant fund."

"Yes, Ascanio is attempting to find evidence of its size. He is working to become Vice-Chancellor, a position that Cardinal Borgia holds now and abuses undisturbed by Pope Innocent. He also believes that the Pope has an agent in our court. Both the Pope and Cardinal Borgia seem to have an uncommon knowledge of our doings that they should not have."

*****

Milan was bustling: the one hundred and twenty thousand people that inhabited the city were seeing an unprecedented improvement in it, one that surpassed even what Francesco had initiated during his reign. Donato Bramante's plan to widen streets was moving forward, especially the street leading to the Castello Sforzesco, which was eventually to have villas on both sides of it. Ludovico envisioned a boulevard of incomparable beauty that would surpass any extant boulevard on the Italian

Peninsular. The canal system was expanding, twenty thousand silk industry workers were now employed and work on the cathedral was renewed. He had also endowed the Universities and Milan and Pavia.

Ludovico had instructed Leonardo to paint a portrait of Cecilia and to begin design for a tribute to his father, a bronze equestrian horse that Ludovico wanted to put on display in a prominent place in the city.

All of this nascent activity permitted Ludovico to concentrate on other projects. One project that had been on his mind was the improvement in his birthplace on the family estate in Vigevano, his retreat about 20 miles from Pavia. The arrival of fall brought thoughts of it to Ludovico and of his vineyard, experimental farm and cattle-breeding station there. On the farm, he experimented with cultivating rice, grape vines, and mulberry trees. He made butter and some of the finest cheeses in all of the Peninsula. The hills and fields grazed 28,000 oxen, cows, buffalos, sheep and goats. His stables housed stallions and mares, and he bred, according to some, the finest horses in Europe.

Near Pavia and started decades earlier by the Visconti, he continued the building of one of the most remarkably beautiful structures in the Peninsula, the Certosa di Pavia (the Carthusian Monastery). Although some people might question the overall beauty of its façade with its myriad, multicolored statutes in marble, of saints in its niches, and an endless variety of foliage, garlands and ornaments adorning the walls, distracting the viewer's eye with no essential focal point, no one can question the individual beauty of each of the pieces, the artistry, devotion and intensity of spirit that imbues each piece.

*****

Darkness descended on the city gradually, like a vine creeping over a bush, slowing the movement of its inhabitants. In a room in the Vatican, the white marble floor tiles were streaked in a pattern that resembled gray-like water dribbling from a puddle. One wall was covered with paintings, the "Adoration of the Magi" begun by Fra Angelico and finished by Fra Filippo Lippi, next to the "Madonna of the Eucharist" by Sandro Botticelli. A fresco of the "Damned Consigned to Hell" by Luca Signorelli occupied the upper half of the opposite wall. On the third wall a large gilded cross hung forlornly facing a desk set between two windows. The small oak desk had intricate floral designs running down its sides and along its bottom. The windows had thick embroidered red curtains of an intricately designed pattern, closed to hide the silent darkness of the night. The bottom half of all four walls were highly paneled in wood with large rosettes centered in an enclosed rectangular wooden design.

The assassin crouched behind the curtain holding his plain hilted dagger, the pommel of a convex design, no silhouette emerging from the thick curtains into the room. The Cardinal entered the room with an attendant walking closely behind him and moved to his desk.

"Put the tray on my desk," he said, "I need a cup of wine," and motioned the attendant to place the gold-plated tray with a cup of lightly aromatic Dolcetto wine, several Ciambella de Monaco cookies and Biscotti on his desk.

Looking pleased, the Cardinal politely dismissed the attendant, walked to the adjoining bedroom, looked in as if to fetch something and quickly went to his desk, pulled his chair out from the desk and sat.

It has been a difficult day, he said to himself as he took his first sip of wine and laid against the backrest of his chair but I have made some progress. He sighed slightly as the hint of sweetness mixed with blackberries in the finish of the wine pleased him. Suddenly, the assassin jumped from behind the curtain and brought the dagger down hard on Cardinal Ascanio's shoulder, prevented, however, by the top of the backrest from plunging the dagger farther into his body. A cry of pain from the assassin and Ascanio went out simultaneously, creating an unusual harmony of agony just as the attendant returned to the room. The assassin rushed the attendant and swatted him with the dagger, laying him down gushing blood onto the white marble floor.

The assassin leaped out of the door, running along the hallway in the dim light. A Swiss guard was after him the moment he left the room. The ununiformed guard chased him in silence along the hall until it ended and turned in a different direction. He was confronted by another guard who thrust his sword deep into the assassin's chest rendering him motionless on the parquet floor. His body was lifeless, on its side, one arm across his chest and blood running from his wound down his stomach into a rich, red puddle. The blood was soon sponged from the floor, leaving it as pristine as it had been prior to the killing.

Without addressing each other, the two guards immediately lifted the assassin and placed him on an old worn rug, rolled him up, and carried him away without anyone taking notice. Back in Cardinal Ascanio's room, the Cardinal was now sitting in his chair slightly hunched over, his attendant sitting opposite him in another chair, the artistry of both chairs now spoiled by each man's blood, and both men soon to be attended to by other people.

The cardinal's attendant, who was only slightly injured, recovered quickly from the attack and after recovering from the shock of it called out for assistance. It took only several minutes for assistance to reach the room. Cardinal Ascanio was carried to the infirmary where he was quickly bathed clean and his wound treated. His full recovery was to take several weeks. The assassin was never found, and the names of the unknown guards were never revealed. It was to remain an unsolved mystery.

As night turned into day, the activity of the Vatican eclipsed the turmoil of the previous evening, leaving only rumors of Cardinal Ascanio's troubles. The incident faded into the dusty shelfs of books and pictures that lay in the hidden parts of the Vatican. I must contact Ludovico, Ascanio thought to himself the following day. I must tell him of this incident.

*****

Ludovico was enjoying Cecilia posing for Leonardo, her portrait nearing completion. He thought to himself, she will be remembered in history, and I as well for this portrait. She is truly beautiful, a pearl in the open shell of Milan. It is painted in oils, a relatively new medium introduced to Italy from the Netherlands. She wears black jewelry around her neck, a reference to Ludovico's epithet, Il Moro. He has a whimsical look on his face as he puzzles over what he believes to be an armorial ermine in her lap. Cecilia, sixteen years old, is seated, pregnant, in a three-quarter profile pose, as distinct from the older full profile pose previously favored by artists, looking out from the picture.

As Ludovico is admiring the painting and Leonardo's technique, a courier enters alongside of Giorgio, both men in a rush. "Ludovico," Giorgio calls out, "there has been an assassination attempt on Ascanio. He was injured but has survived and is recovering from his wound. The assassin has disappeared; there is no trace of him."

"No trace of him! No one saw him."

"Only Ascanio and his attendant saw him, but the attack happened so quickly that they could not identify him."

"I just don't understand how that could have happened."

Giorgio sat down as Ludovico handed him a glass of Vernaccio, dismissed the courier and relaxed in the chair. "Ascanio has also said that he intends to visit you as soon as he is better able to endure the journey."

"Did he give any indication of the reason for the visit other than the attack?"

"No, but it is not the attack he wants to discuss. That much I know."

Ludovico sat in the chair opposite Giorgio and joined him in a glass of wine. Both men sat there late into the day over several glasses of wine, changing to a Chianti later in the evening, Ludovico musing to Giorgio about Leonardo's artistry and Giorgio, always the contrarian, praising Giotto.

"Giorgio, you are one of the most irreligious of men and, yet, you admire one of the most religious of painters. How do you reconcile that?"

"Ah, yes, but Giotto does not just paint Jesus and other saintly people. He paints them in all the agony and pathos of a human. I can feel their pain and see the sadness of the human condition."

At the end of the wine-fest, both men, still lucid after all the wine, still held fast to their initial opinions and could only agree than Cecilia Gallerani was the fairest lady in Milan and that retribution was needed for the attack on Ascanio.

*****

Ascanio arrived in Milan by coach accompanied by his attendant and showing little effect on his health from the long journey from Rome. His wound had healed completely without any noticeable effects on him. "It has been some time since I have been in Milan," he remarked to his brother, Ludovico. "You have created an artistic paradise in Castello Sforzesco. Our father would be proud of you."

"Thank you, my brother," replied Ludovico. He had a warm spot in his heart for his younger brother, younger by three years, and always felt protective of him.

Giorgio and Gianni were also in the room, bright light shining on the parquet floors from the two windows on one of the walls, four chairs arrayed in a circle near the windows. Giorgio and Ascanio traded the kind of affectionate exchanges that one would expect from men who had been raised together harmoniously, jocularly teasing each other of their past transgressions. A warm feeling pervaded the room as Ludovico, Ascanio and Giorgio talked.

Once they were seated, their discussion turned decidedly more serious. Ascanio, taking the lead, first related the assassination attempt and his recovery. After a brief moment of silence between the men, Ascanio said, "I also have information about the monasteries, and it is as we expected. It is not good and portends struggles in the future for many people."

"Just what do you have for us?" asked Ludovico, some concern showing in his voice.

"Pope Innocent is pursuing Sixtus's legacy, hording the funds he is obtaining from the monastery farms, but I have been unsuccessful in determining the accumulated amount. The funds are being placed in Augsburg in the Fugger Bank, bypassing the Medici and other Italian banks. At the same time, he continues to replace the heads of the monasteries with abbots and priors who are beholding to him. Moreover, he is liquidating some of the farms, the land being more valuable since it has been cleared all these years and made more productive. Many monasteries continue to deteriorate over Europe. I suspect he would sell off the monasteries themselves if they had any value." Ascanio had to pause for a minute because he was becoming more animated and clearly perturbed about what he was saying.

"It seems more than possible that the assassination attempt on you has to do with the information you have gathered," said Giorgio, up from his chair as usual like a cat chasing its dinner and, if one had never seen him before would conclude that he was ready to jump on his horse and proceed to attack, someone, anyone that hints at being involved. Ascanio was Ludovico's blood and that meant that his assassin was Giorgio's enemy as well.

"Calm, Giorgio," said Ludovico, he himself more animated than usual in situations like this. Ludovico's intensity was aroused more than in the past because Ascanio's information now hinted at a larger scheme than he had imagined previously.

"Is there more, Ascanio?"

"Yes," Ascanio's continued, "there are rumors that Innocent has been hiring more Swiss mercenaries."

"Ah, more Swiss mercenaries, you say," Ludovico looking for thoughts to place before the men for comment. "Troops mean battles, do they not, not only defense, Ascanio. Do you know of any plans for an offensive attack by Innocent on someone?"

"No, the papal troops have been involved in a few skirmishes but none of great import."

"There is one other oddity. This fund goes back to the time of Sixtus. That is a long time to be accumulating funds. They are gaining interest on the funds, however."

Giorgio could not help himself and had to interject, "I suppose interest gained for the Vatican is not considered usury," then retreaded a step backward waiting for the frontal attack from the others. To his surprise, all three men merely smiled slightly and ignored him, even Ascanio who could still remember Giorgio's sarcasm from his youth but also knew that his sarcasm was not meant to hurt.

"There is a fund, overseen by the Vice Chancellor and several members of the Curia, including Cardinal delle Rovere. I have not yet been able to find it on the books. Cardinal Borgia is Vice Chancellor now. No doubt, he is skimming one ducat of the monasteries' money for himself and one for this secret fund. Meanwhile, Innocent is bankrupting the Vatican with his petty skirmishes and his vast reconstruction program. He cannot secure the normal flow of funds quickly enough to balance his outflows. Power lies in the Vice-Chancellor, and I am trying to maneuver myself for that position."

Rising from his chair, Ascanio continued with his report. "You know as well as I do, Ludovico, that the Popes have been in contention with the secular powers for decades, even centuries. It rises and wanes to the attitude of the man who occupies the Papacy at the time."

"Yes, one can trace the competition between the Pope and secular authorities at least from the crowning of Charlemagne by Pope Leo II in Rome in the year 800, crowning him the Holy Roman Emperor."

Gianni, who had been quiet and reserved all this time, looked utterly absorbed in the conversation and continued to sit with his hands on the table, clasped and relaxed. Giorgio roamed around the room still occupied with the thought of who attacked Ascanio, then suddenly stopped and reclaimed his seat, still not completely involved in the discussions.

Ascanio leaned back against the backrest of the chair. "There was no central authority after the Roman Empire collapsed, the only semblance of an authority was the Church which oversaw the spiritual realm and to some extent the secular realm. The Holy Roman Emperor tried to hold together the northern Italian provinces under his control. This situation made possible the usurpation of areas by local warlords who sought their legitimacy from the Pope or from the Holy Roman Emperor by pledging allegiance to them. In this milieu, it was only natural for the inhabitants to choose to support either the Pope, calling themselves Gwelfs, or the Emperor, calling themselves Ghibellines, often creating a very unstable situation between and within these territories."

"Popes would try to extend their secular control over areas by force, to enlarge the land under their control, called the Papal States," continued Ascanio, reaching for a pitcher of water that had been brought into the room and placed on the table. "To this day this competition continues. No one was ever strong enough to unify all of the provinces. The papacy has been trying to rein in the smaller city states for decades, just as often for political reasons as for advancing their families' interests. Of course, they often allay themselves with the larger states."

Ludovico was aware of the competition. His father, Francesco, was part of it. Nonetheless, Francesco was instrumental in solidifying the Peace of Lodi which brought a semblance of peace between the parties. As Ludovico sat listening to Ascanio, he thought the battles were not simply physical, they often entailed the claims that one ruler would have over another through current or previous marriages, and they would find intricate ways of promoting a claim from some marriage of generations ago.

Ludovico himself was in such a situation. His mother, Bianca, was from the House of Savoy which had French pedigree. Through his mother the French could claim dominion over Milan. Naples, likewise, would have a claim over Milan through Gian Galeazzo and his offspring, his wife was the granddaughter of Ferdinand of Naples and daughter of Alphonse, who would be the next king of Naples.

Ludovico was concerned about these possibilities. His concern was not current, however, Gian Galeazzo being the legitimate heir of the Duchy at present, Ludovico only Regent.

"And just how is Gian Galeazzo," Ascanio remarked, introducing a new subject to the group. "Is he still enjoying his activities?"

Giorgio replied to the question, now settled and sitting again with the group. "Isabella and Gian are still residing in the summer palace in Pavia. He is quite content to hunt and ride and dress in his pompous style. He is unconcerned with state matters. It is his wife, Isabella, who we hear, badgers him about his rights to the Duchy. She can be tiresome, and she has her father and grandfather to take up Gian's claim.

Giorgio was always uneasy about Isabella. From the beginning of her recent marriage, he worried about her being an eventual thorn in their side, creating another troublesome potentiality with which they would have to deal. His solution, one that he never mentioned to Ludovico, would be to eliminate Gian Galeazzo. He knew, however, that Ludovico was not ready for this solution, his use of force was always one of limits. And he would say to himself, maybe, maybe, it will never materialize, maybe Gian would just pass away into oblivion. After all, Gian Galeazzo is not the heathiest of human beings.

\*\*\*\*\*

"Ascanio, Cecilia is holding a soiree this week. You must stay for it. Leonardo is uncovering her portrait. She will have some of our finest musicians there, and Bramante will be decorating the affair. We may even be able to get Leonardo to sing. He has a wonderful voice and loves to sing. Bramante does a fine job with the decorations and always presents a festive and colorful event; Cecilia is a hostess worthy of such wonderful preparations. Moreover, Leonardo will also be showing his drawings for the equestrian statute I have commissioned from him. It is to celebrate our father's career, and he guarantees that it will surpass the beauty and grandeur of Verrocchio's statute in Venice celebrating 'Bartolomeo Colleoni' and Donatello's 'Gattomelata' in Padua, both famous condottiere themselves.

Unlike Ludovico, Ascanio was a pragmatist, always trying to find a solution to a problem, rarely trying to find a problem that needed a solution. He stood with Ludovico and Giorgio in one corner of the room listening to the music soaring through it and subtly elevating the spirits of the guests. Ludovico stared at Cecilia entertaining the guests with her vivaciousness as if he was a teenager again. Leonardo was in another corner laughing at some amusement he had offered the people surrounding him. Even Giorgio appeared to be having a splendid time, unusual for him, although he did seem to be preoccupied with other thoughts on this evening.

Ascanio said to Ludovico in a very serious tone, "Ludovico, have you thought about your succession. Cecilia is to bring you a child shortly, but it will not have the full force of legitimacy, once you assume the title of Duke. Others will have a competing claim for it. You need a wife and a legitimate heir."

Ludovico hesitated for a moment, thinking carefully to himself before he replied. His movements were measured as they most often were. "Yes, I have been considering your question for some time now, and I am about ready to go forward with a resolution."

"Well," said Ascanio, "have you considered anyone in particular?"

'No, but I have people looking."

"May I suggest someone, my brother, from a powerful family, the D'Este of Ferrara. Duke Ercole has two daughters, Isabella and Beatrice. You must have heard of them."

"Yes, I have. They are supposed to be very cultured young girls."

"They are young, that is true, but they are cultured in the arts and literature and able to hold a conversation on politics. They both have been taught all the refinements of a well-educated woman. And they both are said to be quite witty and have already impressed those who have met them at their father's court. Isabella is the older by a year. Both are said to be able to easily handle the affairs of court. They are both said to have the refinement and beauty that would enhance any court."

Ludovico looked at his brother, hesitating for the slightest instance and said, "You certainly give a fine recommendation. Would you also be up to inquiring of Duke Ercole the availability of Isabella in marriage?"

"I can do that for you, Ludovico. As I've said, I believe she would be a wonderful companion for you and welcomed by all of Milan. I would be honored to perform the ceremonies, if the marriage comes to fruition."

Even as Ludovico stared warmly and lovingly at Cecilia dancing around the floor of the ballroom, his mind raced to an image of the unseen Isabella like a butterfly floating around a bush seeking a place to rest and enjoy

*****

"Ludovico, Isabella D'Este is betrothed to Francesco Gonzaga of Mantua and has been for some while. But Ercole has offered you Beatrice," Ascanio said to Ludovico after returning from Ferrara. "If you agree, he is also suggesting that there be a double wedding between Francesco and Isabella and between you and Beatrice."

"A double wedding. That would be unique. But I cannot do it on the dates he has chosen. Are there any other acceptable dates to him?"

*****

The double wedding was not to take place, Ludovico always having a reason for postponing it. Eventually, about a year after Isabella was wed, a double wedding did occur, between the 16-year-old Beatrice and 39-year-old Ludovico and between her brother, Alfonso, and Ludovico's niece, Anna Sforza, the sister of Gian Galeazzo. The marriage ceremony was held in the Cathedral, Cardinal Ascanio Sforza presiding over it. Music was composed by Franchino Gaffurio, the maestro di cappella of the Cathedral, one of the outstanding musicians and composers that Ludovico had invited to work in Milan."

The affair was one to be remembered in the Duchy of Milan. Leonardo Da Vinci orchestrated the wedding decorations and the celebrations, fun and festive, beautiful and sophisticated. He also enchanted the celebrants with his acapella singing. The Castello Sforzesco was decorated in laurel from the entrance foyer up the circular stairway into the ballroom. On one wall of the ballroom a painting of the bride and groom by Donato Bramante, returning briefly to his former painting vocation, faced the attendees as they entered the ballroom. Tables were set around the walls of the room, flowers gracing them in elegant arrangements. The cathedral choir was assembled and led by Gaffurio, his music filling the hall with lively angelic-like tones to everyone's delight.

The new bride and groom were driven from the Cathedral to the Castle, led by troops of street performers dressed in their colored brocaded costumes, floats decorated in floral patterns displaying themes of predicted well-being and happiness for the couple and their duchy. They passed stages ready for the performance of religious plays later in the day and evening. Music could be heard over the roar of the crowd lining the street with Milanese celebrating the royal couple.

Beatrice, newly married but with the grace of someone much older, charmed the attendees with her beauty and innocence but also with her intelligent conversation and her vivacious personality. The celebrations went on into the early hours of the morning. Everyone commented on how impressed they were with Beatrice, and how fortunate Ludovico was to find such a lovely and accomplished bride.

Cecilia Galerina remained in her apartment, lamenting her changed status but accepting it with good humor. Beatrice, too, was aware of her rival, Cecilia, and of the unwonted situation that was now hers in the Sforza castle but held her comments to herself with the grace that was her upbringing, enjoying the evening with no appearance of her disappointment, but with the conviction that the current situation could not last.

In one corner of the ballroom Ludovico spoke to Ascanio and Giorgio while Gianni, wine glass in hand, appeared besotted like a fermenting wine grape with a fair young lady, bubbling over with energy but not yet smooth to the taste. Looking at Leonardo in another corner of the ballroom, Ludovico said, "Leonardo seems to be having a wonderful time, is he not?"

Ascanio spoke. "He is certainly a man of genius, capable of putting this affair together and attending to his painting also."

"Yes, he is a genius in the fine arts, mechanical and engineering methods and even the less serious activities like what we are seeing tonight. It makes one wonder, however, how much of a genius can a man be who eats only vegetables? He does not eat meat. Have you ever heard of something so outlandish? By the way Ascanio, how close are you to the Vice Chancellor's position?" asked Ludovico, surveying the room with contentment.

"Pope Innocent is not well. His condition deteriorates noticeably every day. Cardinal Borgia will definitely be after the Papacy. But it will not be easy for him. Della Rovere is also after the miter. I may have some bargaining power if the Papal Conclave comes to that."

Ludovico stood in silence for a moment, then said to Ascanio, "Were our father only here now." Then softly said to Ascanio, "If money is required, I will be here for you."

The music continued after a brief pause. The guests resumed their dancing and drinking. The conversations grew louder. Gianni stood, barely, swaying like a papier-mache body caught in an unsteady wind.

Pope Innocent VIII was to die within a year of Ludovico's wedding, expiring with a high fever.

*****

The Papal Conclave was called and, as usual, with the gathering of the cardinals, the first ballot was held on the afternoon of the first day. Cardinal Borgia and Cardinal della Rovere were the favorites to win the election and, as expected, received the most votes. No one, however, received the two-thirds majority needed to elect a new pontiff. As was the tradition, two ballots were scheduled on the following morning and one ballot on the afternoon of the second day.

As the cardinals entered the Sistine Chapel on the following morning, the election process followed the ritual of centuries of tradition. Each cardinal was given a paper ballot labeled "Eligo in Summun Pontificem," meaning I elect as Supreme Pontiff followed by the name of their choice to be written. Once a cardinal has written the name of his choice, he goes to the altar for a silent prayer and kneels, then recites the oath, "I call to witness Christ the Lord who will be my judge that my vote is given to the one whom before God I consider should be elected."

The ballot is held high for everyone to see that he has voted, and it is placed on a paten and tipped into a chalice that sits on the altar. After all ballots have been placed in the chalice, it is shaken and one of three cardinals selected as scrutineer removes the ballots one by one in view of the entire conclave and places it in another container. The Cardinal Camerlengo then reads the votes aloud. The ballot is passed to each of the three scrutineers, each of whom also reads it aloud, places the name on a tally sheet and passes it to the succeeding scrutineer to read. After the third scrutineer reads the vote aloud, he runs a threaded needle through the ballot and connects them one by one. If no one has been elected after nine attempts, a pause of one day for prayer and discussion is allowed. A pause is prescribed for each succeeding seven votes.

Cardinal and Vice Chancellor Rodrigo Borgia was in a powerful position to be elected but was opposed by his constant foe, Cardinal della Rovere. Cardinal Sforza was also a contender but his chances for the papacy were thwarted rather quickly. It was becoming increasingly obvious that if an election was not awarded soon, compromise candidates would be offered to the conclave. Cardinal Borgia as Vice Chancellor, however, carried many ways to provide benefices to friends and, as the ballot process went on, Cardinal Borgia was not above offering them to supporters.

After Cardinal Borgia was seen talking individually to several cardinals during a pause in the voting, he approached Cardinal Sforza. "Your support would be especially appreciated," Cardinal Borgia said in a whisper to Ascanio as they walked together around the perimeter of the chapel whose ceiling did not yet have the magnificent frescos of Michelangelo but whose frescoed walls were completed, following the remodeling of the chapel, by among others, Sandro Botticelli, Domenico Ghirlandaio, and Pietro Perugino in 1482.

"I believe you have as good a chance of winning the election as anyone, probably better" Ascanio replied, folding his arms in front of him but not looking directly at Cardinal Borgia. Cardinal Borgia and Cardinal Sforza were not close friends but had a working relationship where they came into contact with each other from time to time and were able to work with each other cordially.

"We seem to be in agreement on most matters in front of the Church," Cardinal Borgia said, he, too, not looking directly as Cardinal Sforza but knowing his devotion to his family and desire for their advancement.

"That is certainly true. We have no strong disagreements. I would welcome the opportunity to work with you."

"Is there a matter of concern that will be in front of the Pontiff of which I could be of assistance to you?"

"No." said Cardinal Sforza, both men now stopped in one of the corners of the chapel, facing each other.

"As Pontiff, I may be able to provide you with monetary assistance, if that will help you. Tell me your needs, and I will attempt to accommodate them. Surely, there must be a benefice I can direct to your or, perhaps, to your family. The Almighty understands our needs are not ordinary and makes provisions for them in the work we do for Him."

"No, thank you. I am more interested in advancing the purpose of the Church, keeping her on firm fiscal footing and helping our catholic flock by attending to their future needs," replied Ascanio.

"Very noble of you. Is there an office that, perhaps, may allow you to pursue that agenda, say, the Vice Chancellorship that I now hold" said Cardinal Borgia, taking hold of Cardinal Sforza's arm lightly and gently moving him even farther into the corner of the chapel? "I can place you in a position to succeed me after my death. Would that not advance your agenda?"

"Well, yes," said Ascanio, pausing for the briefest of moments to mount a reply, not wanting to seem too forward. "That position would be a real challenge for me, especially after the splendid way you have filled it," not revealing his true feelings about Borgia's comportment in the position.

Cardinal Borgia stood silent, waiting for a positive reply from Cardinal Sforza, knowing quite well that Cardinal Sforza could not possibly reply in the negative to his offer. It would make Cardinal Sforza, in effect, Prime Minister of the Vatican, the second highest position, behind the Pope himself.

"I can see…. that the position would do very nicely," said Cardinal Sforza, hesitating momentarily and withholding any show of emotion.

"I can offer you this position, but we would have to talk in private about the duties of the office, some of which may be unfamiliar to you and which you would have to accept. Are you willing to accept that condition?"

"I would feel very fortunate to work under your Papacy."

"Then it is done."

Both men walked away stoically in different directions, each man successful in what he wanted to accomplish. Cardinal Borgia proceeded calmly to approach another cardinal without the slightest hesitation. Cardinal Sforza walked off alone to sit on one of the benches provided for the conclave.

At the end of the day, the ballots were placed in the chapel's chimney with straw and chemicals to produce black smoke, indicating that no pontiff had yet been elected. On the following day, white smoke exited the chapel's chimney from the burning of ballots alone. A new pontiff had been elected. Cardinal and Vice Chancellor Rodrigo Borgia was now Pope Alexander VI, and the Borgia family was now the leading family in Rome and the Papal States that the Vatican administrated.

*****

On a cool, bright day, the sky blue with the beauty of a Spring day, Ludovico traveled to his estate in Vigevano with his new bride. Gianni and Giorgio were to meet him there for discussions. Cecilia continued to live in the castle in her regular apartment, a situation that irritated Beatrice but did not cause her to lose her essentially pleasant nature. The joy of her marriage to Ludovico filled the castle with her spirit, enhancing the atmosphere of everyone there.

"I so enjoy the estate, my birthplace, and leaving Milan for a time. I am eager to learn what, if anything, has come of my experiments, especially those for the wine vines. We have planted several hundred vines on the slope of the hill behind the estate," said Ludovico, looking out from the carriage carrying them to the estate. His mood had been elevated since his marriage, and his new bride was everything he expected her to be.

"Why do you continue to have your mistress living with us," said Beatrice somewhat abruptly but in the softest voice she could manage, ignoring his comment to her. She definitely did not desire to engage Ludovico in any kind of unseemly confrontation but did want to impart her displeasure of the current arrangement.

"Beatrice, Cecilia has been living in the Castello Sforzesco for years. I have loved her for many years and continue to love her, just as I love you. How can I put her out? Would not that be unchivalrous of me? Can you not accept this arrangement?" He knew immediately that he was allowing the conversation to enter a dangerous and untraveled road.

"The arrangement reflects on me, and it also reflects on you. Do not you see the injustice of keeping her in the castle, in her apartment away from the activities of the castle? And further, what do the church fathers see in your unchristian behavior? Won't they find cause to criticize you whenever they feel a need to do so?"

Surprisingly, Ludovico felt somewhat chastened by this conversation. All he could do was to look away in silence at the fertile fields their coach was passing and comment on the beauty of the countryside.

Beatrice remained in silence also, knowing that there was nothing more to be gained at the moment on this topic.

As the coach got closer to Vigevano, Ludovico pointed to the hills south of Pavia and commented to Beatrice, "Our experimental vineyard of 20 acres is on the south side of those hills. I have planted both Barbera and Croatino and some Chiavennasca grapes. There is a Mediterranean climatic influence there, and the Alps shelters the vines from the harsh winter weather. Only on the hills can the vines survive. I am hoping that the Chiavennasca, which is a Nebbiolo grape in Savoy, will someday rival it and that this grape growing region will produce wines of quality to other regions in the Duchy, especially those on the western banks of Lake Garda."

The following morning Ludovico and Beatrice walked together between the rows of vines with Angelo Verdone, their vineyard manager, and with Gianni and Giorgio, only recently arrived. No grapes had yet appeared on the vines, but flowers were making an appearance, the first indication that grapes were not too far away. Beatrice was fascinated with the explanations that Angelo and Ludovico were giving to her. Her mind was as open and interested in this aspect of her husband's life as it was captivated by her devotion to the fine arts.

"See these vines," Ludovico said to Beatrice, pointing to one near them, "now that the flowers have bloomed, the berry will grow and change color for about 100 days before they are ready for harvesting. The size and color of the grape depends primarily on the type of grape. Some grapes are smaller than other grapes. Smaller grapes have more surface skin area relative to the pulp for juice. Wines made from those grapes tend to be more robust, tannic, full-bodied and darker in color than wines made from larger grapes, other things equal. The thickness of the grape's skin will also influence the flavor and body of the wine."

Once they walked through the vineyard, Victorio had a table preset with glasses and various charcuterie set out in an open field by the vineyard. "Let us try a wine from last autumn's harvest," he said, motioning everyone to sit as he poured wine from a pitcher into the glasses. You see the darkness of the color. This wine is made primarily from the Chiavannesca grape which is smaller than most grapes. These are the grapes we have planted in this part of the vineyard. Now, this wine, raising a pitcher and pouring it into another set of glasses on the table is made from the Dolchetto grape, somewhat lighter in color and in body than the Chiavannesca grape."

As the sun began to weaken later in the day and approached dusk, Ludovico and Giorgio sat alone in the vineyard, still sipping their wine. Beatrice, Gianni and Victorio had all strayed away and finally left for the estate, having their full of vines and wines. The pitcher had been refilled several times by a servant who remained behind to accommodate Ludovico.

"Isn't it odd how often the setting sun and the darkness that it portends often has a very relaxing feel to it rather than the feel of foreboding that accompanies the darkness," said Giorgio resting one leg on the long bench he was sitting on with his second leg on the ground? "I like this wine but it needs more aging. The tannins are a bit too strong at the moment."

Ludovico looked in deep thought, staring out into the distance. "Giorgio, Gian Galeazzo's wife, Isabella, has begun to badger him again about his title. He is content where he is, in Pavia, tending to his hunting and social gatherings. She has also resumed her not so subtle threats to us about pursuing the topic with her grandfather and father. This will come to a head sometime soon, and that time seems to be approaching." Ludovico was sober and calm when discussing matters of this nature. He was a kind and generous man mainly but did not abjure violence as a resolution to an insolvable problem or what he perceived to be insolvable.

Giorgio placed his raised foot on the ground and turned towards Ludovico. "We can't have Ferdinand interfering with your reign. Gian Galeazzo has not been in good health lately. You could be fortunate and find him dead one day from whatever is ailing him. His passing would solidify your hold on the Duchy, though you would also need affirmation from another source, like Pope Alexander or the Holy Roman Emperor to certify your title."

"Would we be so fortunate to have such an outcome. Methinks that we may have to hurry Gian's exit along, if Isabella persists in her wanton outspokenness. We cannot linger too long in this kind of atmosphere before it will erode our relationships with the other powers on the Peninsular and encourage their own manipulations."

"I agree," said Giorgio, thinking to himself, why had Ludovico not considered this earlier.

The resolve in Ludovico's face was obvious. Since his marriage, his thoughts had turned to the prospect of his own offspring, and the means to protect their patrimony. "Let's wait for a time, however. I don't want to rush into a decision. In the meantime, device a plan to solve our dilemma so that we can end this chapter of our life in our favor."

*****

Beatrice's subdued demands concerning Cecilia's presence in Castello Sforzesco, which were every bit as powerful as her previous more forceful reprimands, reached a tipping point when Cecilia gave birth to a baby boy later in the year.

"Gianni, we must move Cecilia from her apartment. Her presence has become a distraction in my life and a greater distraction in my wife's life. Set up arrangements to give her Carmagnalo Palace. I am making arrangements with Count Ludovico Carminati de' Brambillo to marry her. I have spoken to her and she has agreed to this denouement."

Ludovico sounded harsh and indifferent in his instructions to Gianni, but Gianni knew the warmth of his affection for Cecilia. He glimpsed a shadow of sadness covering his face like a thin mesh mask revealing only a portion of a man's face but, nevertheless, obscuring his true appearance.

Ludovico sat at his desk and fell into a quiet, reflective mood and said to Gianni, "Life always poses challenges; some, however, are more personal and soul-searching than others. I truly feel that I have been unfair to Cecilia, that I have been less than honest to her but I do love her."

Gianni, being in one of his intermittent spiritual moods, retorted, "On the contrary, you have been fair and understanding with her and, if the Almighty marks this phase of your life as sinful, it will be weighed against all your more favorable actions. Remember, only the Almighty knows the distance from here to heaven."

Slowly, Ludovico recovered from his dark mood and had Gianni join him in a private celebration of his first child with Cecilia.

*****

It was a dark and cold January day two years later when Beatrice produced Ludovico's first legitimate heir, Massimiliano. Ludovico had completed the first step in securing the Duchy of Milan for the Sforza family. His next step was for Ludovico to be vested as the legitimate Duke of Milan which would allow him to pass the regime to his child.

Flags were displayed throughout the city on the day of Massimiliano's birth. They were hanging above the doors of taverns and homes, above the entrances of churches, the emblem of the Sforza's family, an ermine, embossed in red and yellow. Flags fluttered in the wind from the windows of the castle, in the courtyard and at entrances to it, guarded by an array of soldiers in brocaded uniforms.

Merriment was not only in the air but also in the houses bursting with activity, the smell of roasted pork emanating from fireplaces, warm bread baking in the ovens throwing off the aromas of the hearth, people lingering in the streets, greeting their friends with cups of beer and goblets of wine. The noise of friendship ran up streets, around corners, into households. In the baser areas of the city, revelries were also in progress in the taverns and inns, even more riotous than elsewhere, having the appearance of not only joy for the birth of Maximiliano but also for the mere pleasure of imbibing with friends and newly-formed acquaintances. Elsewhere in the city's piazzas "mystery" plays were scheduled for the stages set up in them, religious plays that would have allegorical significance for the Sforza family. Music was heard from the courtyard of the castle and in the Piazza del Duomo, lively music that befit the first-born boy and inheritor of the regime.

Ludovico sat by the side of his wife's bed, holding her hand and patting her brow with a damp cloth. "Beatrice, you have made me so happy," he said to her in the sweetest of voices. "My life is whole now. My life has been whole ever since you entered my life. You have brought joy to a joyless life, lightness to the heavy burden I carry, and freshness to the dull corridors of my existence."

Outside the open door of her bedroom, the soft and melodic music of a dozen violins washed through the doorway and around the edges of the room before it found its way to Beatrice now sitting up in her bed.

*****

"Grandfather, you must confront Ludovico about Gian's patrimony," said Isabella to her grandfather, Ferdinand. She had grown increasingly rancorous about Ludovico's regency, which she considered a usurpation of Gian's right to the Ducal seat. Gian and she neither participated nor were consulted in affairs of state, and while Gian was quite content in the country palace in Pavia, happily unconcerned about state affairs, Isabella was resentful of the neglect in which she found herself. Although they held their extravagant festivities and banquets in Pavia, she saw herself deprived as a participant in the politics of the Peninsular and denied from residing in one of the its most distinguished cities, Milan.

"My daughter, what would you have me do, especially since your husband does not at all seem concerned," said Ferdinand, sitting in his study in Naples. The ride to Naples had taken a particularly hard toll on Isabella, and it showed on her brow-beaten face. She sat in front of her grandfather's desk, looking morose and tired, in outward appearance like an elderly woman ready to collapse but with a hidden resolve to see her troubles through.

"You must talk to Ludovico, even threaten if you must. The throne is Gian's and mine, and it should be given to us. Gian is the rightful heir to it. We have waited too long for power to be handed over to us. I feel humiliated in my present position. I did not marry Gian in order to spend my life reposed in a bucolic countryside, which though pretty, is not as stimulating as the city."

"Why is Gian not here with you, if you are so concerned about your fate?"

"Gian isn't feeling well. He has a fever and has been in a weakened state for weeks. His health has been a continuing issue for quite a while now."

"I will discuss it with Ludovico, but short of creating hostilities with him, I do not envisage an outcome to your satisfaction."

"Gian is the rightful heir. Surely you can threaten him that you will remind the leaders on the Peninsula of our claim."

"Perhaps the best way to approach this problem is to acquire an endorsement for your claim from one of the two people who can legitimize it, Pope Alexander or the Holy Roman Emperor, Maximilian," said Ferdinand, bringing his clenched fist down lightly on the desk, his eyes widening over his newly creative idea. "A Papal endorsement carries a good deal of weight from its centuries of temporal and spiritual rule and might be an easier sell than Maximilian, though I believe that Ludovico is closer to Maximilian than to the Pope."

*****

"Giorgio, Isabella is acting up again and has entreated her grandfather to reprimand me about the Ducal chair. Ferdinand is very good at threatening us in an amicable way. He seems to believe that a threat presented with a smile somehow lessens the urgency of the threat. He has hinted at gaining Pope Alexander's confidence, though I do not have as much faith in that maneuver as he seems to have."

Ludovico just looked up from his desk, waiting for Giorgio's response, which was just as he expected. "A threat is a threat, no matter how it is presented. Wrapping a tocsin in sugar does not reduce the amount of poison in it."

"I suppose we should be careful how we treat Ferdinand," Ludovico said smiling broadly and lightly, clapping his hands once. "It has been reported that Ferdinand has his enemies killed and embalmed, dressed in their usual clothing and displayed for his guests to see. I don't know how well you would look embalmed and sitting upright in a chair. Then again, you would probably look better than you look now, after the way you treat your body."

"I would be the best-looking mummy in his display. No doubt about it," said Giorgio, preening himself mockingly.

"By the way, I see less and less of you, nowadays. Where do you keep yourself?"

"That's because you are so preoccupied with your wife and child," Giorgio said quickly before Ludovico could ask another question. "There is information from Pavia that Gian's health has deteriorated."

"Perhaps we should postpone any action on our part, just to be prudent," said Ludovico. "But, I will not surrender my claim and my son's claim to Milan. It was hard won by my father and I intend to keep it. The Duchy is worth fighting for."

*****

Fall had arrived in Milan. Trees were disposing of their dead leaves to the ground in multicolored piles, the air was turning brisk, the sky was as clear as the spring water that cascaded down the waterfalls in the foothills of the Alps, and the grapes on Ludovico's vines near Pavia were being harvested for pressing and fermentation. Ferdinand had passed away, leaving the Kingdom of Naples to his son, Alphonso, father of Isabella. Gian Galeazzo had died within months of Ferdinand, in October of the same year. And Ludovico was still in danger of having Isabella's claim pursued by her father, Alphonso.

There was a sudden urgency in Ludovico's voice as he called Giorgio and Gianni together in late fall of 1494. "Alphonso has already threatened me and is in talks with Pope Alexander to legitimize his claim on the Duchy. We must preempt him and pursue our own course with Maximillian, the Holy Roman Emperor. I am leaving in the next few days with an entourage for Austria. Gianni, I want you to accompany me. Giorgio will remain behind and quell any disturbances that arise."

*****

Persephone had begun her annual retreat into Hades to satisfy her obligation, leaving snowflakes lightly scattered over the ground. The beauty of nature was overtaken by the importunities of statecraft. Back in Castello Sforzesco from his long journey to meet Maximillian, Ludovico sat relaxed in his office, satisfied with the results of his mission, but exhausted from the hurried return trip to avoid the bitter weather that was soon to arise and cover the mountains in enticing pure white beauty but dangerously life-threatening paths.

Leaning back in his chair, dark shadows under his eyes and a worn expression on his face, with Giorgio and Gianni beside him, Ludovico spoke directly to Giorgio. "The trip was successful. Maximillian has agreed to invest me with the title to the Duchy. I will pay him a considerable sum for his imprimatur. Also, my niece, Gian's daughter, Bianca Maria, will be pledged to him in marriage." All three men lifted their goblets and saluted the good fortune that was theirs, a good fortune that, nonetheless, cost Ludovico a fortune in coin.

Ludovico looked at his two friends, a seriousness covering his face, a mixture of concern and exhaustion. "The danger has not passed. Alphonso continues to press his claim with Pope Alexander, and I do not believe that Maximillian will come to our aid if Alphonso is successful."

\*\*\*\*\*

Brother Matteo, so serene in the monastery, was finally succumbing to old age. In his cell, he rested in his bed, unable to walk very easily. This is where he spent most of his day, except for those times that he was escorted to church. In good weather, he would sometimes be carried outside to rest in the cloisters. His thoughts wandered from his childhood to his adult life, from his pleasures and joys to his regrets and disappointments. He was relaxed within himself now, ready to meet the Almighty and ready to review his life with Him. After a considerable period doubting his vocation, doubting the wanton behavior of some of the clergy, particularly the heads of the church, those who would treat the church as their secular kingdom, those who would act as princes rather than as disciples of God, he was firm in his believe that, at least, he had devoted himself to God's work, that he had taught and inspired a few students. To be honest to himself at these last days of his life, there were only a handful of students that he could remember helping, one in particular was Gianni Cortese. He decided that he would invite Gianni to visit him one last time.

Snow covered the cloistered courtyard of San Gelsera when Gianni arrived. Brother Matteo could reach his doorway to look out this day at the pure, frozen, opaque snow shining from a sun that did not want to relinquish its primacy to a harsher winter. He and Gianni sat in the small cell, Gianni in a plain hard-backed wooden chair facing Brother Matteo sitting on the edge of his bed.

Brother Matteo said to Gianni in a barely audible voice, "Gianni, how glad I am to see you. I have often thought of you. Your appearance has not changed; you do, however, look more confident and hold yourself up like a man of import."

Gianni, concerned over Brother Matteo's appearance, dark shadows under his eyes from the lack of sleep, a skin tone that looked an unhealthy grey, replied, "No, no, brother. I am still the insignificant child I was when I left you and the monastery all those years past."

"You are too modest. I called you here because I think of you as my most prized student and think of our conversations about religion and the religious life. You know, you and Ludovico, for the short time he was here, were the only persons with whom I held those conversations. You were the only person I felt could hear me and understand that I was not condemning the Church, and I certainly was not condemning Jesus; I was condemning many of the people who lead the Church, who decided to move the Church in a way that fulfilled their ideas of Christ and their ideas of what Christ taught."

"Brother, my time with you was one of the most important times of my life," Gianni said, noticing that Brother Matteo was beginning to look tired and dissipated. "Would you like to rest a while?"

"Just for a few minutes."

"I will sit outside. The sun makes for an unusual day on the snow. It is not a combination that we see so often in winter here. When you are ready for me again, just come to the door."

Gianni wiped some thawed snow from one of the stone benches placed against the wall between two of the cells along the walkway. The occasion with Brother Matteo allowed him to consider his own life, one that had taken a far different road than that of Brother Matteo. What have I accomplished he asked himself? What do I believe? It has been a long and sinuous path I have traveled. Am I any better today than I was all those years past?

Brother Mateo came to the doorway and motioned for Gianni to enter his cell.

"Are you feeling better, Brother," Gianni said as he returned to his former chair.

"Yes, I feel somewhat refreshed. Gianni, during our conversations here, I was concerned with the theology professed by the church, but I am reconciled with that now, I am peace with it. Was I able to help you understand the early days of the church? I hope my disaffection at the time did not dissuade you of your beliefs."

"No, brother. I feel that you helped me immensely."

All of a sudden, Brother Matteo's weak, bent body stiffened like a young lieutenant coming to attention in front of his superior. "But I have not come to terms with the dissolute lives that many in our church lead. We have had 20 years of this under Pope Sixtus and Pope Innocent. Now we have an even greater dissolute with the Borgia Pope, Alexander VI. He lives in the Vatican with his illegitimate children and mistress not far from him. And the rumors of Cesare's doings are abhorrent. Surely, he cannot be doing God's work. Dante was able in his great work, the Divine Comedy, to place Pope Boniface VIII in the seven circle of hell. Would that we had a Dante today."

Gianni would stay with Brother Mateo for a week and was in attendance at his death, a death of a man who was at peace with himself, larger in spiritual power at death than at any point in life.

*****

Ludovico sat alone, occasionally rising to look at the snow falling outside his window. It was so beautiful in its pure white form, covering all the blackness under it, but the blackness of the world always comes to the fore, he thought. He had had a propitious life, a wife he was proud of, who was admired by all the courts on the Italian Peninsular, an heir that he so wanted to carry on the Sforza name, the legitimization of his authority by the Emperor and, yet, he could not feel relieved of the pressure constantly weighting on him. He felt as if he was a heavy boulder ready to roll off its craggy ledge to an uncertain doom that he was unable to control or foresee.

The Peninsular was calm but threats continued to break through the false patina of a balance of power. Venice had moved on its "terrafirma" policy, expanding its domain inland by capturing Verona, Padua and Vincenzo and lands to the foothills of the Alps as a buffer to invaders attacking from the west. It remained a threat to Milan and its lands in Lombardy. Pope Alexander was acting aggressively, coveting land in Romagna, which bordered on Lombardy, for his family. Naples, under Alphonso, was continuing to advance its claim on Milan. Ludovico sat pondering these exigencies. He needed to resolve these issues. They were the most important facing him and his progeny in the years he had spent leading Milan.

In France, Charles VIII had a simmering, long-standing, dubious claim on Naples that arose from his paternal grandmother, Marie of Anjou, that preyed on his mind like an insidious idea clawing its way to the center of his ambitious being. He was encouraged first by Pope Innocent, who had a dispute with Ferdinand of Naples himself, then by his successor, Pope Alexander. His ambition was fortified by them, and he was finally ready to advance his agenda.

*****

Cardinal Ascanio had accumulated an enormous amount of overt and covert power as Vice Chancellor. He became privy to much useful but also hidden information about the Vatican. He learned that Pope Alexander was aware, as were previous Popes, of the decaying position of the monastic system in the Church. Each denomination was semi-independent of the Vatican but each was also unaware of the actions of any other congregation, save what each abbot was able to glean from informal contacts. Nonetheless, the Vatican had power over each monastery, and they were allowed to deteriorate under the watchful eye of the Vatican but without widespread knowledge of their condition elsewhere in the church.

Ascanio had gained the confidence of the Pope and was, in fact, one of Pope Alexander's closest advisors, though he was not given access to all of the secrets that the Vatican held. He had brought Pope Alexander into a friendlier relationship with Ludovico, giving both a more secure feeling in the jungle that was the politics of the Italian Peninsular, helping the formation of a silent compact between the Papacy and Milan against the power of Venice in the North, the main rival of Milan, and Naples in the south, the main rival of the Papacy. Ascanio was determined, however, to delve farther into the affair of the monasteries. He knew from the previous attack on him, however, that he would have to be more cautious than ever. He would have to be the garden lizard that waits stone-like for an insect to pass before striking. He did not want to expose himself any more than was necessary.

Ascanio had no associate he could draw into his investigation, but his title gave him access he could use to his advantage. He was confident that his motives were as yet undetected in the swirling cauldron of the Vatican's veiled activities. His wanderings into the archives revealed more substantive material, account books that were available to only a few people, the Vice Chancellor being one.

Late one evening, Ascanio sat at his desk, a cup of tea by his hand, occasionally looking to a crucifix hanging on his wall, composing correspondence to his brother, Ludovico. He knew the information in the letter was vital to the ongoing investigation of the monasteries and that Ludovico was still keenly interested in it. He wanted to have it delivered as soon as possible.

*****

Ludovico sat with Giorgio and Gianni on a cold, windy afternoon, a large fire burning in his office fireplace to ease the discomfort of the gusty wind blowing down from the foothills of the Alps. Each had a glass of young Nebbiola in his hand, fermented only several months-ago from his own vineyards and aged in oak barrels only briefly. They were savoring the fruity finish of the young wine. In the near distance, could be heard the cries of his young son, Maximiliano.

"Maximiliano has a loud voice, does he not? He is as unfinished as this wine," said Ludovico, pointing to the next room with the wine in his hand and smiling profusely to his two friends. "I enjoy hearing him, knowing that he is being well cared for. I can see him bellowing orders out already."

"And how is Beatrice. Has she fully recovered from the childbirth," inquired Giorgio? He was warming the wine glass in his hands as he said this, rolling the glass in his palms, then sipping it with obvious delight.

"Yes, but it was a difficult birth, as you know. She is her bright, youthful presence again. Women are much more resilient than men, don't you agree? They have an inner strength that men lack. Man's strength is all on the outside where everyone can view it and leads to much aberrant behavior. After all, it is the outward appearance of men that attract the opposite sex. It is so in all the animal world, I am told."

"Is that why women were allotted the roll of giving birth by the Almighty?" said Gianni, wanting to enter the conversation.

"Perhaps."

The men were now in a comfortable mood that the wine had brought on with all its complex aromas and not yet developed complex tastes, their bodies relaxing like a sail let out of the wind. Ludovico started, "Ascanio has unraveled some of the mysteries of the Vatican." One could see that he was eager to share the letter with the two men.

"Here is what he has written me in a dispatch that arrived yesterday. It is revealing. There was a vast collection of funds that had been accumulated at least since Pope Sixtus. They had been gathered by replacing many of the abbots with men completely subservient to the Pope, men who had the sae fierce goal and secret ambition as the Pope they served. Where that had not been possible because of strong opposition from the aristocracy of the region, the Vatican would retreat from its policy until such time as it could advance without opposition. The abbots have been able to skim profits from the monasteries and to secretly direct it to the Vatican. The funds lay in the Fugger Bank in Augsburg rather than in Rome. The plan has become more insidious since late in Pope Innocent's papacy. Alexander is advancing the process, probably for his own benefit as well. This much we already knew, but land is now slowly being sold off throughout Europe where possible, especially on the Peninsular because of its turbulence, and the receipts deposited in the bank."

"Yes, we have heard much of this before," said Giorgio, finishing his wine and pouring another glass from the pitcher sitting on Ludovico's desk.

"That is true, Giorgio, but he has also theorized a motive for the accumulation of funds."

"What is that?" said Gianni, keenly interested in the conversation. Gianni continued to mourn the death of his friend, Brother Matteo and felt an obligation to him to understand and resolve the issues surrounding the monasteries.

"Ascanio believes that the funds are definitely for the raising and expansion of a Papal army. He suspected this for quite some time but now has documentation of this scheme. These are monies over and above that which the Popes have usually raised for mercenaries. Furthermore, the scheme has passed down from Pope to Pope since Sixtus. There has been a systematic conspiracy to elect Popes sympathetic to the scheme. And this Pope, Alexander, will and probably is using it for the advancement of his own family as well, Cesare being an example of it."

"Is that surprising?" said Giorgio.

"No, no, it is not. The plan is to someday capture the lands surrounding the territory of the Papal States and expand it whole meal, so to speak, rather than in the piecemeal manner that the Papacy has done in the past. Of course, it would be opposed by the Holy Roman Emperor, Milan, and Venice in the north and the Kingdom of Naples in the south. Wrenching parts of those provinces from their principals takes greater resources than the Papacy has at the moment. The Vatican is the weakest of the major powers. Therefore, the long-term strategy and the need for a large standing army."

Ludovico stopped his dialogue and looked around briefly, thinking to himself that the Vatican could become strong enough to be the major power in the region and threat to him. Turning to Giorgio he said, "We're in a game, Giorgio, 'The Great Game', you may call it, where one's allegiance can shift in an instance, depending only on the short-term outlook for one's self."

"This is how it has been for several hundred years. Why should the future be any different?" said Giorgio, his face turning red from the amount of wine he had consumed but still steady on his feet as he rose from his chair and stood beside it.

*****

Gianni walked alone along the narrow streets of the old city with no destination in mind. The sun was setting, casting a shadow on one side of the street. From time to time he could see several women standing in the shadows, showing no interest in him as a client and he, likewise, took no notice of them. He was only vaguely aware that the usual evening activities, eating, drinking and whoring, were beginning. On this evening, he was only interested in drinking.

Finally, after walking several hours in his dreamy state, he felt he needed a drink, and he decided to go to an inn called "The Broken Arrow" at the end of a street near the outskirts of the city, a place that Giorgio had introduced to him and that Gianni had visited periodically.... where he could be anonymous with his thoughts. He liked the name of this inn, implying as it did both the straightness of an arrow in flight and the tragedy of misfortune. He thought, didn't this say it all about life.

"Hello there, ducky," he heard just as he was about to enter the inn. He took a cursory look at the woman, blonde, slender and attractive with olive toned skin and had to hesitate for a moment to take a second look at her unusual features. Probably has some Norman blood in her ancestry he thought but ignored her and entered the inn.

Gianni proceeded with a combination of walking past and pushing through people to locate an empty table in the back of the tavern. He sat with his back against the wall of the booth he was in and looked around. Women were leaning on their male companions, sitting on tables, some almost lying there, all scantily dressed and inebriated this early in the evening. Some men were in heated discussions about some topic or other, arms flailing, fingers pointed and faces red. The sound of the conversations seemed to reverberate from one wall to the other. Gianni thought to himself, I have no opinion about these people and their behavior. How can I, with what I have seen in my own life.

A carafe of wine was placed on the table by a young slovenly-looking woman with fine features, nonetheless. Gianni could see that with a little attention she would be quite attractive. He nodded at her and immediately turned to his drink.

Ludovico calls it "The Great Game," he thought. What are the rules of this game? All games have rules. He implies that the rules change with the changing fortunes. Surely, one can affect fortune. Man's actions must have some effect. As the night progressed, Gianni become more intoxicated. He found his thoughts flowing like the wine he was drinking to the girl he had seen on his entrance. He walked outside but did not see her anywhere. He walked up the street, then down the street, still there was no trace of her.

In frustration with his search and now as captured by his wine consumption as if he was put in chains by an enemy, he staggered away, only fuzzily aware of his direction but, nevertheless, confident of finding his way to the castle. It did not take long before he was accosted by three rough-looking, bulky brigands as confident of relieving Gianni of his money as he was in finding the castle.

The brigands grabbed Gianni forcefully, wrestled him to the ground with ease and were about to remove his money-belt when he heard through the vague mist in which his mind had settled a woman's voice screaming at the brigands, followed by a trashing of a broom on the heads of the men. Soon, a contingent of women appeared over Gianni, each trashing the men. Recognizing their defeat, the brigands retreated with the speed of Hermes.

Gianni had now somewhat recovered his composure, stood recognizing his embarrassment and was escorted into one of the small homes that lined the street. He found himself with the blond-haired woman whom he had first seen before entering the inn. She was applying a damp towel to his head and tending to the small cuts over his eye from the blows of the brigands.

"Thank you, miss," he said with obvious sincerity, noticing that the woman was even prettier than he at first thought. Then he took the towel from her and held it to his head himself. "What is your name? You saved me from a horrible beating and, possibly, worse. It was my foolish behavior that caused this."

"My pleasure, no one should be attacked by laggards like them. My name is Magdalene," she said as she sat down at her table. "Would you like some water? You should rest for a time."

"No, Grazie. I really should be on my way. I would like to repay you for all that you have done for me tonight."

"There is no need for that. The Virgin Mary will reward me."

The two spoke for a time. Despite Magdalena's protestation, Gianni left a few coins on her table as he left the house. No other transactions were to be consummated tonight.

*****

Spring arrived with all the promise of summer to come, flowers energetically breaking the ground, seemingly testing the propitiousness of continuing their projection toward the sun. This spring, however, Ludovico had the worry of Alphonso and Naples on his mind again. Alphonso continued to press his demand for the Duchy of Milan, and Ludovico was determined to find a solution to this problem.

The solution became clear to Ludovico one evening in his study, staring at a picture by Pollaiuolo of "Hercules and Antaeus". In it Hercules is squeezing the life from Antaeus. Ludovico was aware from previous conversations with Charles VIII that he was interested in pursuing his Angevine claim on Naples and was ready to enforce it. He had a powerful army, perhaps the strongest in Europe. His one obstacle, however, was the journey from France down the Italian Peninsula. His troops would have to journey through Lombardy, Florence and the Papal States to reach Naples. Apart from the length of the journey, opposition from any of them would make it considerably more difficult to accomplish his goal.

Giorgio, sitting comfortably in the study this chilly spring night, rose to place another log on the roaring fire filling the room with warmth. To Ludovico he said, "You appear to have a question on your mind. You have been silent for quite a while. What is bothering you?"

"Ah, Giorgio. I am thinking about Alphonso and how to eliminate my problem with him."

Giorgio stood from the fireplace, "Negotiation will not work with him. He has been too persistent and, while it is easy to accept his threats as empty, he is strong enough to be of concern, especially since he has made an accord with the Pope and Florence. He can surprise us if he has a mind to. It seems now is the time to deal with him."

"What of this, Giorgio, give permission to Charles VIII to pass through Milan. We know he is eager to claim Naples. His army could easily overcome Alphonso, solving our problem without any effort on our part." Ludovico could see the interest on Giorgio's face, his eyes suddenly wider and demeanor suddenly expansive. Action would always excite Giorgio, Ludovico thought. "We know that Pope Alexander would give permission to pass over his land, and we know he can get through Savoy without incident. I think that having our permission would cement the case for him."

"Interesting idea. I like it and it sounds doable to me. Yes, why don't we go forward with it? Do you want me to approach Charles with the idea?"

"No, we can meet him in a mutually agreeable location. Send a messenger to him inviting a conference. I believe the offer of some money would cement the deal. This would be a very cheap way to solve our problem. Other states may join us also in this endeavor."

*****

The meeting with Charles was as successful as could be expected. He heartily accepted Ludovico's proposition, and his advancement into the Peninsular was expected in the summer.

Da Vinci had finished a clay model of the equestrian statute that Ludovico wanted to memorialize his father. Its size and beauty had impressed everyone who viewed it. It would be the largest equestrian statute on the peninsular. Now, Ludovico would have to obtain 70 tons of bronze for its completion and wait for Da Vinci's mood to change before he would embark on it.

Meanwhile, Ludovico could entertain other thoughts, one being a fresco that he desired Da Vinci to put on a wall in the refectory of the convent beside the church of Santa Maria delle Grazie, a building that Bramante had recently partially redesigned. It was to be a painting of the Last Supper and another monument to his father. The work on this project progressed slowly. Leonardo worked sporadically on the project; some days working feverishly all day without eating, then he would not pick up his brush for 3 or 4 days. He was hesitant about the depiction of the faces of Christ and Judas. He could not find a depiction that satisfied him, and it haunted and uneased him, slowing the progress of the fresco. They were the two essential portraits in the Last Supper scene, and he insisted to himself that they must be painted perfectly, that the faces must express Judas's inner turmoil and disgust of himself and the serene mercy and peacefulness of Jesus. He would walk the streets endlessly looking for faces that could fulfill his expectations. Once completed, the painting was destined to become another instant Leonardo masterpiece, admired by everyone who viewed it and the ultimate tribute to Ludovico's court.

Beatrice was in labor again and, after an extraordinarily difficult birth, gave Ludovico another son, Francesco II. Ludovico rejoiced again with parties and banquets and a festive parade through the city decorated with all the imagination and creativity that Da Vinci could elicit from his fertile mind. Ludovico's love for Beatrice lingered on his face as easily and lightly as a bird floating on the wind. His life was happy and fulfilled. His reign, however, was still in danger.

*****

As the celebrations of the birth of Francesco commenced, Charles VIII left France at the end of August intent to enter the Peninsula and intent to capture Naples. He left with a considerable arsenal: siege machines, the first mobile heavy canons capable of bringing down walls, and 25,000 men consisting of French soldiers and Swiss mercenaries. His plan of conquest was completely different than anything that Ludovico and the other parties contemplated. It would eventually frighten each of the states that had previously abetted Charles's ambition.

On his way south, Charles passed through Milan peacefully as had been proposed by Ludovico and dined extravagantly in Castello Sforzesco. Ludovico encouraged his advances and provided what assistance that he could muster, a refreshing respite after Charles's long journey into the peninsular. Soon after his stay in Milan, he entered Genoa, a great port city and sea power for centuries, unopposed. "How large a garrison should we leave?" he asked his second in command, Jean Groppella, a native of Lombardy but long a resident of France.

"A small garrison should be sufficient, I believe, say, about 400 men," said Jean. "Genoa has the most hospitable harbor on the peninsular. Well sheltered. Our supply line should be safe here from Naples and new provisions can enter the country here faster and more efficiently than the land route. It will also enable an escape exit, should we need one."

"An escape route. I don't anticipate an escape route, bellowed Charles, puffing himself up." He was indignant over Groppella's remark.

Jean looked around at the splendid harbor of Genoa, once a great sea power, competitor of Venice and dominant trader in the eastern Mediterranean, now seeing its economic power slowly ebbing away after its disastrous conflicts with Venice for dominance at sea. "We should also establish smaller garrisons on our way south."

"Where should they be established?"

"About three days' march between them," said Jean, gazing at a map of the peninsular, pointing to a series of locations about 50 miles apart. It, of course, will also depend on the topography of the area." Naples had now been alerted that Charles was moving south and bent on enforcing his claim. Knowledge of the French strength that Charles had retained had reached Alphonso, and he was alarmed at it. With the encroaching French army nearing Naples, Alphonso was soon contemplating abdication. Before abdicating, however, Alphonso decided to test Charles's resolve. Believing that he could deter Charles by destroying his primary base of operation in Genoa, he responded first by sending a combined force of Neapolitans and their Spanish allies south in a sea born invasion of a nearby town, Rapallo, as a first step in ousting the French from Genoa.

On a dark, moonless night the ships of Naples and Spain slipped into the small harbor of Rapallo with a contingent of soldiers aboard. The soldiers were unloaded on the shore and easily captured the small town with its pretty curving shoreline and perfect white sand. From here they would be able to represent a constant threat to Genoa and the French's main supply line. For the Neapolitan and Spanish troops, it was time to relax, rest and enjoy the local pleasures of Rapallo.

Charles VIII was outraged when the news of the capture of Rapallo and the threat to the Genoa garrison was reported to him. "They will pay for this," he shouted in his gravelly voice to his advisors. "Prepare to vacate your positions and march to Rapallo." The march to Rapallo was replete with angry commands and expletives, instilling his men with a hatred for the Neapolitans that did not exist before, energizing his men almost to a frenzy.

Charles's army easily routed the enemy from the town and chased them into a nearby village where the French shelled them into submission with their large canons. "Level the town, if you must," shouted Charles from his horse as he viewed the battle, a battle that showed the Peninsular forces easily overmatched. "I want all of the Peninsular on notice that we are not to be trifled with, and the punishment I mete out will be severe."

The Neapolitan and Spanish troops trapped in the town were then submitted to excesses which the peninsular forces were unaccustomed. French troops ran through the town in a frenzy, slicing and shooting their opponents with abandon, establishing a reputation for themselves of ruthlessness that would follow them down the peninsular to Naples. It was the first massacre of the first "Italian War." The news of the outcome and the hideous manner in which the French accorded themselves percolated throughout the peninsula. This type of warfare, the viciousness in which it was waged, was unknown to the Italian states. Most often their form of warfare was an easy-going battle of essentially border skirmishes where small armies met on a level field and men fought, some were killed, others captured and ransomed off. Massacres were not the norm. The French and Swiss, on the other hand, were used to fierce battles and astonishing bloodshed. It had been a part of their history for the hundred years of the eponymous named war. The news unnerved all of the southern Peninsular states.

Marching farther south Charles encountered a combined Papal-Neapolitan army marching north to combat him. Unsurprisingly, Charles shattered the army with his heavy artillery, chasing the remnants of the army into a nearby town. Again, Charles shelled the town mercilessly with artillery and, when he entered it, massacred everyone, blood staining the street as if spilled wine. What remained of the army fled south to guard Naples's borders? With them went the fear of the French and their well-deserved and growing reputation for viciousness.

As Charles approached Florence, the city emptied, and the aristocracy of the city fled to their country castles and estates. They were not to be spared. Their castles would be devastated as routinely as were the towns previously entered by Charles. Their aristocratic blood would stain the street and show as red as those of the other towns that Charles sacked. He entered Florence uncontested and moved on farther south.

To reach Naples, Charles had to pass through the Papal States. He called Jean Groppello to his tent, offering him a goblet of wine from a bottle of Barolo that Ludovico had gifted him. "Jean, rather than fight our way through Rome and the countryside, and incur the wrath of the Pope--he still has the spiritual power to condemn us—I'm considering offering him some recompense."

"Splendid idea. Even though our battles, thus far, have not been exhausting, the men deserve a rest before we have perhaps a pitched battle with Naples."

"And," said Charles looking at a map of their route to Naples, "the money comes from the Florentine treasury. We lose nothing."

Charles looked pleased with himself. He showed that he not only understood military power but also understood the game as played by the city-states. He bribed the Pope's condottieri. They were eager to accept it, not desiring the results that had so far been accorded to previous cities that Charles had entered. Charles entered and exited Rome harmlessly.

He was now ready to face Naples and establish his claim. On the news that his army was in tatters, Alphonso finally decided to vacate his throne and flee. The subjugation of Naples took only a few sieges and small massacres along the way, massacres that were becoming commonplace. The battle was easily won, his large canons were no longer needed for victory, the French army just walked into the city unmolested. Charles entered a city devoid of people.

"Charles, you must see this. Follow me," said Jean after having surveyed the castle. "It's below ground."

"What is it?" replied Charles in a soft, contented voice. His demeanor had calmed noticeably in the last few days. It was less necessary for him to project himself forcefully.

"I want you to see Ferdinand's enemies. People have always said that he liked to keep his enemies close to him but this is outlandish and macabre and, certainly, counter to Christian values. He enjoyed giving this tour to his guests himself," I am told. Jean's voice conveyed a slightly high-pitched tone, somewhere between an excited teenager and a shrieking bird. He caught himself before his excitement became overbearing and foolish.

Charles followed Jean down unlit stairways into the below ground caves and cells, away from the sunlit upper floors of the castle. Finally, they came to the room, the "museum of mummies". Upon entering a large, dark, dank room with little light illuminating the figures sitting at a large rectangular wooden table, upright and still, no sound breaking the eerie silence, were the mummified remains of Ferdinand's erstwhile enemies. Charles, a participant in so many bloody and grievous scenes, had no way to express himself, stood dumbfounded and speechless for a moment, eyes dilated, mouth ajar, until he broke into a large bellowing laugh. Jean could only follow suit. The laughter echoed through the cavernous walls and hallways. Each mummy of a man was dressed in his earthly clothing, seemingly ready to dine, dinner plates and wine goblets in front of him, looking straight-ahead with what could be interpreted as slight smiles on their bony, desiccated faces.

Charles was to remain in Naples only 3 months before he learned of the Holy League arrayed against him. His position was precarious, and he knew that his journey northward to France would be contested by the combination of city-states who had grown to fear him and loath his army. The viciousness of his advance had troubled many rulers, even those, like Ludovico and the Doge in Venice, who had initially welcomed him into the peninsular. Charles alarmed them with the power of his army, and he threatened the existence of each of them. They had suddenly realized that their states were in danger of becoming mere provinces of France, and they also recognized that they would have to unite in order to stop him.

The leaders met in Venice and became signatories, without the usual squabbles, to the formation of a Holy League, composed of Venice, Milan, the Pope, the Spanish King, the English King and Maximilian, the Holy Roman Emperor. They engaged Duke Francesco Gonzaga of Mantua to form an army with the purpose of expelling Charles from the peninsular. Once formed this army began to threaten and take the garrisons that Charles had opened on his advance down the peninsular.

Hearing the news, Charles immediately knew that his return to France would be contested and also knew that he must leave Naples immediately if his return was to be possible. "Jean, we must make ready to quickly leave Naples and proceed home. It will be a long journey, longer in effort and more dangerous in opposition than the one we took to reach here."

"Yes, we have information that the League has taken the Genoa port and the one at Livorno. The remaining forces are moving swiftly westward from Venice where they were grouped. We can be ready to move in two days."

*****

Gonzaga and his commanders stood over a table in the Doge's palace in Venice looking intensely at a map of the northern Peninsular. "We must move west from here and set up a position to block Charles's route north. From our scouts, we have learned that he was moving towards Genoa in an attempt to leave on a sea exit to France. We have removed that option. Venetian ships have captured the port. His only exit now is north over the mountain passes."

"Should we not send troops south to harass and disrupt his supply posts," said Ludovico, raising himself from the bent position he held while viewing the map.

"Yes," replied Gonzaga, he, too, standing straight, which revealed his hunchback more prominently. "There is some talk of sending the light cavalry south to harass his rearguard which is carrying the booty that he has pillaged from us on his trek south."

Ludovico, always hesitant about mercenary troops, thought to himself that the prominence of mercenaries in the League forces might put it at a disadvantage to the French whose force was primary composed of French professional soldiers. Only quick victories were the way to stabilize a mercenary force. This was not the time to raise this question, he said to himself. Better to remain quiet now.

"We have time to coordinate our attacks," said Gonzaga. "Charles is hampered by moving his siege machines and canons and his trains of booty. His progress will be slow. We will meet him here in the plains of the north before he reaches the mountains. After we dismantle his garrisons, his troops will acquire a sense of loss that they have not yet experienced in this adventure of Charles. They will become dispirited when their provisions are expropriated by our troops and may be a less effective force when they finally realize that they are fighting far from their homeland."

*****

Giorgio led the Milanese force to the French garrison town of Grosseto. His goal was to destroy the garrison and then to proceed on to the next garrison at Orbetello. There was a total of 8 garrisons between Genoa and Naples. Allied forces were tasked to handle the remaining garrisons. The men were enthusiastic to reach Orbetello, eager to avenge the massacres and eager to share the spoils of the battle as they had been promised.

"We will stop here tonight," he told Gianni who was Giorgio's aide-de-camp, a position that Ludovico had given to Gianni after much thought. Giorgio acquiesced without question. He had confidence that the instructions Gianni had taken in the use of weaponry over the last several years had prepared him for battle despite his limited experience in actual warfare. Giorgio was impressed with Gianni's courage and loyalty, and he believed that courage and loyalty would prove more beneficial than his shortcomings.

The garrison at Orbetello was small, occupied by less than 150 soldiers, all footman with no heavy artillery. The camp sat in the town center some 30 miles from the sea, the small oval main piazza consisted of a pretty village-sized church which anchored one end. Several inns and large homes circled an oversized fountain, one more appropriate for a town three times its size, statutes of putti in flight sprouting water into a large circular basin. It was the focus of much of the town's activity. French officers and staff were being housed in several of the more attractive homes while foot-soldiers opened their tents on the outskirts of the town near the stockade of provisions.

A partial moon lit the piazza as the clouds moved over it when a small contingent of Giorgio's men advanced on the town. They had already dispatched the guards, easily overcome since they were partially intoxicated and totally uncoordinated from the wine they had appropriated from a citizen's home. Giorgio's Stradioti scouts, rugged mountain mercenaries from Greece and Albania known especially for their light cavalry, had stealthily come upon them and quickly relieved them of their duties and their lives. Nary a sound was heard in the darkness of the night.

Giorgio motioned the remainder of his troops to move to the house each was assigned. Five other men waited outside, ready to attack when the French exited the house into the piazza. The cavalry was left in a nearby clearing to wait on their mounts until the signal was given to ride through the stockade, expected to be in disarray and easy prey for a cavalry charge after the French were aroused by the noise emanating from the piazza. Gianni led this group, somewhat nervous of the responsibility he was given by Giorgio. Ludovico had instructed Giorgio to expose Gianni to battle, and there was no better way than to place him at the center of an expected rout of the French.

Creeping into the homes, Giorgio's men were surprised at the number of men living there. Several were slain in their sleep, silently and efficiently. Before long, however, the remaining French were up and armed, led fighting into the piazza by Giorgio's men. So many French were slain as they passed through the doorway that dead bodies blocked access to the piazza by others. An unexpected comedy ensued when hostilities ceased, the French in the houses and the League soldiers in the piazza. No one seemed to know what to do next. League soldiers could be seen leaning on their swords with the tip of their blades in the ground.

The French soldiers at the stockyard were aroused by the noise, as expected. With swords in hand they ran from their tents headed to the piazza excitedly. Gianni's cavalry charged, slicing through the garrison easily and viciously. Men lay bleeding on the ground, moaning, only to be killed where they lay. Arms and a few heads mixed with the dead bodies, motionless under the rising sun. League soldiers reached a frenzy of killing, stabbing bodies that were already dead or dying.

Gianni stood among the carnage, shouting commands to discontinue the attack. No one listened. His commands flittered into the air among the moans and shrieks of the dying and the yells and screams of the living. The attack stopped only when all the pent-up anger that League soldiers had been carrying with them since the reports of French massacres was released. Gianni walked from the scene in a daze of disbelief, his face covered in agony, his heart bleeding sorrow.

The League troops were mercenaries, many Stradioti, but they were as incensed over the French massacres as were the Peninsular forces. Many mercenaries had families with them on the peninsula, and they could visualize their own slaughtered as well as could the native troops.

Some French soldiers scampered into a nearby olive grove, running among the trees to escape the massacre. Ladders rested by trees yet to have their olives harvested; nets were spread under them to capture those olives falling from the trees. Men screamed as their lives were taken from them among the trees which resembled gnarled old men looking down at their dead bodies.

Gianni recovered his poise and ran into the grove after the remaining French soldiers, hoping he could stop the slaughter. He was pushing his troops off of dying men with all the vigor of a zealot while the Stradioti were decapitating French soldiers, as was their habit in battle. Suddenly, a tattered and blood-soaked soldier jumped from behind a tree, hatred in his eyes, to knock Gianni down, ready to thrust his sword into Gianni's immobile body. The soldier fell over onto the ground dead, a sword plunged into his back. Giorgio, looking battered himself, knelt down by Gianni and lifted his head until his senses recovered.

The battle was over, bodies scattered over the town center, blood mixing with the soil of the unpaved streets. Troops were sitting exhausted by the fountain, plopped up by its walls. Talk was minimal. It seemed that they had expended the energy of a month in one hour. It seemed that nothing could interest them now.

"Gianni, you had me frightened for a while." said Giorgio, sitting with Gianni in one of the homes on the piazza.

"Thank you, you saved me," whispered Gianni in a hoarse voice.

"When I heard your anguished cries, I knew something was awry. It took me a while to get to you through the fighting that was going on around me. Then, I saw you run into the grove."

"The carnage is disheartening…. no, immoral," said Gianni, expressing his true belief, more in exasperation than in anger. His anger was exhausted, released while he was killing Frenchmen. He knew the limits of anger and had no more to expend.

"Gianni, I suppose in one way, war is immoral. But it can often support a greater good."

"No, not the fighting, the savagery, the unmerciful manner in which it is fought."

"Gianni, it's difficult to be merciful when your life is at stake. I suppose there are some who can rise above the savagery, but there are not many saints in the world. Most of us merely want to get to the next day. Perhaps, you are just calling for a better way to kill, something more efficient and clean looking. To me, who has been a soldier all his life, one way to die is as good as any other." He hesitated, not willing to continue the conversation. Looking at Gianni, he said, "We must get ready to leave tomorrow."

Giorgio surveyed the piazza, then walked over to the stockyard. Seeing one of his captains there, he said, "Restock our provisions with what we need, distribute the remaining food to the locals, burn everything else."

*****

Charles left Naples in May knowing that a sea escape from Genoa was not possible and that a French relief force was driving southward towards Milan with the intention of meeting up with Charles's army. He was forced to change his original route along the coast to a more inward route through mountainous areas, slowing his advance.

In Venice, the Holy League consolidated its plan to approach Charles. Once they were informed that a French relief force was heading south and near to attacking Milan, urgency of action came to the fore. The debate over whether negotiation was the better approach with Charles ended swiftly.

Ludovico stood and urged an attack, telling the participants, "We can wait no longer. We must confront Charles's main force immediately. Not only is Milan in danger but he has overrun the League's garrison in Pontremoli, again slaughtering all of our men, and he is in Pisa now expelling the Florentines, leaving a garrison behind to help the Pisans against the Florentines. He means to be as disruptive as he can be on his exit from the peninsular. He must be repaid for these atrocities. We must stand up and stand together. Now is the time. Now is how we will be remembered. Now is how our future will be defined."

Agreement was reached in short order after Ludovico roused his compatriots. Plans were easily made to move the whole of Gonzaga's contingent west to block Charles's path north which they did at Fornovo, about 20 miles from Parma. The 12,000 French soldiers with 3,000 Swiss mercenaries and 28 heavy guns settled on the right bank of the Taro river. The 20,000 League soldiers with 16,000 mercenaries including 4,000 Stradioti cavalry stopped on the left bank of the river. There the situation rested on July

Charles sat in his tent the evening of July 4 and called his second in command, General Louis II de La Tremoille to meet with him. "General," he said as he sat in his oversized, heavily padded and wood carved chair, legs propped up on an ottoman and a goblet of a fine claret in his hand, "Ah, it is so nice to relax with some of our fine wines. Our provisions are running low, are they not? Good reason to get back to France as soon as possible."

General de La Tremoille sat in an adjoining chair and accepted the goblet that was offered him by one of the attendants. "Yes, we have not been able to replenish our supplies since we left Naples except for what little we have taken from those small towns we have sacked."

"Are the men still in good spirits?"

"They are holding up but are anxious to reach France and their homes. They have been away longer than most of them expected."

Charles paused for a moment to look over his back, exhibiting the nervous apprehension that so often appeared in him in times of stress. When he noticed his attendant behind him, he relaxed noticeably. "Without provisions, we will not be able to move very far. We still have a distance yet to reach France. How long will our provisions last?

"Perhaps a week, no more than 10 days. We have lost much from the overrunning of our garrisons. The League has been very efficient in taking them down."

"Let's try to negotiate with Gonzaga for free passage into France. Otherwise, we will have to make our stand here in Fornovo. Make arrangements for a meeting and make ready for battle as an alternative. I want to be prepared. Begin to array our guns at them. Perhaps, that may discourage them somewhat."

"I have some doubt that they will be in a mood to negotiate. Their leaders may be but the troops seem to be in a hostile mood. I have gotten word that the overrun garrisons have not been treated well."

"It is Gonzaga and the others that count, not the troops. And give the men an extra portion of wine tonight.... enough to raise their spirits but not to inebriate them. We may need them fresh tomorrow."

\*\*\*\*\*

"Your Highness," Gonzaga's condition for free passage is the return of all of our booty and territory that we have accumulated."

"No, we cannot accept this condition. That would be humiliating. We must prepare for battle," said Charles walking to the opening of his tent and looking at the rain falling. "The muddy ground should prevent their cavalry from crossing the river. This should give us an advantage. It should neutralize the Stradioti."

Both armies waited in anticipation for the rain to abate, anxiety growing in each camp. That night the low murmur of conversations could be heard in the darkness. It seemed few men was asleep. The following day the rain did stop,

251

leaving a cloudy sky preparing for the newly risen sun and soggy river banks with unsteady footing and nearly impossible passage across the river. Nevertheless, both armies prepared their battle lines.

Charles formed three battle lines on his side of the Taro. He led the second largest group and thought his troops were in good position to repel the League forces. Artillery was arranged in front of the first line. "Prepare for their charge," he cried out to his troops, as they waited for the attack to begin.

Gonzaga arrayed League troops in nine lines. His plan of attack was to first advance his cavalry on Charles's first two lines, waiting for them to become disorganized and outflanking the remaining line in the turmoil. His troops were eager to begin, dispelling their anxiety in the daylight after being told again that they could retain much of the spoils of battle.

As the sun rose through the cloudy slate-grey sky that July morning, Gonzaga released his light cavalry across the river, both the Venetian contingent and the mercenary Stradioti. Loud war cries broke the morning quiet, mixing with the far away soft chirping of birds. Ludovico waited in command of one of the reserve lines in the background, impatient to enter the flay.

The French artillery was unable to fire, only now noticing that their powder was wet. Charles's troops waited to counter the onslaught of the League, stiffening their resolve. Horses slowed to a walk to keep their footing in the wet, slippery, muddy ground, fortunate that the French heavy guns were inactive. Both sides had lost an advantage. Men and horses slipped to the muddy ground to be encased in a brown carapace.

Finally, the League's reserve forces were signaled to attack Charles's flank. Ludovico and his men raced into the battle, clashing swords punctuating the air. Ludovico narrowly missed being felled by an arrow but continued leading his men even as he could hear the moans of the fallen over the sounds of battle, human limbs and horses' legs entangled in a mass of flesh soaked in bright red blood and muddy brown loam. Taken off his horse by an attacker, he swung his sword furiously at his enemy rushing into battle. His left arm now had a deep wound from an enemy sword but ignoring it, he tried to rally his men, calling out for continued resistance. Men fell wreathing in agony, leaving their companions to continue the battle. The advantage was flowing to the League when the Stradioti light cavalry noticed an assigned troop of League cavalry attacking and driving away the French from the rich baggage train in the rear of the French line. The Stradioti detached themselves and joined the skirmish over the train, looting it after driving the French away.

After an hour of fighting, the French were pushed back to a hill in retreat, but the outcome of the battle remained indecisive. Two thousand League troops were killed, 1,200 French troops. The following day amid the fallen a truce was called so that bodies could be removed from the battlefield. Ludovico walked through the battlefield among the fallen. He did not feel victorious among the broken bodies.

The French, having lost all of the prizes of their expedition, were allowed to continue unmolested on their way to France, leaving Charles, however, with the knowledge of the vast wealth that existed there. The battle was indecisive. It did not deter the thoughts of another incursion into the Peninsular. The League disbanded and resumed their usual bickering and machinations over borders and other matters.

*****

Milan was relieved that the French had departed. Ludovico, alone in his chambers, thought of the last few months and the precariousness of his situation at times but was pleased that his position was stronger than ever. He was recognized as the Duke of Milan, thanks to the support of Maximilian, Naples had been put on notice that its meddling in Milan affairs and its threats would not be tolerated, his ties with Florence were as strong as ever, Venice was neutralized, his relationship with the Pope was shaky but he had Ascanio as an advocate to the Pope and the one mistake he had made, enticing Charles to enter the peninsular, had been rectified.

He rose to close the opened curtains that were allowing the morning sun to enter his chambers unmolested. He turned to view Leonardo's painting of Beatrice hanging on the wall, a new painting that very few people had seen. That is the way she wanted it. Although she encouraged the arts throughout the realm and enjoyed discussions of the artistic life, she was private and modest about her personal life and wanted the painting to be only for Ludovico's pleasure. His love for her was no less than it was on his wedding day. Beatrice still illuminated his life as the sun does the day, bringing otherwise hidden feelings to life.

The painting reminded him to see Leonardo's progress on the "Last Supper" in Santa Marie delle Grazie. "Find Giorgio and Gianni", he shouted to his attendant at the door "and tell them to come here." Then remembering that he also wanted to speak to Tomasso Vermentino, he asked the attendant to find him also.

"Tomasso, are our finances in order? I hear that some people are grumbling about taxes, complaining about them. They do not understand the need for them to sustain the court and our resident artists. Our tax burden is less than the French would have enacted, had they remained in the city. Do they not know that it was with their tax money that we were able to expel the French?"

Tomasso replied, "We are running a slight deficit. The expense of the recent war with Charles was an expense that was not expected in the accounts. But with some slight retrenchment, we can attain balance."

"Good, good, I do not want to go back to the people so soon after our last tax increase. We must moderate our expenditures. Thank you, you may go."

Giorgio and Gianni entered soon after Tomasso's departure. "Let's ride over to Santa Marie delle Grazie and see the Leonardo. I've asked Beatrice to accompany us."

"It's beautiful and full of the love of Christ.... what is finished," remarked Beatrice. "When will the remainder be completed," she said to Leonardo, knowing immediately after she spoke those words that Leonardo was displeased. He just mumbled with a faint scowl and continued on with his painting. He was usually a well-tempered person.

"I see you are painting on a dry wall," she continued, not bending to his peevishness. "Does that not jeopardize the durability of the painting? Will it last as long?"

"No, no, no. I need the extra time to insert the features I need in the picture, especially those of Christ and Judas. I have spent days wandering the streets, looking for the perfect combination of features. Their faces will be a composite of the many that I have seen, and I cannot just dash them off with impunity."

"But I understand that dry wall will not hold the paint as long as a fresco, that the paint will deteriorate faster."

Leonardo replied in an uncomfortable voice. "True, fresco requires one to paint before the plaster dries. Therefore, one must paint quickly. I need the time to visualize what I want to do. I can ponder my strokes. I cannot paint quickly; I simply cannot paint this picture quickly. Dry wall allows me that time. I am seeking a luminosity in my colors. Dry wall permits this. It will be a painting that will honor Ludovico's father and honor the court of Milan. People will consider it the most beautiful painting in Europe. Can you not see the brightness of the colors?"

"Yes," said Beatrice, moving closer to the wall but keeping out of Leonardo's space. "How do you accomplish this result?"

The sun was now moving away from the painting, retreating to a corner of the dining hall, throwing different shadows on the wall. Leonardo placed his brushes down and walked to Beatrice and the others. He sensed he would not be able to do more work until he answered Beatrice's questions. In any case, the light was no longer adequate for him; answering her questions would show deference to her. "I place an undercoat of white lead to enhance the color of the oil and tempera. Does not the color shine with life? Does it not show the luminosity of spirit of the soon to be martyred Christ?"

All of them agreed with him and stood before the painting mesmerized as the sun moved around the adjacent wall, leaving Beatrice completely mollified.

*****

Ascanio sat in his apartment composing a letter to Ludovico, sipping a glass of Frascati fermented and bottled on the outskirts of Rome. The Trebbiano grape can sometimes make an amiable wine, he thought to himself. Nice for sipping but not something I would serve to a guest. A wine for me on a lonely, overcast night like tonight. He wanted to update Ludovico on his progress on the monastery question. The letter would say he had found that Bishop Mario Grignolino, the Assistant Director of the Papal Camera, the treasury, had sympathies similar to theirs, sympathies that abhorred the reckless, selfish, and frivolous expenditures that were made in the Vatican, especially for the benefit of the Pope's relatives, sympathies that were also resounding distressingly in the north in the Holy Roman Empire. It was a behavior, he

257

thought, that brought dishonor to the clergy that had taken vows to serve their flocks, a dishonor that fell on all the clergy, guilty of irreligious activity or not. Ascanio could not but feel that the news he was hearing from some in the Holy Roman Empire would someday lead to a crisis in the Church.

Ascanio rose from his desk and walked to the window in thought, opening his drapes to peer down at the street. He thought, who am I to disavow the Vatican. Do I not use the benefices I obtain from my office to pay my gambling debts? What justification do I have? He thought for a moment. Only that I do not benefit my relatives. His noticed his wine glass was empty and filled it, thinking, if I am so profligate and sinful, why do I purchase such inexpensive wine? He looked at his wine glass and smiled.

Ascanio was able to confide in Bishop Grignolino on the long-standing situation at the monasteries. Grignolino was not only shocked but offered his service without solicitation from Ascanio. He was a true believer. Ascanio explained to Ludovico that even though he was Vice Chancellor, there was much that was hidden from him, financial accounts that were unknown but to a few people. Bishop Grignolino, on the other hand, could, given his position, weave his way through all the camera accounts and, perhaps, find information that revealed a conspiracy and its purpose, although a purpose was becoming clearer.

The letter went on to say that Bishop Grignolino confided to Ascanio that he had found an account book amongst hundreds of retired account books, and it had confirmed funds were held in the Fugger Bank. This book had current information but is now missing. He had searched the shelfs several times for it but was unable to locate it. Ascanio concluded that we must now assume that the perpetrators of the scheme are aware of our efforts to expose them, and we all should proceed with our activities with this information in mind.

Ascanio leaned back in his chair, rolling the glass of Frascati in his hands. The papacy has been competing with the secular princes ever since Charlemagne. Isn't that why the Pope is often called the Prince of the Church, a title matching that of the princes governing their own lands? These two forces have been at odds for centuries. The Papacy desires to safeguard its territory, the Papal States, just as fervently as the Holy Roman Emperor, the King of France or the Duke of Milan does their territory. The means to achieve that outcome are the same, military power, diplomacy, and, more often than not, treachery. The Pope has one advantage. He can invoke Christ and St. Peter, and Popes have used the power of excommunication often to achieve that advantage. People have become even more dedicated to the Church in the last century, fearing the Black Death that has so decimated the cities and countrysides. The fear of the Plague still lingers in the minds of the populous.

Ascanio decided to walk outside in the gardens to clear his head, the wine had begun to cover his mind in a veil of ambiguity. The night air was welcoming, relieving the pressure that he felt in his apartment. How a different venue sometimes magically unseals thoughts that elsewhere remain hidden, he said to himself? The Vatican has the use of all the funds that come into it. The Pope can use them in any way he desires, and popes have taken monies from general revenue to fund their expeditions. Their attempts at aggrandizing more territory is, in many cases, not for the benefit of the Vatican but for relatives. Pope Sixtus had done this as did Pope Innocent. And Pope Alexander has this in mind for his son, Cesare.

Why the Fugger Bank, though? After walking, then sitting under the overcast sky, the half-moon partially hidden by clouds and mirroring the content of his mind, he rose again and walked towards the exit. "Ockham's razor" should apply, he thought with a light jump to his steps, the principle posited by William Ockham in the last century that the easiest explanation is more often the correct explanation. And here the explanation that fits easily is that there has been a continuing conspiracy since Pope Sixtus's time to promote and execute a larger military effort, perhaps one on several fronts at the same time. This kind of adventure would require a reserve fund if ordinary revenues were insufficient and, perhaps, unavailable. In a long-lasting conflict, one could expect that the affected parties would be less agreeable to delivering benefices to Rome, if their lands were in jeopardy. The Fugger bank was out of the jurisdiction of any of the peninsular states and the account would not be jeopardized if a conflict arose.

The conspiracy would require collusion between successive popes. Could that be the reason that the last three Popes, Sixtus, Innocent and Alexander seemed so close? Could that be the reason I did not gain the papacy, he asked himself? Innocent was elevated to Cardinal by Sixtus and was independently wealthy, capable of influencing his selection with his own wealth. Alexander had been elevated to Vice Chancellor by his uncle, Pope Calixtus III, which made him the benefactor of enormous wealth from the selling of benefices and would provide him an advantage that many Cardinals did not have. He also had enormous influence on Innocent, and the Vice Chancellor would have to be a party to the plot. Every cardinal knew that Alexander was outwardly interested in advancing the territorial claims of his family, which he could do through the papacy. Ascanio convinced himself that there was sufficient information to substantiate his theory. I must get this information to Ludovico. He must send someone to the Fugger Bank for more details on the fund.

\*\*\*\*\*

To Ludovico's triumvirate of Giorgio, Gianni and himself was added his finance minister, Tomasso. The four men discussed Ascanio's letter. He had included a second letter that he wrote as Vice Chancellor of the Vatican, a Vatican seal attached to it, giving the holder of the letter the authority to discuss the account with officials of the bank.

Ludovico was vitally concerned about San Gelsera. His concern for the other monasteries was less compelling, but he, nonetheless, had an interest in them. It was just that he did not have the same conviction for them. Looking at Gianni, he said, "Have you been back to San Gelsera lately? Has the condition of the monastery deteriorated severely since last you saw it?" Gianni noticed an urgency in his voice, one that he very seldom had heard.

"My last visit was to see Brother Matteo. I have not returned since his death. The condition then was very

E. F. PALERMO

disheartening. In addition to the physical deterioration, the monastery had not been gaining novitiates, hence those passing on have not been replaced. It is a sad condition."

Giorgio spoke up, more in jest than in earnest. "Perhaps the loss of land was providential since they do not have the manpower to sustain it. The losses balance themselves out."

"Giorgio, there is more often bombast than realist in you," retorted Ludovico. "You are so often the bombast that we do not know when you are the realist. I know where your heart lies, and it is not with the hierarchy of the church. You are more an earthy presence, tied to those good, hardworking peasants and monks, I might add, that you admire so much."

Gianni took up the mild berating with a smile and joined in, "You have always shown the same urgent interest in the issue as me, just not so openly. You have a genuine ability to hide your true emotions, one that you seem to never unleash. But I have peeped at you from time to time, and I can see the emotion on your face. It is one of anger for the position that the monks have been put into, not one of sardonic posture for their position. You would as soon strike a bishop than despoil the unselfish work of most monks."

"This conversation is becoming much too serious for me," said Giorgio. "Ludovico, at least give me a glass of wine, a good one if you please, so that I can fend off your sarcasms with aplomb, if not truthfulness."

"We are nearing a resolution of this issue," said Ludovico running his hand through his hair nonchalantly and turning to pour Giorgio a glass of wine, "one in which we can all be proud, the restoration of the monastic life in, at least, these parts. Our agenda cannot, of course, include monasteries all over Europe. We just do not have the resources for that. Even our little adventure is still fraught with danger to us. We cannot be indifferent to it. We must be alert. Giorgio, I want you to go to Augsburg with Ascanio's letter in hand and speak to the bank officials. Get the true history of the account, names of those involved since Sixtus, amounts deposited over the years, times and dates of withdrawals and any other information that they care to offer you."

\*\*\*\*\*

"Ludovico, your title is no longer in danger and you are one of the accepted leaders on the Peninsular," said Giorgio, strolling with him along the ramparts of the castle. "So, what is your next digression, something pleasant, I hope."

"Giorgio, I have taken up with a lady-in-waiting to Beatrice, a woman named Lucrezia Crivelli, a beautiful, mature woman. I did not actively pursue her. It happened almost without knowing how attracted I was to her. This all occurred after Cecilia left."

"Is this wise, you know how unhappy Beatrice was about Cecilia and the trouble you went through to marry her off."

"She knows and is not happy about Lucrezia. But please, can I not love two women at the same time? Beatrice is my true love, the one I want to have for the rest of my existence, the one who satisfies all my desires from a woman, the one who complements me in my personal life and public life. Did you see how professionally and astutely she behaved at the peace conference last year? She was as helpful and attuned to our position as any of the so-called diplomats there. She is like an appendage of me. I could not exist without her."

"Yes, she was excellent," said Giorgio, "but how is Beatrice taking your new arrangement? She was quite forceful last time about dispatching Cecilia. Remember, with you one plus two equals three, with her one plus two equals zero."

"She wants me to exile her from the castle but I just cannot do it. The situation is at a standstill, and she is pregnant now. What complicates the situation is that Beatrice is also pregnant, a nervous trill in his voice." Ludovico stopped and looked pass the city streets surrounding the castle wall, retrieving fond memories of his youth. "Remember when we could walk the streets with impunity. Now we need accompaniment to leave the castle. The city has changed. We have made great improvements: the canals, the streets and the promenades lined with beautiful villas, many with a Florentine architectural touch that has become so prominent today. It is an accomplishment I am proud of."

"Well, you may need accompaniment, but I can still walk the streets alone with my own thoughts. It is the way I like it. I can wander the streets without concern. Yes, the city has changed but I will always be there for you."

*****

Deep in the night, the moon obscured by the clouds of an impending storm, two men walked along silently, dressed in dark cloaks avoiding the turmoil around them, drunken men leaning haphazardly against walls, women clinging to them barely able to stand themselves, the noises of the night mixing in the usual cacophony of this corner of Milan. They stop at a doorway, then move along the adjacent alleyway, scale a wall into the rear garden, quietly pry open the rear door and enter the darkened house. Their silent entry speaks of wonted experience, steeled by years of similar activities. The small house has two bedrooms. They freeze for a moment before advancing any farther like two statutes not quite in their appropriate places but ready to be put on display by the curator.

They open a bedroom door with the minimum of effort, silently entering and stopping over the two individuals sleeping in bed. Without discussion, they draw their daggers and with a sweep of their arms the blood of the occupants' spews from their necks. Giorgio Falanghina and his wife, Magdalene, have their blood mix together in a pool of red on the wooden floor. In the next bedroom, their child cries aloud in the darkness.

In a house, far from this corner of Milan, the two darkly cloaked men arrive at the rear door. A knock opens the door by a well-dressed man with dark circles under his eyes. "The deed is done, Tomasso. Cesare should be happy."

The following day Ludovico is struck by anger alternating with sorrow, his body tense with the news of Giorgio. His mind races through all the events that he and Giorgio experienced together. He was my closest confidant, he thinks. No, he was more than a confidant. He was a true brother.

"Gianni, we have to find out who is responsible for this outrage. Who could it have been? Who would have struck us so severely?"

"Perhaps, it is best to start with the question, why was he assassinated?"

"We have no conflict we are engaged with at the moment, Gianni. But Giorgio was set to leave for Augsburg soon. The information he gathered could rattle the Vatican. They could be a suspect."

"The Vatican is certainly capable of it. Cesare is well-known to have an assassin's immoral attitude, and he is rumored to have been part of many. And slaying a man in bed is within his modus operandi."

"You knew, Tomasso knew. No one else knew directly. I suppose someone could have deduced it somehow."

"Could it not be coincidence?

"It is not a coincidence, Gianni. The simplest explanation is always the most likely. And that is, we must keep an eye on Tomasso. He has to be the prime suspect."

"Gianni, you will have to go to Augsburg in Giorgio's place. No one is to know. We have to keep this secret to ourselves, but you must leave immediately."

Once the two men completed their discussion, the atmosphere turned to somber blue, thoughts of Giorgio and of his newly discovered secret wife and child. They finally learned why he had been so often missing from the castle. Both men could not understand why he did not want them to participate in his private life, but pleased that happiness had entered his life, and they hoped that he had found at least a modicum of contentment. The secret would forever rest with Giorgio, and his image would always rest with them.

The following day Ludovico learned that Tomasso was missing, his home vacant and his whereabouts unknown. His anger was frothing like hot oil over fire. He's in Rome, he thought. We can get to Rome. It's not like we have no influence there. My reach is as extensive as is the Vatican's. I must inform Ascanio immediately. He may be in danger also, although we never used Ascanio's name as far as I remember.

It was not long after his letter to Ascanio was sent that Ludovico received a letter from Ascanio relating that Bishop Grignolino had been reassigned to the court of Maximillian I, the Holy Roman Emperor, as Papal Envoy. Ludovico and Ascanio were to lose their valued informant.

*****

"Gianni, Beatrice is in labor. I am to have another child soon," Ludovico said one day as he and Gianni were walking in the garden fronting the castle. The sky was clear and the crocus were exposing their tips for another year. He was as excited about this birth as he was about the birth of his previous children. "I think a daughter this time

267

would round out my family, if I am so fortunate. The Almighty has been kind to me."

Near the birth date, Ludovico paced his office while reading his correspondence, his mind not entirely focused on the correspondence. His concern for Beatrice was elevated, given the difficult time she had had carrying the child, his worries causing an unusual lack of focus for him.

"Ludovico, you must relax," said Gianni who had returned from his journey to Augsburg several months prior. His journey had confirmed the minutiae of the Vatican account held in the Fugger bank.

"You should know, Gianni, that child birth is not an easy or safe procedure for a woman. One must always be cautious and pray to God that both the mother and child come through it unharmed."

"You have fine doctors here, Ludovico, and your pacing and excessive anxiety does not a thing to lessen Beatrice's encumbrance." Of course, no words could reduce his concern, but they were necessary to show common cause with him.

The weather outside of Ludovico's window spoke of a fine day, cloudless and mild, a day made for hiking in the forest outside the city or along one of the canals. He was intent on taking a walk but thought the better of it after the doctor sent word that Beatrice was struggling with this birth.

Hours passed without additional word from the doctor. Ludovico and Gianni sat together on a bench in the garden, each with his own silent thoughts. Ludovico thought of his wedding day, his pretty, young, petite wife by his side at the altar in the cathedral, the Duomo choir arousing thoughts of angels singing from heaven, filling the church nave in an exquisite expression of love. He thought of his wedding reception, Beatrice charming the guests like she had been a host for years, the beautiful and unusual decorations of Leonardo receiving everyone's plaudits; all capping a glorious day for him and for Milan.

Finally, Ludovico was called by the doctor. He ran into the bedroom to be told that the unthinkable had occurred. Beatrice was dead and his baby son had died stillborn before her. The agony exploded within him like a lightning bolt, rolling his mind in unimaginable contours, colors muting together like a Leonardo pallet fallen to the ground, unheard of sounds clashing in his ears. He fell to his knees by Beatrice's bed, clasped her hand one final time, holding it tenderly with all the love he had had for her in their short 6 years of marriage. Tears flowed from his eyes, washing down his face, wetting his shirt in narrow streams of sadness. He knelt and prayed.

Ludovico was inconsolable. He could do no work; he was hardly able to walk, so shaken was he. For several days after the funeral, he lay in bed, no thought in his mind except those that dealt with his life with Beatrice. No one was able to move him from his bed chambers. He just rewound and rewound his thoughts, stopping at some particularly happy moment to try to give life to the memory. Her body was taken to Pavia to be buried in the Certosa. The pain within him would not subside. It kept bubbling outward, giving substance to his inner grief, attending mass every day, praying to the Almighty most of the day in the chapel, trying to absolve himself from his belief that he had contributed to her death, abandoning his duties even while there were threats rising for Milan over the mountains in France.

*****

"Ludovico, Charles VIII has died in France from a freak accident. He struck his head on the lintel of a doorway and succumbed several days later," cried Gianni, walking quickly into the chapel. "He has been succeeded by his cousin, Louis XII. He is no friend of ours, and we should be prepared for an adventure from him. You must concentrate your powers on him."

"Yes, yes, I know," Ludovico replied softly, turning toward Gianni from his kneeling position in a pew near the alter. "I will not be surprised by anything he does. Massimo, our agent at the court, tells me that Louis is already contemplating an attack on the Peninsular. But I cannot move. I cannot survive without my Beatrice. My muscles seem to be tied to the earth she walked on here."

Gianni looked sternly at Ludovico, steeling himself to be forceful to him. "Your sons," he shouted, "what about your sons? Do you not want to leave them your Duchy? Do you want to abandon them? Would not Beatrice want you to protect their patrimony, to be the father and mother that they need? Is she to be the cause of your defeat, of your humiliation?"

Ludovico stopped his prayer and leaned back in the pew, some color returning to his pale face, some life returning to his lifeless limbs. "Yes, Beatrice would want me to resist

Louis; she would want me to defend Milan." Then rising from his pew, he grabbed Gianni's arm and led him from the chapel. Once outside of the chapel, he said, "Louis believes he has a claim on us through his grandfather's marriage into the Visconti family who ruled here before my father, and he is obsessed with it. His cousin, Charles, apparently described too vividly the wealth that exists on this side of the Alps, and it is too enticing for him to ignore. He will be a formidable force but one we can overcome. We've done it before. I would be so more confident if I had Giorgio here with us. We must form the League again to repulse Louis."

"There is no league to form," said Gianni several weeks later. "No one is willing to come to our defense. There is a sense that we invited the French onto the Peninsular 4 years ago, and the bitterness from that has not subsided. He will come with all the equipment and men that Charles had. That means 80 heavy mobile canons, more than enough to destroy any wall in Lombardy, and 25,000 men, including Swiss mercenaries and the elite French lancers. He means to show his strength by leveling any fortified town that resists him, just as Charles had done. He is recruiting more Swiss mercenaries and has concluded an agreement with Savoy to allow free passage through its territory into the Duchy as well as allowing him to purchase provisions. We may not be so fortunate as to have it rain on French gunpowder this time. Providence is unlikely to be with us a second time."

"Call Leonardo here. We must devise new defenses. We must hear what Leonardo has to say. His 70 tons of bronze for the equestrian horse is in storage. We must melt it down and produce our own canons."

\*\*\*\*\*

Louis wasted no time in sending his army into Lombardy, eager to start the campaign and redeem what he believed was his rightful inheritance. The first town his army, under the command of Marshall Giacomo Trivulzio, approached was Rocca di Arazzo in western Lombardi. He had instructions from Louis to capture the town at all costs. Stopping in front of the walls, he said to his second in command, "These walls will crumble like the walls of Jericho, and their God will not be able to help them."

Canon were brought up and aligned facing the western wall. Once the first shots flew into the wall, the troops resting atop the wall and residents inside the wall were amazed at the power of the shots. Large chunks of grey stone fell apart in the air, falling to the ground in dust and shards. For hours, this display of power overwhelmed the eyes of the inhabitants. The town was seized without use of the cavalry or foot-soldiers. "Massacre everyone," Marshall Trivulzio called out to his troops as he entered the town, "leave no one alive." It was meant to be warning to other towns in Lombardi that resistance was futile. It was a strategy that the French had used in the 100-years war of the last century.

Ludovico, only mildly recovered from his despondency over Beatrice's death, faced the prospect of encountering this French force alone. He was quickly assembling a Swiss mercenary contingent but knew that he could not confront the French without heavy guns. "Gianni", he said soon after the news of the attack on Rocca di Arazzo reached him, "we must hurry the production of the canon. The French seem to be in a hurry to annihilate us. We simply cannot face them without it."

Gianni looked at Ludovico's face, the disappointment clearly visible. Abandoning the statute dedicated to his father was just another blow to that aging face that had become apparent since Beatrice's death. His life, so full of the nuances of politics and military adventure, the appreciation of music and the arts was ebbing away even as they discussed their future.

Louis XII army, meanwhile, was advancing on Annone, duplicating the massacre that they had perpetrated in Rocca di Arazzo. Succeeding towns surrendered without resistance; they had gotten the explicit message that Louis intended. Louis's army was ready to take on Milan.

*****

"Pope Alexander has sent his son, Cesare, with his French mercenaries borrowed from Louis at your niece, Caterina, in Forli," said an excited Gianni as he entered Ludovico's study. "He is now laying siege to her castle, and she is resisting as best she can and refuses to surrender. She is a true tigress." Gianni, as had many other men, had a more than warm spot for the beautiful, accomplished, and earthy Caterina. She had already shown more courage in her young life than most men twice her age. "Cesare is trying to annex Forli as well as Imola into the Papal States."

"Yes, we've known that Alexander wants to give his sons a patrimony and wants the province of Romagna for the Vatican. This is, I believe, part of the papal conspiracy to add territory to their realm. I would send assistance but cannot with the threat of the French so near. We need every man to defend Milan." Ludovico could only listen to Gianni's account without offering any alternatives. "She is resourceful. She can survive."

"I hope that is the case," said the forlorn Gianni. "I fear for Caterina at the hands of Cesare. His reputation for cruelty is not without merit. He is cruel with impunity and only for his own advancement, not for the betterment of the people. Caterina is too appealing and charismatic a person to lose to such a cruel and sinister person." Gianni was clearly affected by the news of Caterina. Ludovico wondered how Gianni had come to this feeling.

"We cannot hold Milan, Ludovico. Louis sits calmly in Lyon while his army is here. He is simply too powerful for us. We must retreat and wait for a better time."

"Let us call together our troops. We cannot have Trivulzio destroy our city with his big guns. The loss of people and property can be prevented, as it should. We will evacuate to the safety of the Holy Roman Empire until we can resume our campaign against Louis. Then send word to our agent in Rome that the Tomasso affair must come to an end. Give him notice that you will be there soon. We must uncover from Tomasso who set him upon Giorgio."

Louis XII troops entered Milan without a battle. The inhabitants met them with equanimity, having lost faith in the administration of Ludovico by the high tax burden he had placed on them in recent years and confident that the French would not treat them as they had other cities. Once in the city, the French needed the cooperation of the Milanese as much as the Milanese needed the mercy of the French. It was an implicit bargain that served each group at the time with each knowing that bargains are made in heaven but disassembled on earth.

*****

Ludovico's trek to Aachen was a mild affair, the French so preoccupied with solidifying their hold on Milan and Lombardi that they had no resources to expend on the chase after Ludovico. He was not the man of past years but continued to have the stamina to contemplate a return to Milan with another army. The failures of recent years had not yet led him to abandon his ambitions.

Riding at a slow trot on his horse, Ludovico said to Gianni, "Once under the protection of Maximilian, we should begin to rebuild out forces so that we can return to Milan. There is still victory in the air for us." He looked around at the jagged, grey mountain peaks surrounding him, trailing off into lush green valleys, the sound of cow bells ringing in the morning air, the images combining to whisk away his thoughts of the last few months, giving him the confidence that only a bright, sunny day and clean, fresh air can give to a person. "With God's help, we will prevail."

Gianni, too, had his thoughts overtaken by the beauty of the day, briefly laying aside his contempt of Louis. Will I ever be able to reconcile belief in Christ with what I see in Rome, he thought to himself. There are rumors of discontent over the Alps in the regions of the Holy Roman Empire about the venal manner in which the Vatican has been operated, and they are increasing at every report I receive. There is a cataclysmic change coming to the Church, I fear, one that will shake the Church to its roots.

"Once in Aachen, Gianni, we must negotiate for our own troops to counter Louis's troops. The Swiss always have mercenaries available. They will be our starting point."

"How many troops do you believe we need," replied Gianni, riding comfortably on his horse, a far cry, he thought, from his early days wobbling on a horse. "Some of the French troops have withdrawn from Milan, I hear."

"We need about 6,000, I believe, to supplement our troops that we have left in Lombardy and that we will gather on our way to Milan. And then it will take some propitious circumstances for us to defeat the French. We must hope that they will stretch their forces too thinly, neglecting Milan for other areas."

*****

On a clear, brisk, spring day with the sun streaming through the nearly cloudless sky, loud commands could be heard hanging in the air over the long, treeless flatlands at the northern foothills of the Alps where Ludovico's troops gathered for the march to Milan. Six thousand plus Swiss mercenaries, well-trained in warfare stood in rows waiting for the command to begin. At the head of the group was Ludovico, back stiffened on a horse replete with the ornamental accessories and caparisoned gold cloth appropriate to the commencement of a journey of this kind, one last flourish before the mastery of appearance relents to the savagery of battle. Gianni held steady the reins of his horse by Ludovico's side.

"Gianni, you will leave us as we get closer to Milan. Try the best you can to relieve Caterina's situation. It will be an almost helpless cause I'm afraid but we must try. Antonio Pigato will assist you. He is to meet you outside Forli and has some resources in the area."

"I will do my best."

"Of similar importance is your task in Rome. Do not forget Tomasso? Are you up to the chore? Giorgio must rest in peace. His elimination will b e a gift from God."

"A well-deserved gift, I'd say."

"Yes, well-deserved and much looked forward to. May God's providence advantage us."

*****

"Antonio, Cesare's men are in the Forli Castle. When did that takeover occur and where are they hiding Caterina?" said a surprised and uneasy Gianni immediately upon meeting Antonio.

"She was taken away in chains two days ago by Cesare......to Rome I believe, after resisting so valiantly. The odds were against her. Her fame and standing in the public is spreading even farther through the peninsular, even as she is dragged to Rome. She was betrayed by her condottiere. Word is that he was bribed by Cesare and opened the gates to Cesare's men in the darkness of night.

The battle was short-lived, more like a surrender than anything else. Caterina had only a small contingent of trained soldiers; the remainder were untrained village men. She was the fiercest of the lot and held the castle for three weeks with the forcefulness of her character. Before he departed for Rome, Cesare made peace with the officials of the town, vowing to treat them fairly. They assented to his conditions and laid down their arms. At the moment, there is a sense of calm over the town and surrounding area."

"I fear for Caterina's life. Cesare's reputation for cruelty does not preclude a person's gender. He would be as cruel to a woman as to a man."

"His accomplice, Antonello, is a vicious assassin and does Cesare's bidding with alacrity. The town awoke the morning after their departure to the halved body of the town's leading dissenter on two poles at opposite ends of the town's piazza."

"Then it is to Rome for me, Antonio. Wish me god-speed."

*****

After breaching the walls with his newly formed force, Ludovico entered Milan with the acclamation of the city's inhabitants. In an unexplainable move, the French did not leave a sufficient number of men to secure the city. It had not taken long for the residents to despair of the French and pine for the return of their former ruler. He accommodated them eagerly. He had raised another 6,000 men on his journey to Milan, doubling his force, enough to intimidate the sparse forces that Louis had left behind. The

French evacuated the city to Ludovico who entered it with the aplomb that a reigning Duke was expected to display, in full dress regalia of his own person and of his horse. He resumed his place at the Castello Sforzesco and began to give commands for the defense of the city.

His elation lasted as long as a strange noise on a summer evening sinks into the silence of the night. Word spread quickly that Louis was approaching Milan with his full force, the strength in numbers and equipment that had ravished all before him on his previous venture into Lombardy. The sound of his canons still reverberated in the minds of the Lombardi.

Ludovico was determined to face the French this time, even though abandoned by his fellow royal brethren for his intemperate welcome of the French in 1494. He met the French alone in a field outside of Milan, the snow-capped Alps looking down once again at a scene that it had seen too often in the past, the memory of blood-spattered fields tainting the pure white snow like wine dribbling from the mouth of the inebriated.

Louis's canons, lined up across the battle field, faced Ludovico's troops. Louis expected Ludovico to send his troops in a frontal assault. The assault came with little hesitation and with loud cries ringing in the air from the Milanese troops contrasting with the deathly silence just seconds before the charge command was given. Birds in the forest trees adjoining the field discontinued their chattering, finding the situation so disorienting that black clouds of them swirled away toward the foothills. The enthusiasm of the Milanese troops dissipated, however, as soon as the arms and legs and bodies of the fallen impeded the progress of those coming from the rear, as soon as the cries of the fallen challenged the sounds of the cannons, as soon as the air absorbed the putrid smell of death. Despite the earnest entreaties and harangues of Ludovico, his army was in full retreat. His dream of recovering his Duchy died on the field like a tiny insect facing a giant predator. His only recourse was to retreat towards Novara, his base of operations and wait a final encounter with the French.

*****

Gianni had reached Rome and met with Sergio immediately, desiring to end the inner torture he felt over the murder of Giorgio and his wife, a woman who looked familiar to him when he saw her body, but whom he still was unable to place. "Sergio, have you followed Tomasso's movements?"

"Yes, I have tracked them intensively. I know his intimate associations."

"Is there something of particular importance that I should know, something that exposes a weakness of his, that we can exploit," said Gianni, the exhaustion of his journey showing on his face as palpably as writing on a page.

"Ah, yes," replied Sergio, eager to relate to Gianni the secret that Tomasso must have been hiding for years. "Our Tomasso seems to have a predilection for pretty little boys. He visits the streets often trying to satisfy his urges."

Gianni's eyes seemed to expand to cover his whole face. "Perfect. I want this affair over with quickly. I have been harboring my own urge to put an end to him for much too long. I want him to recognize who is dispatching him to hell."

"We can set up a scheme as soon as you desire. Do you need some time to rest after your journey? You look exhausted. You do not want to jeopardize your mission from lack of sleep."

"You're right, Sergio. But not much sleep. One night of sleep is sufficient. Meanwhile, keep an eye on him?"

Gianni awoke the following morning fresh and impatient to put a plan in motion. A pleasant night's sleep seemed to heighten his senses and attune them to the task at hand. Sergio entered his room early that morning, waiting for instructions.

"Sergio, can you find one of these urchins that Tomasso likes so much? Let us offer him compensation for leading Tomasso to a room of our choice. A discrete boy. Yes." Gianni's body seemed to visibly expand with the importunity of his words. He walked around the small wooden table that sat nearby the window of his room. Scattered on it were the leftovers from his meal of the previous evening. He placed his hands on the backrest of a chair that was pulled away from the table and leaned towards Sergio.

"I can find a room. Perhaps across the Tiber in the Trastevere section which is accustomed to untoward incidents in the night."

"Let us do it then. Tomorrow night. Is that sufficient time to arrange it?" Gianni was impressed with the efficiency and composure of Sergio, feeling more confident with his colleague than he had expected to be prior to meeting him. "Also, I will need some poison. Some potion that will accomplish our task with alacrity but allow Tomasso to know what is happening. And we must extract one piece of intelligence from him. Who hired him and to whom did he give his traitorous information?"

"Belladonna. That's what you want. A sufficient amount will paralyze the muscles leading to death. Although many parts of the plant are poisonous, the berries are exceptionally poisonous. I can easily obtain it. Do you mean to trick him into swallowing it?"

"No, by no means. I plan to shove the berries down his throat while you hold him down."

"About ten berries should do it. I will get a handful in case more are needed."

Enticing Tomasso to a room proved an easy task, his appetite for young boys being so exceptional that his usual prudence floated away like water vapor on a cold wintry day. He entered the first floor of a small house in Trastevere near the Tiber that the boy claimed to Tomasso belonged to an acquaintance that was away. His spirits were high, the boy telling him that a room would provide a more intimate and memorable experience and asking a larger price than usual for this enhanced meeting.

Gianni and Sergio waited in the darkness of the street until Tomasso and the boy had entered the room. The door was left unlocked. After several minutes, they rushed into the house into the small bedroom where they were undressing, as surprise and fear mingled on the face of Tomasso like two combatant soldiers vying for supremacy, each having its moments.

"Hello, Tomasso," said Gianni in his softest but most threatening voice, his hatred in full view.

Tomasso was almost speechless, mumbling some inaudible words, his legs wobbling noticeably, a quick sweat forming on his forehead.

"We finally meet again. Did you think that Ludovico and I would let your treachery and maliciousness go unpunished?"

"What do you want from me?"

"Nothing much, just a name. The name of the person who paid you to kill Giorgio. The coward that you are; you had to kill him and his wife in their beds, Giorgio's hatred spewing out in full force now."

The young boy was paid and told to go on his way. No remorse showed on his face as he left the house.

Sergio and Gianni immediately forced Tomasso into a chair, tied him securely, and began questioning him. Fear continued its grip of Tomasso, his denials flowing from him in ever increasing speed as if the speed of his response was more important than the response itself, his cries muffled by the noises of the street, his face red with blood from the blows of Sergio. Finally, he gave up Cesare's name, somehow holding onto the belief that it would save his life.

Tomasso was exhausted, his head dangling, his chin resting on his chest. Gianni beckoned for Sergio to hand him the belladonna. It was not difficult for Sergio to hold Tomasso's mouth open as Gianni forced Tomasso to swallow the crushed berries. A small smile appeared on Gianni's face, followed quickly by his own physical exhaustion.

Watching Tomasso go into delirium and convulsions was more difficult than Gianni expected, and he had to turn away from Tomasso's death throes. Once finished, however, Gianni sat and felt not anger, not remorse, but relief, relief that his obligation to Giorgio was partially satisfied, relief also that he had discovered who ordered Giorgio's murder, Cesare Borgia. The information confirmed his belief that Giorgio's slaying was connected to the Vatican slush fund.

Gianni turned to Sergio. "Cesare Borgia is back in Rome, Sergio, is he not?"

"Yes, that is the word on the street."

"And he is holding Caterina Sforza, is he not?"

"Yes, she is being held in the Pope's dungeon in the Castel Sant' Angelo. It is the Pope's defensive fortress, its Passetto de Borgo, a raised, narrow, open air passageway that runs over a moat that surrounds the Castel is connected to the Basilica San Pietro. It also includes a covered passageway beneath it. It was used, among others, by Pope Alexander to escape Charles VIII when he entered Rome in 1494. The Castel is a very difficult building to break into."

"I am certain that Cesare is molesting Caterina, that is his nature. She is a strong woman but we must try to free her," Gianni's nervousness showing in the tics of his face.

"I will inquire about the Castel and Caterina, but I cannot hold out any encouragement to you. It is heavily guarded, the only access being from the narrow Passetto. There is no place to hide on it. If you did manage to enter the Castel, Caterina is probably located in the dungeon area beneath the Castel, no doubt in the last cell on the block. You would have to walk the length of the corridor to reach it. The only escape route is to return the way you entered. Impossible. One would have to rely on complete secrecy to pull it off. It is foolish to try."

"Well, perhaps we do not have to break in," said Gianni. "Perhaps, we could rescue her from the Passetto itself or better yet when she is brought to the street. Yes, I believe that is the better way. On the street."

"What do you mean?"

"Cesare must have her escorted into his apartment from the Castel, if he has plans to molest her. If we know when she is to be escorted, perhaps we can rescue her from her guards on the street. We would not have to enter the Castel. Would that not increase our odds of succeeding?"

"He does have an apartment in the Vatican. But perhaps, he also has an apartment in the city. We would have to monitor him for a while to determine if that is the case and, if so, know when she is being moved and on which route she is escorted," replied Sergio, sounding more interested in the plot the more the conversation continued.

"True, she probably is not moved every evening. We can employ someone to monitor the Passetto in order to determine if there is a pattern to Cesare's evil," said Gianni moving away from Sergio and moving around the room, pensively stroking his hair from time to time.

*****

If Cesare holds to pattern, tomorrow night is the night for our rescue of Caterina thought Gianni, enjoying a mid-day glass of wine, a blend of Trebbiano and Malvasia, with his plate of cheese and crusty bread sitting on the table. When finished, he stood and opened the door of his street level room, bare of any of the luxuries that he had grown accustomed to, only a bed, a table and several chairs furnished it. He stepped outside and looked around a few minutes. A change of venue eases my mind when I am anxious, he thought to himself.

The narrow street was lined with small houses and several taverns. Noise was a constant reminder all hours of the day that Gianni was in the tenderloin section of the city. During the day children ran along the street unwatched and ragged with the dirt of the city on their undernourished faces. The agony of their life did not show in their eyes and did not show in their voices. It lay hidden deep down within them, not yet ready to show itself. In the evening the patrons of the taverns staggered along home unconcerned about their coarse behavior and the effect of their rowdiness on the inhabitants of the street. Their life was an endless series of drinking and whoring, night mixing with morning until neither lightness nor darkness were distinguishable.

Sergio arrived mid-afternoon with news. "Our plan is no longer viable, Gianni. Caterina is being transferred to the Belvedere and negotiations have started on her release." Sergio sat at the table opposite Gianni, and the two men bent over it in conversation. "She, being the stubborn Sforza that she is, continues to resist signing an agreement ceding Forli and Imola over to Cesare. Once this is signed, she will be released, according to my informants."

This was comforting news to Gianni but not without a sense of cheerless expectation. Gianni was so intense in his desire to gain the approbation of Caterina that he was temporarily stunned by the news of her possible release without his assistance. He and Sergio had prepared for a rescue twice previously and were disappointed when Caterina and her guards did not show. Each time they guided her through a different route than usual, and Gianni and Sergio had missed her. Now, it seemed that there would be no rescue of Caterina by Gianni.

"Who is negotiating for her release," remarked Gianni, visibly pondering his next move.

"Abbot Lauro Bossi."

"Ah, an abbot. Why not Cardinal Ascanio, her uncle?"

"Cardinal Ascanio is not well-received by the French and he has joined his brother in Milan. Cesare's troops, who captured Forli and Caterina, were mainly French, borrowed from Louis XII. The French have not forgotten Ascanio's role in bringing the Pope into the Holy League with Milan to expel Charles VIII from the Peninsular in 1495. Their memories are long and bitter."

"But an abbot," questioned Gianni, looking through the one window in the room at the twilight encroaching on the narrow street. "What do we know about this abbot. Can we trust him to fulfill this obligation? There are abbots I would not trust with anything temporal or spiritual. They are as deceiving as a chameleon changing its color to deceive its prey. However, there are abbots I would trust with my life, so god-fearing and honest are they."

"He is a long-time friend of hers from Florence, said to be honest, trustworthy and clever."

"No, I am not willing to leave her destiny in his hands. We must retrieve her from her abductors. Sergio, have a boat ready on the Tiber and a ship at Ostia. We'll continue with our own plan. Once we whisk her away from her captors, we can take her on the Tiber to Ostia and then sail her to Livorno, thence by horse to Florence. She is a Medici by marriage. They will find a place for her."

The rescue of Caterina proved easier than expected three nights later as she was being transported. Perhaps it was just the goddess Fortuna, so long missing from Caterina's life, that finally afforded her an opportunity to return to a normal life after the harsh treatment she had experienced over the last year. Her four guards, escorting her by wagon to Cesare's apartment, had imbibed sufficient wine to be less than stellar guardians this night, wine provided them the previous night by a pretty young girl of Sergio's acquaintance. They were overcome without much difficulty or harm to anyone. The real harm to them would come from Cesare.

Gianni looked at Caterina by the barge that was to take her down the Tiber to Ostia, pale and haggard with dark shadows under her forlorn brown eyes, weakened by her confinement in the dank cell of Castel San Angelo, close to the heavenly body of Christ, yet so far from Christ's everlasting mercy.

"Caterina, do you remember me? My name is Gianni. I am an aide to your uncle, Ludovico. He has sent me to help you. We will be placing you on a ship to Livorno and then have you delivered to the Medici in Florence. We met several times some years ago during your stays at Castello Sforzesco."

She looked at Gianni, hope slowly seeping into her eyes, a slight smile finding a place on her face after a long period of disuse. "Yes, Gianni," she said in a faint voice, so unusual for her but appropriate for the physical state in which she was. "I remember the good times we had."

Gianni saw in Caterina's face not the beauty that he remembered from the past but the misfortunes she had endured in the present. He readily understood her current appearance. Nursed back to health, he was confident that she would return to the vibrant, strikingly beautiful woman he remembered. "You will have time to rest on the barge that will take you to Livorno. Rest and peace of mind is what you need now. I will leave you in Livorno to return to Milan and Ludovico where your uncle is now. Milan is threatened by the French again, and Louis vows to punish your uncle."

To himself he lamented that he could not personally deliver her to the Medici. Nor did he have the time to find Cesare. He vowed, however, that he would return to Rome to do so sometime in the future.

After a long day relaxing by the Tiber to relieve the pressures of the last few days, Gianni returned to his room to be greeted by an anxious sounding Sergio at his door, "Gianni, I have received an inquiry from Ascanio's servant on your whereabouts. He must see you with an urgent letter from Cardinal Ascanio. He will be waiting by the Coliseum to deliver the letter to you."

"This is very enigmatic, Sergio."

The letter was delivered by Ascanio's trusted servant, Umberto. In it, Ascanio simply said that they must meet immediately upon Gianni's arrival in Novara. This is very puzzling, he thought to himself.

*****

Louis's French troops had not yet reached Novara, a town about 20 miles west of Milan, when Gianni arrived exhausted but in good spirits from his journey from Rome. Defense of the city was in the process of being set up. Military commands could be heard shouted from the walls of the city. Soldiers could be seen hurrying around, pushing the few canons that they possessed, placing them in strategic places in the piazzas around the city and along the city wall. It is a fine day, Gianni thought, the sky bright blue, the white clouds a perfect palette of intriguing patterns. If I am to die, this is the kind of day that I would pray for.

He stopped at a livery, dismounted from his horse, as equally exhausted as Gianni, and tied it by a water trough, went inside to fetch a bucket of oats for him and soaked his own face in a handful of water, hoping it would refresh him. "Board my horse for me", he called to the owner, and threw him a few coins. "Where will I find the Sforza headquarters," he asked matter-of-factly, then realized he sounded curt, turned and said with a gentle smile, "I have had a long journey on the road."

"His headquarters are near the north gate. Walk up this street here, pointing to a street that veered off at a forty-five-degree angle."

"Thank you."

Walking toward Ludovico's headquarters, he wondered where Caterina would be now. He was hoping that the Medici would care for her, perhaps in one of their villas outside the city. They owned several. After all, her child, Ludovico, also was a Medici, he thought. He could not resist the warmth congealing around a sensual pleasure he got from thinking of her. She was as lovely, charismatic and strong as her reputation that followed her. I must put her out of my mind. I must concentrate on our survival here.

When he found Ludovico, Ascanio was not with him. He had moved on to the local church to speak to the pastor there. "Gianni, it is better that Ascanio tells you the information he wants you to have," Ludovico said, throwing his arms around Gianni a second time and hugging him.

"We have a strong position here but Louis's guns always give him an advantage. We cannot outrun him. We have to stand and fight here. You have freed Caterina. You will be thanked all over the Peninsular, or at least most of the Peninsular. She is a true heroine. There are few lovers of Cesare here, a pathological killer who disguises his horrid activities for advancing the Church's duties."

"He will be repaid someday. Caterina will need some rest to rejuvenate herself but a woman of her capabilities will find a way to regain her former luster," replied Gianni, finally taking a seat. "When is Ascanio expected to return? I am anxious to hear what he has to say. I have been musing over his message since I departed Rome."

"Soon. Meanwhile, let us relax and enjoy a glass of this Valpolicella. War should not deprive us of enjoying a few sips of heaven in the midst of hell. Salute, my old stalwart."

"Gianni, welcome," Ascanio said as he entered the room where Gianni and Ludovico were sitting, a half empty carafe of wine on the table, glasses in their hand and smiles on their faces. He hugged Gianni as he raised himself from the table, then pulled a third chair to the table and inquired, "So where is my glass, gentlemen? Is this the way you treat a holy man?"

Wine was quickly poured into his glass and the conversation continued. "No doubt, you are curious about my purposely worded enigmatic letter, are you not, Gianni?"

"Yes, yes, I have been mulling it in my mind since I left Rome."

"Well, you know about the accounts held in the Fugger Bank in Augsburg."

"Yes."

"Those are monies specifically siphoned from the monasteries for 20 years. It is considerable and dedicated for the sole purpose of the Pope's agenda of advancing and defending his temporal authority, i.e. adding territory to the Papal States. It has been tapped on several occasions to supplement its regular wartime finances since Borgia became Pope but is still a substantial amount. We are all agreed, I believe, that the money belongs to the monasteries. Before Bishop Grignolino was transferred, he and I had identified the multiple accounts in which the money is held, all in the Fugger Bank. As Vice Chancellor, I have wide ranging authority to administer Vatican activities. Some cardinals sitting in the Curia have oversight on some of my activities. But it is not all that difficult to manipulate the books to our advantage without incurring their curiosity. Gianni, I have a list of the accounts and the amounts held in them. I am the administrator of certain of those accounts." Handing Gianni a piece of paper, Ascanio said, "This is a list of the accounts over which I have authority. As you can see, I have placed your name as my assistant with the authority to handle the accounts with my permission." Handing Gianni a second piece of paper with the Vatican stamp on it, "This is a letter introducing you to the officials of the Fugger Bank that you met previously and indicating that you have the authority to transfer the funds."

"Gianni stood speechless. I do not know how to handle money. What am I expected to do?"

"All I and Ludovico want you to do at the moment is to go to Augsburg and transfer the funds in these accounts to Banco di San Giorgio in Genoa, a very substantial bank that is competing with the Medici banks now. These accounts amount to about 75 percent of the total funds at the Fugger Banks. They are aware of this forthcoming transaction as is Banco di San Giorgio. You have nothing to worry about. We will eventually allocate these funds to the monasteries in some proportion. There are no records of the amounts taken from specific monasteries, and, when the time comes, we will have to develop a formula to decide the amounts that should be returned."

"When do you want me to complete this transaction? I am available at your pleasure. However, I would like to participate in the coming battle."

"As soon as possible…. tomorrow," said Ludovico, entering the conversation, "before the French lay siege to Navara. Let us toast a good journey for you. Ride fast and successful and may God go with you." With that the three men toasted each other as the true friends that they were.

*****

The siege began soon after Gianni departed. It came on a cold, wintry, late winter day, words hanging in the air encased in the vaporous mist emanating from the mouths of soldiers, puffs of white breath fading into oblivion. Ludovico walked along the ramparts encouraging his troops, many of whom were Swiss mercenaries. Across the ramparts the Swiss mercenaries in the French army shouted entreaties to their countrymen on the ramparts to abandon their posts. "We do not want to slay you. Follow us home. Our valleys will soon be painted green with spring, cowbells will soon be ringing over the hills, our women will soon be churning the milk which will be turned into cheese. Do not die in this foreign land, forgotten by your loved ones. Follow us home. The government of the Swiss Confederation has forbidden Swiss to fight Swiss."

For three days, not a cannonball was shot. The only sounds were the murmurs among Ludovico's troops debating whether to leave. Eventually, the Swiss mercenaries on both sides departed their posts and could be seen marching away northward toward their homeland.

"What am I to do," he asked Ascanio. "We were already outnumbered and outgunned. Now we are losing more troops than Louis. We cannot possibly compete with him. It is fruitless to try.

"Ludovico, we have no choice. We must try to slip away as best we can, replied a dejected Ascanio.

"Tomorrow, we will try to infiltrate the citizens who are leaving the town. With some luck, we can, perhaps, elude the French," Ludovico rejoined, trying to sound as positive as possible.

A large group of citizens were grouped together at the gate to leave the following morning, their conversations floating away on the white condensation of their breath. The air was still cold, the sun bright and the sky clear. Expectations were high in the French camp. They could feel victory was nearby and the spoils of victory theirs to enjoy. Ludovico and Ascanio in peasant flocks mixed with the exiting group. Their emotions were bubbling over internally; they could only hope that it was not obvious on their persons. Ludovico's hand, carrying a bag of old, ragged cloths, shook. He tried to put the thought of capture out of his mind to steady his nerves. He was a courageous man but had never been in this kind of situation before. The group stopped in front of the French guards and was given a cursory examination before it was allowed to pass. "Thanks be to God," Ascanio whispered.

In a low voice, Ludovico said to Ascanio, "Once over the rise ahead, veer off to the right across the field and make for the forest."

Midway across the field, loud shouts could be heard coming from the French guards in front of the walls. "He's escaped" roared one guard. "After that group," pointing to the recently exited group. Ludovico looked back and saw a Swiss mercenary talking to the guards. Turning to Ascanio, he said, "An informant must have given us away. Run to the trees."

A cardinal's life had not prepared Ascanio for this sort of exercise, his was much more of talking and consulting. He faltered well short of the trees, on his knees panting excessively, sucking the air as quickly as possible.

"Ascanio, can I help you," shouted Ludovico, turning to run back to him.

"No, go ahead, my capture is less a trophy for them than you. God speed."

The trees came upon Ludovico. He dashed between them, zigzagging, in an attempt to be less visible but realized that it was not an aid. He wished that he was not unarmed but had carried his sword. That, however, would have been a blunder, he knew. Peasants do not own swords. He thought, what am I to do if the forest ends. No time for such considerations. Run, just run, Ludovico, he said to himself.

He could hear the voices of the French pursuing him, instructing each other on the direction to take. They appeared closer to him. He stopped briefly, surveying the area, saw what appeared to be a large hole by a row of shrubs. He advanced on it, saw it was sufficiently deep to cover his body. Shoveling with his hands the remainder of last winter's leaves, he laid in the hole snugly, pushing leaves and small twigs over him until he felt that he was well covered. May God cover me with his mercy, he commented to himself. He relaxed and waited for whatever his fate was to be.

Suddenly, the thought of his dead wife, Beatrice, entered his mind. She had been an almost constant presence with him since her passing. He offered a silent prayer to her.

Even if I am captured, her two sons have a chance to become Duke, he remarked. His anxiety was relieved and his body, tired from the preparations for battle and the exhaustion of the chase, fell into a deep, comforting sleep.

When he awoke, all he could hear was the sound of crickets chirping as if they were introducing themselves to him in unison. Brushing off the leaves, he could see the rays of the moon breaching the forest intermittently as clouds passed under its light. Time for me to move along, he said aloud to himself, rubbing himself to shake off the cold. But where. Perhaps, I am better off remaining here for the evening rather than walking in the darkness. I hear no soldiers around.

After an hour's walk the following morning, he exited the forest. He was walking north. He could see the Alps in the distance rising from the ground in all their jagged majesty. It was hours before he reached a group of huts sitting by a newly plowed field, large brown clops of soil in neat rows, ready for sowing the following spring. Two cows moped along in an unplowed portion of the field, stopping occasionally to ingest the remaining grass. Riding on the unpaved road running alongside the field and providing access to the huts, Ludovico could see two horsemen dressed in French military garb.

They have noticed me he cried to himself. The horsemen halted their steeds a moment, shifted and raised themselves in their saddles slightly to view him. Turning their steeds, they approached him at a trot. I cannot outrun them, he said. Steady, don't panic. Continue walking. Once they reached him, Ludovico looked up at the men. He greeted them politely, trying to keep his anxiety at bay. They were definitely French soldiers. A farmer came from the opposite side of the house and walked toward him and the horsemen.

"Good morning," the farmer said, addressing Ludovico and the horsemen.

One of the horsemen inquired of the farmer about Ludovico. When his reply was negative, both men dismounted with hands on the hilts of their swords, surrounding Ludovico. After a few more questions to the farmer and Ludovico, it did not take long for the horsemen to realize that Ludovico was foreign to this land. Looking at him and then his hands, the horsemen became convinced that they had found the Duke of Milan. Ludovico's journey was ended with a murmur.

Back at the French camp, Ludovico joined Ascanio. Both men were unharmed and compliant with General Trivulzio's commands. Several days later Ascanio was first handed over to the Venetians, later to be returned to the French for incarceration.

*****

Gianni returned to Milan from Genoa, completing the transactions which made him administrator with Cardinal Ascanio Sforza of the funds transferred to the Banco di San Giorgio. The French were occupying Milan, troops dispersed throughout the city to restrain any uprising. The residents seemed content, however, with the occupation. The sun continued to rise each day, the night continued to twinkle with the stars of heaven, and Louis had wisely reduced the taxes that Ludovico had instituted; all was forgotten and forgiven by the Milanese. As far as Gianni could calculate, he was some two weeks behind the capture of Ludovico. Ascanio had been hauled off first to Venice, then to Lyon, France, he learned. Gianni doggedly tracked the group of soldiers transporting Ludovico, closing the initial distance between them to three days. They ended their journey in Berry, France where Ludovico was held in the Castle Lys Saint George.

Gianni was alone, friendless, and without knowledge of the language. He was an obvious foreigner in the town and knew he could not stay very long without exposing himself to questioning by the authorities. His principal purpose, he had to constantly remind himself, was to discover Ludovico's location so that he could return with a plan and support to extract him from his impoundment. He learned that Ludovico was able to move about most of the castle area. At least he is given freedom of movement in his confinement, he thought to himself. What I need are some French-speaking mercenaries and a few good Milanese to return with me to secure Ludovico's freedom. He traveled back to Milan with the objective to return before the weather grew severe.

*****

Gianni's return was delayed until summer. A large storm swept in, laying snow across the northern peninsula and closing the paths across the mountains. He contemplated moving across the narrow path southwest by the Mediterranean but rejected that approach because it made a longer journey to Berry. By the time he departed, it was summer, the sun not yet the scorching ball of energy that wilted anything exposed to it for long but sufficiently enervating to cause a slow, uncomfortable pace for men and horses. The evenings, however, brought a cool, welcome breeze from the sea that refreshed the band.

The delay proved to be advantageous to the expedition. Gianni was able to recruit Sergio from Rome and to enlist several French-speaking Swiss mercenaries who did not return to their country when the other Swiss departed Navara. Together with five Milanese, there were ten men in the band including Gianni.

Knowing they would be conspicuous together, they entered the town in three groups over the course of a week, each group with a French speaker in it. One of the Swiss mercenaries knew the configurations of the castle and through casual contact with a guard discovered that Ludovico was allowed to roam the courtyard at leisure, his movement not tightly controlled. He also learned that on Sundays there were fewer guards in the area, many being allowed to attend church services together.

"He is not guarded very well," said Jacque, meeting Gianni outside of town by a clear, flowing stream, both relaxing by it to avoid appearing other than two friends enjoying a sunny, warm day together.

"Will it be difficult to enter the area," asked Gianni, placing a blade of grass in his mouth, then swatting a fly who decided it wanted closer contact with him.

"The courtyard, which is behind the castle, is a large rectangular space enclosed by a wall, of course, not very tall, maybe 12 feet. There are two gates on the same wall, perhaps, 80 feet apart. There are no obstacles beyond the walls, although there is a vast clearing before one meets the forest. The town is on the front side of the castle, but Ludovico is never allowed there."

"Your description does not sound very imposing. An escape seems very doable. Can the guards be overpowered on a Sunday?" Gianni had risen and was standing by the stream now, looking down at the small swirls and soothing sounds that it was making as it passed over some small rocks in the middle of the water. "It is mesmerizing, isn't it," pointing to the stream.

"I believe it is very possible," said Jacque, looking up at Gianni.

"Let us plan for next Sunday. We must infiltrate two people into the yard first. We can disguise them as merchants making a delivery. Will we be able to overcome the guards at the gates? We need to take both gates."

"Yes, take the two guards at one gate with three men. When the other two guards respond, send four men from around the corner of the wall to attack them."

"What about the two who have entered the yard," said Gianni, shading his eyes from the sun which had moved in his path.

"They can snatch Ludovico and lead him away."

"Keep this to yourself until Sunday."

Everything was set for Ludovico's escape. The men were to meet in the town Sunday morning. Before then, each would try to stay as hidden as possible.

The town was surrounded by low lying mountains on one side, rock strewn trails leading from the town into the hills, enticing Gianni to hike into them. The summer had brought out wildflowers which were sprinkled over the rocks, clinging to whatever soil they could find. The juxtaposition between the brightly colored flowers and the ashen grey of the rocks for some reason reminded Gianni that a well-lived life was made of contrasts. Is that what his life has been, he asked himself. Am I weighting my own life more favorably than others? Can I even assess my own life? Was Brother Matteo's life, so even and uneventful, so mono-colored, of lesser value than his own? He, at least, had affected other lives... my own, for example. What life have I affected for the better? Am I just an over-inflated windbag, spewing platitudes and underwhelming observations? Enough, enough, this is leading nowhere. Move on.

The Sunday of action came. All the men were positioned. Ludovico, not aware of the coming attempt to liberate him, was in the courtyard, walking nonchalantly around it, showing obvious signs of restlessness. The two men assigned to enter the courtyard as peasants were easily permitted into the yard without incident. They stopped their cart by the door leading into the castle, blocking access from it. With shovels in hand they removed plants from the cart and moved toward the garden area where Ludovico was standing. One of them leaned toward Ludovico and quickly moved away. Ludovico's face reflected an almost imperceptible smile, had anyone been focused on it.

Suddenly, with great force the two guards on one of the outside gates were overpowered and fell to the ground. Sufficient commotion was made that the two guards on the second gate ran to assist their comrades. They were followed swiftly by four assailants and subdued. Ludovico and his rescuers made for a gate to run for the forest where horses were secreted away for them. Their path of escape, however, was blocked by many French soldiers pouring through the gates. Looking behind him, Gianni could see that the cart blocking the door was overturned and more soldiers were entering the courtyard. There was no escape route other than fighting their way through the defenders. His Swiss mercenaries quickly relinquished their swords and knelt down in submission. Gianni and Ludovico were left with only their five Milanese comrades.

"Let us fight our way out," shouted Gianni to Ludovico and the others.

"No, no," came the reply from Ludovico. "It is useless. No benefit can be achieved. Surrender."

Gianni and the Milanese released their swords but stood in defiance to the French troops surrounding them. They all were shackled and lead away by the captain of the guards. One Swiss mercenary walked away without shackles in the company of the smiling captain.

Betrayal is never easy to accept, Gianni thought, but even less so when it is caused by one's own misjudgment.

The following day Ludovico and Gianni were brought in front of Louis XII's secretary. "Where is the King?" shouted Ludovico in anger. "Does he not have the courage to face me?" he added in exaggeration.

"Has he seen you since you were first captured? No. He has no time to waste on someone who would first invite his cousin, Charles, into your province to fight your battles, then to turn against him with your own enemies."

"Charles was sowing fear throughout the Peninsular, massacring whole towns with impunity. His agenda became much more horrid and widespread than he at first let on. It is I who was misled by him."

"Well, have it your way, if you like. But your future is in the King's hands now, and you will suffer under his memories, not yours."

"What does he have in store for us?"

"You and your friend here will be transported to the Castel in Loches, not so very far from here. There is a dungeon cell awaiting each of you. Your freedom will be much more restricted there. The only freedom you will have is the freedom of your own thoughts."

Ludovico looked resigned to his fate, holding his chained hands together in front of him, turning his head and smiling slightly at Gianni. "Before you leave, can you tell me where my brother, Cardinal Ascanio, is?"

"He is with the Venetians. That is all I know."

\*\*\*\*\*

Time passes very slowly when you are confined to a cell alone, thought Gianni. One year seems like 10, he murmured to himself as he sat at his table, the sun slithering through the bars of his window onto his one opened book, "Dante's Inferno." Perhaps Dante should have placed me in one of his circles of hell. Could it be any worse than what I have experienced for the last year? My jailers do not even permit me to see Ludovico. We apparently are let out to the yard at different times. I would not even know if he has been transferred elsewhere.

The dampness of his dungeon cell made his bones shiver, his only recourse, to try to catch warming from the small slivers of rays that passed into it. It's the smell of the dankness that bothers me the most. It has the smell of death.

His door clanked open and two guards stepped into it. One looked at him scornfully, "The king wants to see you Come with us."

"What does he want with me?"

"How should we know, you miscreant," said one guard pushing Gianni out of the door, "just follow us. You will know soon enough."

Gianni followed the guards through the narrow, dark corridor lined with cells. He tried to glean whether Ludovico was in one of them, but was unable to see into any of them, the doors covering the entire doorway except for a small slit about three quarters of the way up. Neither did he hear a sound coming from any of the cells. As he was taken to the upper levels of the castle, guards lined the corridor walls full of magnificently designed tapestries. I would never have been able to escape this castle, let alone break Ludovico out, assuming he is still here, he thought. There are just too many soldiers in it.

"Hurry up," the guard walking with him said as he yanked on Gianni's chains. "The King does not have all day to wait for you. Affairs of the state weight on him."

Gianni entered King Louis's great hall. The captain of the guards was present, standing alongside of the King's advisor, Pierre de Rohan. He surveyed the walls which were covered in mirrors encased in gilded wooden frames, the ceiling displayed a heavenly scene of angels circulating around the Virgin in clouds, the pale blue of the sky contrasting with the deeper blue of the Virgin's cloak. Impressive, but nothing that I have not seen in Milan and better done there, he said to himself smugly.

Louis sat in a high-backed chair, his advisors on either side of him. "I would ransom you, if you had any value to anyone, but I see no one interested in your release, he said sarcastically. However, there is one task that could be of value to me. So, let me come straight to the point, Gianni. I need your assistance and am willing to release you for it.

"And Ludovico. Will you grant his release?"

"Well, that depends on you. If you successfully complete this task, I will consider releasing him," Louis said as he

307

looked disdainfully at Gianni. "As you can see, there is no way that you can escape."

"What exactly is this task that you deign to offer me," responded Gianni, silently trying to restrain the rising anger that he felt, partly for the treatment accorded him today but also for the frustration and ignominy of the last year.

"Cardinal Ascanio has been released by the Venetians to attend the conclave for selecting the next Pope. The Venetians apparently have come to terms with Ascanio. You would not know that Pope Alexander VI has died and was seceded briefly by Pope Pius III for 26 days before he also passed away. Ascanio always was a good diplomat. He will be considered for the Papacy himself. He is one of the strongest contenders and, if he succeeds, will make this assignment much more possible. I want you to convince Ascanio to mediate an agreement with the Venetians on my behalf, a non-aggression pact between us. I do not desire to have Venice always threatening my northern boundary on the Peninsular. I will be willing to provide a financial consideration to them and to the Vatican."

"Why can't you negotiate this agreement yourself?"

"Ascanio is a good diplomat. He will have more import than me, at least with this current Doge. And he has departed the Venetians on good terms. They have mended their disagreements. I do not want to be turned down personally by them."

"And for this you will grant my outright release," said Gianni, already dreaming of his release.

"Yes," replied Louis rising from his chair and approaching Gianni who was standing but still shackled and rubbing his right wrist with his left hand. "But only a successful conclusion will see the possible release of Ludovico."

"But why would the Venetians be so willing to negotiate with Ascanio?"

"As I said, Ascanio has a peninsular-wide reputation for diplomacy. And since you were one of Ludovico's close advisors, they see you as having some legitimacy with the Milanese. I find some worth in having your involvement in the agreement. Sort of a surrogate for Ludovico."

Louis stood by Gianni and said, "Do you and I have an agreement?

Gianni replied with a simple, "yes." To himself he thought I must be free before I can develop a plan for Ludovico's release, a plan that was already hatching in his mind.

*****

Gianni was led into Ascanio's quarters in Rome. He had never been in the Vatican previously and on his way to greet Ascanio was overwhelmed by the sheer luxury of its decorations, the magnificence of its artwork, the decadence of its furnishings, the sheer beauty of its reconstruction. They greeted each other with the warmth that only exists between two men who have been through a similarly painful situation, exchanging the story of their capture and the dreadful, almost deathly, life that they led in captivity. This was all done with a glass of Valpolicella

Ripasso, savoring its soft tannins and raison-like flavor as they now laughed over their former life.

"It is so easy to laugh about it now," said Ascanio as the men sat in his office. "It seems you had it much worse than I. And no sight of Ludovico?"

"No, I do not even know if he is still being held in Loches. I heard no word of him during my imprisonment there."

"Well, what is it that Louis wants you to relate to me? And what are the conditions. Louis seems to believe that he is the next Alexander the Great. His ambitions go to the whole peninsular."

Gianni leaned back in his chair and looked at Andrea Mantegna's 'Christ as a Suffering Redeemer' on the wall. It must be a new acquisition, he thought, as he rolled his wine glass in his hands. He had become very proficient in the niceties of life before his imprisonment, good wine, fine art, ballroom activities and women that only the aristocrats of society could enjoy. He sometimes missed Giorgio who disdained this life and more often sought the earthier pleasures. "Is this a new acquisition? It is beautiful and haunting," he inquired, pointing to the Mantegna.

"Yes," replied Ascanio, sitting up in his chair and turning to view the painting himself. "It was only recently completed. Does not the starkness, the elimination of all extraneous elements, rivet your attention to Christ? Mantegna is the court painter for the Gonzaga's of Mantua. He graciously agreed to do this painting for me, and it has become one of my favorite."

"That it does. It always astonishes me how great painters can elicit such emotions from the viewer. As to Louis, he's hoping you can sway Venice to accept a non-aggression pact with him. Now that his troops are in Milan, he is concerned about his northern border. I suppose he is no longer concerned about your brother recovering Milan. And with Ludovico in a French cell, he has the upper hand. He offered to consider, merely consider, releasing Ludovico if an agreement can be had. Also, he offers remuneration to both Venice and you."

Sitting back comfortably in his chair, Gianni related his idea of a released exile for Ludovico that could be proposed by the Venetians. "The Venetians have never had an outright hatred for Ludovico; they were only concerned about the possibility of him threatening them, as would any leader on the peninsula. A released Ludovico would not be a threat any longer. He has been out of the public eye for these two years. He no longer has the support of the Milanese, has no army nor the funds to purchase an army. Moreover, they seem to have abandoned their "terra firma" policy that so concerned Ludovico. Perhaps, the Venetians would also negotiate for his release, a release that would have him exiled from Milan, perhaps to Florence."

"Since my own release, I have managed to develop a rapport with the Venetians. It just may be possible. And remuneration is always welcome. This is the Italian way, not Alexander's way. Louis is becoming a real Italian." Then with a smile, Ascanio added, "At least, he learned something from his time here. I will make a good-faith attempt, but I cannot hold out any encouragement for either Louis's proposal or for yours."

"Even if you are successful, it is an effort without any certainty of acquiring our objective. We have to put our trust in Louis to release Ludovico. It is as if we take aim at a target we cannot see."

"Now, about our account at the Banco di San Giorgio," said Ascanio. "Are we at a point to disperse the funds as we agreed on?"

"Now that I am free, I can arrange an appropriate system to do so. I will set myself up in Milan, hire a trustworthy lawyer to be our administrator and liaison. And, as we agreed, the funds will be dispersed to the monasteries, San Gelsera primarily, but to others on the peninsular. We will restrict ourselves to those. I will determine an appropriate dispersal period, either annually or semi-annually."

"Yes, yes, I am anxious to advance this plan," said Ascanio, a satisfied look on his wine-red face. "I am enjoying you and this wine too much, Gianni. It is so nice to see you," as he tried and failed to raise himself from his seat. He leaned back and said, "There is one other item I want to discuss with you. I have now placed you as the sole executor of the account. We must look to a future without me. That day will inevitably come. I trust you as I would trust my brother. I know that honesty runs in your blood and know that you will fulfill our ambition."

*****

The Venetians were not receptive to the French proposal. They feared the expansionary policies of Louis and saw themselves as a counterweight to it. As for remuneration, they were quite content with the wealth they were generating from their many trade routes across the Mediterranean Sea. They were now and had been for some time the sole maritime power in the Mediterranean; Genoa and Pisa, former competitors to Venice in the Mediterranean, had long since been vanquished from the eastern part. Their main foe now was the Ottoman Empire, that rising power in the east which had captured Constantinople 50 years ago, the site of the eastern branch of the Church and consolidated their hold on southeastern Europe. It would be a constant threat to western Europe for some time to come.

Meanwhile, Ludovico languished in his cell, not heard from since his capture. Cardinal Ascanio resumed the Vice Chancellorship of the Vatican and attempted one final time for the Pope's miter but lost his bid to Giuliano della Rovere who took the name of Pope Julius II at his consecration, the nephew of Pope Sixtus IV. He would forever be known as the Warrior Pope.

*****

The sun glittered off of Lake Como, highlighting the deep blue of the water and contrasting with the paler blue of the sky. Boats slid over the water, leaving a noticeable wake in their passing. The villas on the shoreline stood tall and magnificent in the sunlight, surrounded by their perfectly manicured and statute-laden lawns. People bathed off their docks and tanned on their patios. The aristocracy was in full pleasure mode, enjoying life like Venus enticing another suitor.

On one slope a smaller villa clings to it like a vine clutching a trellis. A short distance away a field of mulberry bushes

313

in perfect rows descend the slope almost to the shoreline. A man sits at a table sipping a glass of Arneis wine from Piedmont, staring at the mulberry field and reminiscing about his time at San Gelsera with Brother Matteo whose family owns the adjacent field. He thinks, I have come a long way since then, since Brother Matteo taught me about topics that showed me a different aspect of life, of living a life, who taught me to respect others and offered me a life far from the meagre existence of my ancestors, not necessarily better in the spiritual sense but full of the wonders of learning and, certainly, full of many of the material comforts of life.

Approaching the sienna-colored villa, a well-dressed man enters through the gate, multi-colored inpatients and red geraniums planted on both sides of the walk complementing each other and brightening the entrance. A large fountain slightly off the entrance bubbles with water flowing from the angelic figure in its center, seemingly giving a heavenly essence to the home. The visitor enters the premise and is escorted to the rear main patio that looks out over the lake. The patio surrounds a swimming pool, a table with chairs sits by the bar under an overhang, a serving cart by the side with a carafe of wine on it. Smaller nooks of the patio provide individual sheltered sitting areas. Overlooking the patio as if a bridge of a ship, bedroom apartments look out onto the lake also. The men greet each other cordially, with a genuine familiarity of friendship and sit at the table.

"Good day, Gianni. How are you today?"

"I am fine, Giuseppe, and you? A glass of wine before we begin." He pours the wine simultaneously with an answer from his guest.

They sip from their glass of wine and converse before Giuseppe says, "Gianni, the funds were transferred to San Gelsera on Monday last. The next installment will be delivered in six months. I have a list of additional monasteries that you should review to decide if you want to support them also. I will leave it with you."

Gianni glances at the list and says, "You are certain that San Gelsera does not know where the funds originate. To divulge my name could bring tragedy to our program. You were a monk before you resigned to become an attorney. You know how much need there is in the monastery."

"Yes, and you know how much I support what you are doing. As to the other affair...... Cesare."

"Yes, tell me about Cesare. I have heard he is in poor health and is in Spain. With the death of his father several years ago, his fortunes have declined?"

"Yes, they certainly have. As you know, Pope Julius II was a bitter enemy of the Borgias and has succeeded in thwarting Cesare's ambitions and excluded him from Vatican affairs. He is with John of Navarre now and seems to be in slightly better health. Have you set in motion some plan against him?"

"Oh, yes. I can never forget Cesare. I have employed three Spanish soldiers in Count Lerin's army to target him.

Cesare is now a commander for John of Navarre's troops in Spain.

Just then a flaxen haired, once beautiful but still striking woman stepped out of the house. Gianni turned to Giuseppe and said, "This is Caterina Sforza di Medici. She is visiting me from Florence."

Behind her ran a child of perhaps 10 years of age toward Gianni. Gianni shouted, "Giorgio, come here, let's walk down to the lake."

# Afterword

Ludovico Sforza died in 1508 in Loches, France where he is buried. He never saw Milan again. His two sons would each become Dukes of Milan briefly later in the century.

Cardinal Ascanio Sforza died in 1502 in Rome. He is buried in the Church of Santa Maria del Popolo.

Caterina Sforza di Medici died in Florence in 1509. Her son by Giovanni di Medici would become a renowned condottiere. Her grandson would become the first Grand Duke of Tuscany. Other descendants would become Queen of France and Queen of England.

Leonardo Da Vinci was employed for 17 years by Ludovico. In 1500 when Ludovico was captured, he fled to Venice. Cesare Borgia employed him as military engineer and map maker in 1502. He moved between Florence and Milan until 1513. He died under the employ of King Francis I of France in 1519 and is buried in the Chapel of Saint Hubert in Chateau d'Amboise in France.

Cesare Borgia died in 1507 in Spain, slain by 3 soldiers of Count Lerin's army.

# Question

All of the fictional characters have something in common. What is it?

Hint: It has to do with their surnames.